"My guest room or my bed? It's your choice."

As she listened to Reed's words, Ellen felt a rise of anger against him. "What if I choose neither . . . ?"

"Then I'll stay here." Reed glared at her. "Somebody may be trying to kill you, and I will not leave you alone tonight."

If only he'd asked to stay instead of hurling commands and treating her like an infant.

But he hadn't.

Ellen turned away from the memory of his gentle embrace, and said firmly, "I have fought too hard to become a complete person, Reed. I just can't risk getting involved with another man who won't let me breathe. So you can stay or go, it doesn't matter anymore. . . ."

ABOUT THE AUTHOR

California author Suzanne Ellison has written twelve Superromance novels, as well as several mainstream books.

The idea for this story came from a newspaper article describing how a family had found a time capsule in their home and tracked down the originator. Suzanne enlisted the aid of family members in researching the backgound. Her husband, Scott, is an environmental planner and her brother-in-law, Michael, a cartographer.

Books by Suzanne Ellison

HARLEQUIN SUPERROMANCE
420–HEART OF THE WEST
423–SOUL OF THE WEST
427–SPIRIT OF THE WEST
452–A DANGEROUS LOYALTY

HARLEQUIN INTRIGUE
46–NOWHERE TO RUN

Shifting Sands

SUZANNE ELLISON

Harlequin Books

TORONTO • NEW YORK • LONDON
AMSTERDAM • PARIS • SYDNEY • HAMBURG
STOCKHOLM • ATHENS • TOKYO • MILAN
MADRID • WARSAW • BUDAPEST • AUCKLAND

Published February 1992

ISBN 0-373-70488-7

SHIFTING SANDS

For Michael,
the family cartographer,
who helped me map out this book

CHAPTER ONE

IT WAS FOUR O'CLOCK on a hazy, rain-splotched afternoon when Ellen Andrews tripped over the coffee can behind the Chumash Mountain cabin.

At first she thought it was a rock, a fallen branch or an exposed root, any one of which might have ambushed her after this exhausting day traipsing through these densely wooded hills. But as she caught herself from falling, she glanced down and spotted a yellow plastic lid atop a red one-gallon can.

Out of habit, she stopped to pick it up. It didn't matter that this entire stretch of magnificent Apache pines might soon be dotted with construction markers. Ellen had too much respect for nature to let any man-made trash spoil the pristine ambience. She wasn't sure that her partner felt the same way; in fact, all she really knew about John Neff after three days as his rod man on her first field survey for Zamazanic & Eagleton Consulting Engineers was that she desperately wished she'd been teamed with somebody else.

But one glance at the rusty tin forced Ellen to exonerate John, who was only two years older than her first-born son and had surely been a child when the can first fell to the ground.

As she squatted to retrieve the rusty can, Ellen's forty-four-year-old muscles, already shaky from an endless day hiking, measuring and recording these steep ridges and draws, seemed to groan in protest. Once Ellen had been as limber as John—who had fairly galloped up the last hill to beat her into the cabin—but that was before twenty-five years as a housewife, three difficult pregnancies and two surgeries for a slipped disc in her lower back.

All things considered, it had not been a terrific day. In fact, the only good thing Ellen had to say for it was that she herself had chosen to live it this way. And that small victory—no, that enormous, incalculably marvelous victory!—seemed to make it all worthwhile.

Ignoring her creaking bones, she reached for the can and was surprised to find it firmly wedged in the wet ground. Apparently it had been buried until the week's rain had washed away enough top soil to allow it to protrude. Ellen took hold of the visible top with both hands and tugged, only to find the can veritably glued to the waterlogged soil. All that came up was the yellow plastic lid.

"Oh, come on, Ellen!" she groused at herself, wondering why those thrice-weekly workouts at the Kansas City gym had done so little to strengthen her biceps. "How hard can it be to pull one lousy can out of the ground?"

In the old days—three years ago...four?—she would not have made a further attempt. She would have called Howard or one of the boys, or simply waited until her "men" got home. None of them expected her to do anything that wasn't strictly "women's work"; none of them wanted her to. Certainly none of them wanted her camping out in a drafty old mining cabin while she surveyed a forest, nor did any of them—especially Howard—understand why on earth she'd left the oppressive security of her posh midwestern home to take on such a physically demanding job in southern California. But then again, Howard had never understood any of her dreams. He'd only understood her fears. In fact, he had worked hard to *create* them.

Thrusting away the dark memories of life with her ex, Ellen reached for the can again, perplexed by how firmly it was wedged. But just as her hands cupped the sides, she realized that the coffee can wasn't an ordinary piece of discarded trash. It was heavy because it had a very large rock inside.

But it wasn't the greenish-black rock that quickened Ellen's pulse, nor the neatly folded newspaper page. She also bypassed the soggy business card clipped to it as she tugged out the real prize. To the untrained eye, it was just a collection of wiggly lines on yellowed paper, but to a proud possessor of a recent degree in geography, it was obviously a blurred photocopy of a geological map. It had no title, but after surveying every nook and cranny of this area on her blistered feet, Ellen was certain that she'd be able to figure out the exact piece of ground represented by the map...and the secret that made it special.

Unwilling to sacrifice her discovery to the rain, Ellen grabbed the can and hurried inside the cabin. She knew that her find wasn't really enough to justify the sudden upswing in her mood, but the simple truth was that she was lonely at night when John disappeared over the hill to see his girlfriend at the forest service camp, and an enticing little mystery was just the thing to chase her blues away. She loved reading detective stories and watching them on TV; she always kept a

crossword puzzle by her bed and a thousand-piece jig-
saw puzzle on a card table in the kitchen. Tracing the
source of this buried map would be just her cup of tea.

Under the dim light of the Coleman lantern, she
studied the squiggly lines. They revealed pockets and
veins of assorted geological material, coded to a legend on the right. Unfortunately, most of the legend had
dissolved in subsoil moisture, and about all she was
sure of was which side of the map pointed north.

"What do you make of this, John?" she asked the
young man who was pumping up the gas in the porta-
ble tabletop stove. He was of medium height and medium build, still struggling to feel at ease with a woman
old enough to be his mother.

He raised his eyebrows without much interest.
"Make of what?" he asked.

She handed him the map. "I found this in a rusty old
coffee can outside."

He gave the wilted paper a cursory glance. "It's a
geological map. Probably tossed out when somebody
else stayed here during some other survey. I think some
previous owner had Z & E—" he used their firm's
common nickname "—check this site out for possible
development about twenty or thirty years ago. And the
first railroad survey was done way back in 1948."

"I know," Ellen repeated tersely, not appreciating
the way he said "1948," as though it were the high
point of the western movement instead of the year of
her birth. "But this map wasn't just tossed out at random, John. I found this newspaper neatly folded beside it." As she pulled off the paper clip that held the
newspaper and the business card together, the card
flipped over on the table. On the back were scrawled

the words "Has to stop... fault." There was probably
more to the original note, but the pencil marks were
badly faded and the edges of the card were shredded
off. "I got the feeling they were all buried together for
some reason."

He shrugged. "What's in the newspaper? A story
about a fire up here or something?"

She scanned the paper quickly. Moisture had eaten
away at the folded edges, but most of it was still legi-
ble. The front side included a random collection of articles: the foreclosure of a local bank, a gushy write-up
on a young girls' basketball team, and the donation to
the Westhope Historical Museum of some nonagenar-
ian's turn-of-the-century clothes. On the backside was
a full page ad for a massive new development of "luxury" houses, with a streak of red crayon next to the
tiny street map. The curious mixture of subject matter
suggested the pages were probably from a small-town
weekly, but Ellen couldn't find the name of the newspaper or the date. She did, however, find several references to Westhope, a rural community not too far
from Bentbow.

Bentbow was home not only to the headquarters of
Zamazanic & Eagleton, but also to the numerous
county offices with which the firm did business. It was
also the location of a two-bedroom apartment that was
currently stacked with Ellen's half-unpacked boxes but
didn't yet feel at all like home.

"Nothing about Chumash Mountain or Bentbow
National Forest at all," she told John, who was now
heating up some soup on the Coleman stove. She didn't
need to ask if he'd thought to make some for her. If she
didn't eat for a week he wouldn't be likely to notice it.

Ellen picked up the business card and read out loud, "Reed Capwell, Assistant Planner, Environmental Resources Agency, County of Bentbow." She peered at John expectantly. "Mean anything to you?"

"Nope. Of course I haven't been with Z & E long enough to know all the guys at County. Or he might be somebody new."

Ellen shook her head. "Oh, I doubt that. In fact, he's probably long gone by now. I'd guess this stuff has been buried for a good twenty years."

Plopping his steaming bowl of soup down on top of the fragile newspaper, John asked, "How's that?"

Ellen picked up the bowl, retrieved her prize and thrust the flip side of the paper at him. She pointed to the price advertised for the luxury houses. "Nowadays you couldn't buy a driveway for $50,000 in L.A., let alone a magnificent five-bedroom house on a half-acre lot! The price of the houses alone give the age of the paper away."

John shrugged. "I guess you'd know."

It was just a casual comment, but it reminded Ellen all too keenly of her age. Ellen didn't think that John actively disliked her; he made no particular effort to act obnoxious. He was just a self-centered young man who had better things to do with his time than worry about the feelings of a woman old enough to be his mother, and he was probably bored and slightly embarrassed by their temporary assignment as a team.

As she took the items from the coffee can and retreated to her sleeping bag by the cold fireplace where logs had yet to be laid, she asked herself, for the thousandth time, if she'd made a terrible mistake insisting on fieldwork at Z & E. The twenty-five years she'd spent out of the work force, under Howard's thumb, were lost to her; they could never be regained. She was older now, her body grew tired more easily, and she had nothing in common with the other rookies at the firm—all in their twenties—who relished climbing hill and dale all day. And, when night fell in the mountains, she was lonely. In fact, with only young John for company during her work hours, she was also lonely during the day.

She shook off the maudlin feelings and reminded herself what she was about. She'd spent too many years seething with resentment as she rattled about in her cotton-candy cage to give up now! Here, in this wild terrain, she was free. Free to work hard, free to cope with loneliness in her own way, free to pat herself on the back at the end of a long day in her chosen field because she'd done the job she wanted to do, and done it very well.

As John wandered off into the night after an indifferent farewell, Ellen picked up the can again and pondered its contents. Nothing had been stuffed inside in a casual manner. Each item had been neatly placed as though whoever had buried it expected it to be unearthed again—which either meant that somebody had intended to come back for this impromptu underground file, or intended for somebody else to dig it up later. As Ellen studied the note again, she realized that it could either have been a message from the man whose name was on the front of it or a message that somehow involved him. In any event, whoever had written the words seemed to be confessing to something…or maybe casting the blame on somebody else, somebody who might be long dead and buried by now.

Suddenly she sat upright. Of course! How obvious! It was a time capsule! A message from days gone by. Memories of—she plucked the moist and muddy business card and squinted through the cabin's dusk at the small print once more—Reed Capwell! Whoever he was.

A fresh wash of excitement whisked away the rest of Ellen's aches and pains. Of all the puzzles she'd ever tackled, none could compare with this! She'd read about time capsules, of course, and seen a fascinating show or two that dealt with them. But she'd never met anybody who'd left one buried, let alone somebody who'd found one in the ground!

Suddenly Ellen knew that she *had* to find out everything there was to know about her hidden treasure. Not just the area covered by the map, but the significance of the note and the newspaper page. Which one of those articles had been crucial to the man who'd buried this? Or had he merely been trying to capture the flavor of the period? How unfortunate that the date had rotted off! And not one of the articles specified a date. Obviously a young girls' basketball team would have played in the winter, but the games were reported as "last weekend" and "the Saturday before last."

She wondered how old Reed Capwell had been when he'd buried this collection of memories. She wondered how old he'd be now. She wondered if anybody at the County would remember him. Thank God he'd left her his card as a clue! On Friday, when she was scheduled to return to Bentbow for the weekend, she had planned to stop by the County offices for some old railroad maps of Chumash Mountain. While she was there she could ask if anybody remembered Reed Capwell.

With him or without him, she vowed to ferret out the site of the map... and whatever secrets might be hidden there.

"HONEY, I DON'T REALLY think you need a new car," Reed Capwell patiently counseled his stepdaughter as he gripped the phone with one hand and rubbed his greying temple with the other. "I know you're really trying, but I'm already paying for your apartment and school expenses. And I think—"

"But Daddy, you know I can't concentrate on school if I'm worried about anything!"

Reed rolled his eyes, grateful that Jackie couldn't see him. Her repertoire of excuses for her shortcomings was quite extensive, and he didn't bother to analyze her reasons anymore. She was a good kid, but she was slow coming to adulthood, despite her short-lived marriage. The boy she'd chosen was as immature as she was, and had an infant daughter by a previous marriage to boot. Jackie adored the little girl, as did Reed and his ex-wife, and they were glad that Jackie's ex still let her bring Sherry over to visit from time to time. But Jackie's efforts to play wife and mother were largely a thing of the past, and at present all Reed wanted was for her to grow up. Yet he couldn't bear the thought of tossing her out of the nest.

He had always bent over backward to be a perfect parent, a goal that was doomed to failure. His shortcomings in that regard would not have bothered him so much if he hadn't made a deathbed promise to Jackie's father to take care of her... or if she hadn't become so precious to him in the years that had passed since then.

"But Jackie, your Camaro is only nine years old," Reed reiterated patiently. "My T-Bird has been going strong for twenty-six—"

"But you're a *man,* Daddy!" Jackie wailed. "You know how to fix it if anything goes wrong. And if you're stranded somewhere it's not nearly as dangerous!"

Straight for the Achilles' heel, he told himself, recognizing her skillful ploy but not certain how to work around it. The truth was that he did worry about her safety—and he would even if she were driving a brand new car. He was grateful when he heard a knock on his office door.

"Come in!" he called out, then said to Jackie, "Somebody's here to see me, honey. Gotta go. We'll talk later. I love you." He hung up before she could start to wheedle him again.

With a quick smile he greeted his spunky, redheaded secretary, Sandi Ipswitch, who'd been at the County almost as long as he had. At the moment she was grinning one of those boy-have-I-got-news-for-you smiles that heralded a new piece of office gossip. Sandi considered it her duty to keep Reed informed of such juicy tidbits; otherwise, he would have been totally oblivious to the daily scuttlebutt.

"Well?" he prodded with a smile.

Sandi laughed. "There's somebody here to see you, Assistant Planner Capwell."

Reed, whose official title was now Supervising Planner, Residential Permits Section, hadn't heard that designation in years. He cocked one eyebrow and asked, "What's the punch line?"

"There isn't one. This isn't a joke." Despite her denial, she was grinning. "There's a very attractive female at my desk. Personnel sent her over here when she asked if they had any records on an assistant planner named Reed Capwell. She's even got one of your cards."

"One of my assistant planner cards?" He was stunned. "I don't even have any of those left. I haven't been an assistant in—" he tried to remember "—hell, Sandi, probably twenty years!"

"Seventeen, to be precise," she corrected him. "And the card in her hand looks every day of it."

Reed was intrigued. "Does she seem, uh, normal?"

"You mean, is she some *Fatal Attraction*-type female who's going to tell the whole office that you secretly married her twenty years ago and forgot to mention your six kids to Clara?"

The sudden vision of the shock on his ex-wife's face made Reed laugh out loud. He had a reputation as the world's most reliable old shoe. Nobody—not even Clara, who so often thought the worst of him—would imagine that he had an old buried secret.

He did have one, but it had nothing to do with an attractive American female or with the days when he was an assistant planner. It was a secret he would gladly have given his life to change, but there had never been anything he could do about it.

"Send her in, Sandi," he told his friend. "I've got a meeting at eleven, but I can spare ten or fifteen minutes." It was all he needed to say. He knew he could count on Sandi to discreetly dislodge his visitor in time for the meeting if he had any difficulty doing so.

But a moment later, when the woman in question appeared in his doorway, he had the strange feeling that telling Sandi to bail him out later had been a mistake.

"Mr. Capwell?" his visitor asked, sounding perplexed. Her gray eyes sparkled with verve, and her smile was gracious and subdued. She looked about his age, though her shoulder-length hair was dark and wavy, and his was already leaning toward gray. She was wearing a clean pair of jeans and a turquoise camp shirt, topped with a black ski parka. He couldn't get much of an impression of her figure, but he had no trouble registering that she was all female. "I didn't expect to find you here after all these years."

He wasn't sure what to say. If she called him "Mr. Capwell," they couldn't have been close friends, let alone lovers. And he certainly had had no lovers—except for Clara—between the time he'd come home from Vietnam and last year when Clara had finally left him. Actually, no woman had roused his passion since he'd lost Su Le.

Reed struggled to remember some nuance of this new woman's appealing features, but he was certain that they'd never met.

He stood up and held out his hand. "I'm sorry, Ms...."

"Andrews. Ellen Andrews." Her shake was firm, confident. Her hands were unpampered—freshly blistered—yet subtly feminine. "We haven't met, Mr. Capwell. I didn't mean to give your secretary the impression that we had."

He motioned for her to sit down, and he did likewise. "She said I'd given you a business card...many years ago."

Ellen shook her head. "I *found* your business card."

As she handed it to him, he decided that Sandi was right; it looked as though it had spent a decade or two in a landfill. He couldn't imagine why Ellen Andrews had bothered to track him down. People stumbled upon old phone messages or business cards all the time, didn't they? At least if they kept house the way he did.

"It looks like mine. It's been so long since I was an assistant planner that I don't remember exactly how my card was printed, but I see no reason to question its authenticity."

She chuckled, showing firm white teeth. For a moment her eyes danced, and the sight made Reed want to do some dancing, too. "I'm not questioning its authenticity, Mr. Capwell—"

"Reed," he corrected her.

"Reed." She followed his lead easily, still smiling. "I just happened to be in the building today and thought I'd see if I could find some trace of you. I didn't think you'd still be working here."

That much made sense to him. What didn't was why she'd come looking for him in the first place.

"You see, I'm currently doing a Chumash Mountain site survey for Zamazanic & Eagleton." She paused expectantly. When Reed did not respond, she finished on a note of triumph, "I'm staying at an old mining cabin up there. I found this—" she tapped the card in his hand "—in a coffee can out back!"

She perched on the edge of her chair with such enthusiasm that Reed began to feel uncomfortable. She obviously had no doubt that he would understand her reference to this old cabin in the Chumash Mountain area, but he had no idea what she was talking about.

The County often contracted Z & E for specific sections of environmental impact reports, and he was quite friendly with about half a dozen members of the large staff. But he'd never done any work related to Chumash Mountain. In fact, he'd never even been there—except for a camping trip in Bentbow National Forest when Jackie and his son had been in elementary school.

Apparently sensing his inability to recall anything important about Chumash Mountain, Ellen leaned forward and flipped over the card in his hand. He could barely make out the words, but he could tell that he hadn't written them. "'Has to stop'," he quoted. "Looks like 'my fault' or 'your fault,' but the card's torn there. In any case, it's not my handwriting, Ellen. And if I ever received a note like this, I don't recall it."

Ellen stared at him soberly. "A note on the back of a card is usually written by the person whose name is on the front of it."

"Not this time," he repeated. "Any number of people could have had access to my business card. If one of them was working on a project up there—or even camping nearby—I guess they could have tossed my card into the trash."

Disappointment instantly darkened Ellen's lovely eyes. The dark wavy hair feathered her jawline enticingly as she shook her head. "No, it wasn't in the trash. It was in a time capsule with some other interesting things—a geological map, some newspaper stories and a big rock to hold the whole thing down."

Reed's mouth dropped open just a tad. "A *time* capsule? Why on earth would anybody put my old business card in a time capsule?"

Ellen shrugged, looking sheepish now. "I don't know. I thought you would know. I mean, I figured it was *your* time capsule. It seemed like something that a young man would do. My sons are about the age of my partner up there—" the tightening in her voice revealed that she had mixed feelings about the man "—and I can see any of them leaving behind a memory of their manly youth."

He watched her closely to see if she were teasing, but he wasn't certain. She didn't look old enough to have adult children, but maybe that was because her outfit looked so fresh, so casual, compared to some of the high-powered suits and dresses he so often saw in the bureaucratic business world. There was something else youthful about her. Something that gave him the feeling that she was just starting out.

Suddenly he realized why. If she was assigned to Chumash Mountain doing fieldwork, she was a novice, and it was very rare to find a novice in her forties. How long had this woman been working? When had she gotten her degree?

Quickly he dismissed the questions. Ellen Andrews' background had nothing to do with the situation at hand. In fact, there wasn't even a "situation" to be dealt with. There was only a very attractive woman sitting in his office moments before he was due at a meeting. She had a mildly intriguing mystery that she wanted to solve, but it was hardly something that required his attention.

It was the woman herself, not the mystery, that aroused Reed's curiosity. Her assignment of fieldwork at Chumash Mountain—a controversial piece of land that its owner hoped to develop as a hot springs resort—was in itself an anomaly. A woman her age doing fieldwork *period* was pretty unusual. Working up in the mountains with one partner and no phone didn't seem appropriate to him, let alone safe. He certainly wouldn't have allowed his daughter, let alone his wife, to do it. Of course, Clara had always chafed under his "cloying chauvinism" as she'd disparagingly referred to his concern. She'd always accused him of treating her like a child.

She'd never understood that all he'd ever wanted was to keep her safe. It was a promise Reed had made, not to Clara, but to Nathan, and if he'd failed in his endeavor, it wasn't from lack of will.

He had also failed to satisfy Ellen Andrews' curiosity; that much was certain. He wanted to tell her something that would make her feel that she hadn't wasted her time in tracking him down, but he couldn't think of much to say. After all, he didn't owe her any favors, and her quest was hardly a matter of life and death.

"Do you recall what projects you worked on when you were an assistant planner?" she suddenly asked. "That might be a place to start."

Reed tried to recall and came up empty. He had a notoriously poor memory; Clara harangued him about it all the time. He'd have been hard-pressed to recall what project he'd been working on last year at this time, let alone in the late sixties.

"Sorry," he told her honestly. "I work on twenty or thirty projects a year. I could have given my assistant planner card to a half-dozen people during every project. I have no idea who they might have been."

"There must be some way to find out," Ellen persisted gently. "Can't you check your old files?"

There was a quiet urgency to her words that startled Reed. Again he studied her face, trying to read the curious blend of innocence and experience he saw there. And trying to understand why it affected him.

"Ellen," he said kindly, "I suppose I could dig through the fifty or sixty cases I handled as an assistant and come up with some names, but it would take a lot of work. If somebody's life inheritance hung in the balance, or the police needed to solve a murder, I'd be willing to take the time. But just to satisfy your personal curiosity as to why my old business card ended up in a coffee can in the mountains?" He shook his head. "I just can't see it. Can you?"

He regretted the words as soon as they left his mouth, because a slow crimson stain bloomed on Ellen's cheeks. He knew he'd humiliated her, which hadn't been his intent. He was just a busy man, with too many things on his mind to indulge in historical fantasies. Even for a very appealing female.

But that very appealing female was suddenly looking fragile...almost wounded. Reed didn't know why this time capsule thing was important to her, let alone why her feelings should be important to *him*. But he never could bear to see a woman unhappy, and it was obvious that he'd stripped all the magic from this one's pretty eyes today.

He was struggling to come up with some way of making amends when Sandi knocked on the door and poked her head in. "I'm sorry to interrupt, Mr. Capwell," she announced with the mock formality she used to impress strangers, "but Mr. Hawkson is waiting for you in the conference room."

Ian Hawkson was the section's newest employee—an assistant planner preparing for his first presentation to the board of supervisors—but Sandi said his name as though he were some powerful curmudgeon whom only Reed could placate. Taking the hint, Ellen rose at once.

"I don't want to keep you, Mr. Capwell," she said quickly, almost, but not quite, concealing her disappointment. "Thank you for your time." She barely met his eyes as she shook his hand and stepped away.

The feel of her soft but sturdy fingers lingered against Reed's skin as he said apologetically, "I'm sorry I couldn't be of more help, Ellen." Before he could stop himself, he added, "And it's still Reed."

Her eyes widened for just a second. Her glance seemed to take in his whole face—silver-sprinkled brown hair in need of trimming, glasses that were due to be replaced. She seemed to regret the end of their meeting as much as he did.

"Reed," she said softly.

Long after she'd left him, he could still hear an echo of the way she said his name.

BY THE TIME ELLEN retrieved the old railroad grading maps for Chumash Mountain—the reason for her trip to the County office—it was nearly lunch time. Since she wasn't expected back at the Z & E office until one-thirty, she decided to drive over to nearby Westhope—population six thousand and four—to check out the weekly newspaper.

She found its offices sandwiched between a mom-and-pop shoe store and a homey dress boutique on the main street of what looked like a turn-of-the-century town. On the front window, Westhope Herald was hand-painted in old-fashioned script, right under the proud announcement, Serving the Community for Over a Decade.

Ellen did some quick mental arithmetic and realized that the *Herald* might not have been in business when the time capsule was buried, but on the other hand, she hadn't asked Reed Capwell exactly how long he'd served as assistant planner. Shrugging, she decided it was worth a try.

The front office of the *Herald* was full of computer terminals, stacks of printouts and mounds of newspapers. Several phones were scattered across half a dozen mismatched tables. The desk next to the front counter was empty, but near the back a fashionably dressed woman in her forties held a receiver between her shoulder and her ear as she took fervent notes with one hand and tapped nervously on the rim of a photograph with her other. It was a picture of a lovely young woman about the age of Ellen's sons.

She glanced up at Ellen, grinned a merry hello and mouthed the words, "I'll be right with you." Ellen smiled as she leaned against the counter, deciding it would be more courteous to face the outer window and watch the world go by than to stare at the woman as she talked on the phone.

Alone with her thoughts, she found herself replaying those few moments with Reed Capwell. Despite his courtesy, the interview had been a disaster, and the memory of it left her flushed.

It didn't help any that the man was so appealing. He'd struck her as a kind man, a man of simple tastes...a man who was casually attractive and utterly oblivious to it. Any fool could see he wasn't married—a wife would have made sure that he didn't wear a shirt that had been stuck crookedly on a hanger and jammed in the closet so long it had an angled crease across the front pocket. And she would have made sure he got new glasses when they started to wobble, and kept after him to cut his hair.

Ellen knew that Reed hadn't meant to belittle her, but it had been evident that he found her interest in the time capsule somewhat amusing, and his secretary had hinted broadly that Ellen's frivolous inquiries were taking up time from his busy day. She knew that both of them wondered why the time capsule was so important to her; so did John. But she wasn't about to explain that she had never been able to leave a puzzle unsolved. Let alone that spending night after night alone in a gaslit mountain cabin—or worse yet, spending it with a young man who made it clear that he'd sooner have shared his dwelling with an iguana—was bringing her down, as her sons would say. So were the weekends alone in her half-settled apartment. She needed something else to keep her occupied.

"So sorry you had to wait," the bubbly brunette greeted Ellen as she hung up the phone. She stood up swiftly and walked the few steps to the front counter. "Carol's out to lunch, and I'm sort of holding down the fort. Did you want to drop off an ad?"

Wanted: information leading to the whereabouts of the person who buried a time capsule at remote Chumash Mountain cabin twenty years ago.

Not a bad idea, Ellen decided as the notion struck her. If worse came to worse, she'd try it.

"Actually, I'm looking for information," she told the pleasant woman. "I found a newspaper with several references to Westhope in a time capsule buried up at Chumash Mountain. I was wondering if anybody here could figure out what year it might have been printed, based on the articles."

Rapt intrigue sparkled in the woman's blue eyes. It was precisely the expression Ellen had hoped to see in Reed Capwell's kind brown eyes but hadn't. "A time capsule! How exciting! You say you found it up on Chumash Mountain?"

Encouraged, Ellen answered her eager questions with all the information she had about the capsule, while the other woman began to scribble notes. Ellen told her about her dead end with Reed, omitting the way his gentle touch and virile voice had left her feeling. And finally she asked if she could look through the old copies of the newspaper for the years in question.

That's when the woman—Shannon Waverly, a longtime reporter for the *Herald,* as it turned out— shook her head. "I'm so sorry, Ellen, but the *Herald* only goes back to '78, and it sounds to me as though you're dealing with the late sixties. You can look through our morgue if you want to, but I don't think you'll find what you're looking for." She paused a moment, tugging off her glasses as she pondered. "Your best bet is to go to the local library and ask for the old copies of the *Trailblazer*. It was the weekly here for almost thirty years and didn't go out of business until about ten years ago. Chances are good that's where that page came from."

The suggestion made good sense, but after Ellen had agreed to let Shannon write up an article about the time capsule for next week's *Herald,* she decided that she should take advantage of the reporter's enthusiasm. Maybe one of the articles would jog her memory. "Have you lived here a long time?" she asked.

Shannon nodded. "All my life."

"Would you mind glancing at this to see if anything rings a bell?"

The other woman grinned. "I thought you'd never ask!"

Returning her smile, Ellen dug out her prize—carefully preserved in a file folder—and showed it to her new friend. Shannon studied it with care, making comments as she read. "I remember the bank foreclosure, and it had to be after 1969 because that's when my sister-in-law quit working there. My daughter played on our girls' basketball team when she was ten or eleven—" she pointed to the picture on her desk as though the beautiful girl were in the room "—but she's not in this team photo, and I don't recognize any of the other girls, so that only eliminates...um, let's see...'76, '77, somewhere in there. Now, as to the museum, dear old Sara Mae Rafferty passed on years and years ago, and her family has given so many things to the museum that I don't think anybody would be likely to remember this particular donation."

Shannon shook her head, then stopped a moment, chewing on the earpiece of her glasses, as she added, "But if anybody would, it'd be old Edwin Thompson. He's been the curator over there forever, and he knows the Rafferty family as well as anybody. You could ask him if he remembers or maybe wrote it down someplace. It's worth a shot."

When another customer came in—a young woman with two whining tots—Ellen thanked Shannon and started to fold up her prize. As she reached the door, Shannon called back, "Look, is there somewhere I can get in touch with you if I find out anything else?"

Ellen gave her a business card, trying not to reveal the burst of pride she experienced. It was ludicrous, but this was the first time in her life she'd ever given anybody such a badge of her professionalism. She ought to send one to Howard, just to prove to him that out in the real world, people took Ellen Andrews seriously.

Then she reminded herself that she was no longer in the business of proving anything to Howard, and all memories of his expectations should be purged from her mind. Surely her disappointment with Reed Capwell's reaction to her inquiries was only a step removed from the old pattern—dependent Ellen longing for the approval of some big strong man.

I don't need Reed Capwell's approval, she told herself fiercely. *I don't need anything from any man.*

But another voice, hidden more deeply within her, squeaked, *But when I solve the mystery of the time capsule, I'll have a reason to go see him again.*

Instantly she extirpated the notion before it had a chance to take root.

IT WAS THE FOLLOWING Thursday afternoon when the puny *Westhope Herald* appeared on the supervisor's desk along with a pile of junk mail. He subscribed to the *L.A. Times* for news, but the *Herald* served two other purposes. Its down-home flavor was entertaining, and its gossip—particularly tidbits unearthed by nosy Shannon Waverly—often lent him ammunition to help get things done. He'd grown rich cutting corners and manipulating the weak. Other people's dirt, he'd often learned, could be translated into cold hard cash. His own dirt he kept tightly undercover. No loose ends. No trouble. Nothing leftover to trip him up.

Which is why he found himself slack-jawed when he read Shannon Waverly's tongue-in-cheek headline: Mapmaker Finds Time Capsule Linking County Official To Mysterious Past.

Actually, it wasn't the headline that left him stunned, but the first paragraph.

Last week, Ellen Andrews, a geographical consultant for Zamazanic & Eagleton Consulting Engineers, discovered a twenty-year-old time capsule near the site for the proposed Chumash Mountain hot springs resort eighty-six miles northeast of Westhope. The rusty coffee can contained several newspaper articles, a real-estate ad, a large, greenish-black rock, a geological map of an unidentified location and a business card for Reed Capwell, supervising planner for the Residential Permits Section of the Planning Department of the Bentbow County Environmental Resources Agency. The soiled business card identifies Mr.

Capwell as an assistant planner, a position he has not held in seventeen years....

The supervisor read the rest of the article with haste, then reviewed it more slowly a second and third time. Reed Capwell and some damn geological map. After all this time! This was one knot he'd been certain would never come unraveled. He'd considered getting rid of Capwell back then, but he'd thought the squealer was lying when he'd claimed that he had told Capwell what he'd discovered and left evidence for him as well. A man facing death is likely to say anything, and the squealer had understood, in those last few seconds, that he was going to die. But the supervisor didn't believe that the man had had time enough to tell Capwell what he knew. Apparently he *had* had time enough to bury his evidence! Maybe he had told Capwell after all!

Had he made a mistake trusting fate... trusting Capwell's ignorance or fear? Should he have killed him, too? At the time, the supervisor had felt that getting rid of both of them would have roused too many suspicions. Capwell was known for his steadiness; nobody would have believed that he'd just up and wandered away. But no one had questioned the fate of the other one.

But he'd left damning evidence behind. Evidence that this snooping newcomer had uncovered and seemed determined to examine!

Maybe Reed Capwell's fear had kept him silent all these years; maybe he'd never known a thing. But it was not a chance that the supervisor could afford to take at this late point in his career. If Capwell showed the slightest interest in Ellen Andrews' "time cap-sule," he would have to be silenced.

As to Ellen Andrews herself, it was unlikely that she'd pursue the subject any further, but the supervisor would have to watch her very closely. If she gave up her treasure hunt before anybody else paid attention to what she'd found, she could live.

CHAPTER TWO

"GOT A REAL CELEBRITY on our hands, don't we, Sandi?" joshed one of the other planners as Reed walked into the office on Friday morning. Bearded Bill Hazlett had been Reed's first supervisor in Residential Permits years before and still treated him a bit avuncularly. Nowadays Bill was running Commercial and Industrial Permits—counting the years to retirement, from what Reed could tell. His underlings called him the "stealth planner" because he was so hard to find. And no wonder; it was common knowledge that the cafeteria was the only place where a diligent case planner could run him to ground, assuming it wasn't the opening day of some benighted species' hunting season.

"I tell you, Sandi, when that skinny ex-GI started to work for me in his salad days I never thought he worked for the CIA." Bill winked at Reed as he sailed on by. "Or is it the FBI?"

Reed managed to grin at Bill; he even managed to grin at the next four or five associates who found their way to his office to make similar jests. By nine o'clock his smile had faded, and he was fairly certain that every damn person who worked in his building had managed to read this week's *Westhope Herald*. A copy was already pinned up on the staff bulletin board with

Reed's name underlined in red. Some jester had added
a blank sheet inviting additional jokes, clues and potential theories; it was already half full.

Shannon Waverly's information about his business
card had been fairly straightforward, and he couldn't
really find much fault with the *Herald's* use of his
name. But he found he was disappointed that the article had told him almost nothing new about Ellen Andrews, except that she was a "recent transplant from
Kansas" and had been working for Z & E for less than
a month.

It had not mentioned her dark wavy hair or quiet,
vibrant smile. It had said nothing about her intriguing
gray eyes. It had shed no light on the fact that he'd felt
a strange tremor each time she'd said his name.

Reed's errant thoughts were cut short by a call from
Jackie shortly after he'd gotten his day's work underway.

"Daddy, my old car broke down!" She was crying,
but he wasn't convinced that her tears were genuine.
He'd had too much experience with the crocodile kind.
"You've got to come get me!"

"Tell me what happened," he asked calmly, fighting the mixture of fear, guilt and resentment that always gripped him at moments like this. He couldn't
bear the idea of Jackie being stranded somewhere, especially at night, and when something like this happened, he always wondered if he should give in and buy
her a new car. But he serviced her Camaro himself—
had done so just two months ago, in fact—so he knew
it was in reasonably good condition. He also knew how
much she wanted a new sports car. He hated to accuse
her of crying wolf, but it was hard to avoid the feeling

that the car's mechanical malfunction was being, well, exaggerated.

"I drove to school in the morning without any problem, but when I came back after my class, it wouldn't start."

"Did it turn over? Idle low? What?"

He was greeted with more sniffles, but no enlightening information. "I don't remember. I just tried a couple of times and it wouldn't go, so I called you."

Reed sighed. He'd have to go fetch her; it was inevitable. "I've got a meeting in ten minutes I really shouldn't miss. Could you go to the library or something for an hour or so?"

Suddenly the tears were history. "Sure, Daddy. No problem. I just need to get Sherry by four o'clock. I only get her till eight, you know."

Reed had no argument for that. Jackie's visits with Sherry were rare, and solely at the whim of her ex-husband. It was vital that she give him no cause for complaint.

"If I can't get the Camaro running, you can borrow my car this afternoon," he offered.

Jackie choked. "You've got to be kidding, Daddy! I wouldn't be caught dead in your old clunker!"

"Hey, it runs," he insisted. He'd explained to Jackie dozens of times that thirty years ago a girl her age would have killed to drive a turquoise T-Bird, but his Beach Boy stories had fallen on deaf ears. She was equally immune to the argument that the classic car had once been her biological father's most prized possession.

It was the death of Jackie's father, Nathan—Clara's first husband, Reed's best army friend—that had brought Clara and Reed together, but it was his memory that had always kept them apart. As Nathan lay dying, Reed had promised to do everything in his power to take care of the wife and baby daughter Nathan was leaving behind, and the easiest way to do that had been to marry Clara. At the time, it had not been a great sacrifice for Reed. She'd been young and pretty and truly nice. And with her, at least, he had not had to hide his sorrow. Besides, at their somber wedding he'd still been too numb by his other loss in Vietnam to imagine himself ever falling in love again. Making a life with Clara made more sense than grieving in solitude.

It had been enough for Reed, but in time Clara had longed for more than he could give her. No matter how lovingly he carried out his role as her husband and lover, he could not force himself to love her the way he had loved Su Le. Even the birth of their son, Nate, had not changed his feelings.

"I tell you what, Jack. I'll take you out to lunch and we can talk about cars," Reed conceded reticently. "I'll pick you up at the library at twelve."

"Oh, Daddy, you're the greatest!" she gushed before she hung up the phone.

Reed growled at himself as he gathered up the papers for his meeting. "I'm doing my best, Nathan," he said softly, fighting memory's knot in his stomach.

There was no one in the room.

IT WAS A SLUSHY, sloshy Friday morning when Ellen ducked into the lobby of the County offices—exactly a week since her last visit. This time she'd dropped by to pick up a list of owners of properties adjoining the Chumash Mountain site, since she and John were spreading out toward the south and would soon be close enough to some outlying summer cabins to cause some possible consternation. The smart thing to do was to avoid any problems by notifying everyone of their whereabouts in advance.

She'd spent the previous weekend unpacking, so she hadn't made any progress unraveling the capsule mystery. Secretly, Ellen had been hoping that Shannon Waverly's article might flush somebody out of the woodwork. She'd read the story last night and had no complaints. If anybody knew anything about the capsule, there was certainly enough information there to let them know it was time to come forward.

But Shannon had left a message on Ellen's answering machine reporting that while everyone was intrigued by the time capsule, nobody had any clues as to where it had come from. "If you find out anything, be sure to drop by and let me know," Shannon's cheery voice had urged her.

Well, she didn't know anything yet, but she was determined to find something out this weekend. She was just thinking about her first clue—Reed Capwell's card—when her eyes widened at the sight of Reed himself. He looked much the way he had when she'd seen him last—boyishly dimpled and slightly rumpled. But the last time she'd seen Reed he'd been sitting behind a desk, and she hadn't had the pleasure of watching him move.

And it *was* a pleasure. His legs were Tom Selleck-long, and he moved with the easy grace of one who spends a lot of time outdoors. Ellen was surprised. She'd expected a County bureaucrat to be a genuine couch potato.

Ellen noticed his new glasses—dark, distinctive frames that added character to his handsome face— and realized that she was entirely too pleased to see him. After all, they were likely to have professional dealings from time to time. Considering the silly impression she'd made on him at their last meeting, it would hardly do for him to find her gawking at him like a love-struck teen.

Ellen couldn't decide whether it would be better to speak to Reed or pass by unnoticed, but she was certain that the choice would be hers. The last thing she expected was for him to spot her and break into a wide grin.

"Ellen!" he greeted her, as though they were old friends. "Back for more clues?"

Ellen wasn't sure just why he was grinning so broadly, and she wasn't sure she liked it. Oh, she loved his smile—it ranked up there with fudge brownies—but she wasn't sure whether he was grinning with her or laughing *at* her.

"I'm here on business, Mr. Capwell," she said almost coolly. "I need a landowners' list for the parcels adjacent to the Chumash Mountain site. Don't want anybody shooting us as trespassers, you know."

His smile melted so quickly that Ellen regretted her frosty tone. Had he been smiling just because he was glad to see her?

He pointed to the left. "Down that hall, third door to your right." His tone had no expression, and he didn't tell her to call him "Reed" again.

Against all logic, Ellen felt compelled to bring back that magic smile. Wildly she tried to think of a topic that would pull down the bars he'd just snapped into place, but all she could think of was Shannon Waverly's article. "I hope you didn't mind becoming a local celebrity," she gently teased him. "I didn't expect Shannon to tell everybody your whole life history when I told my story to the *Herald*."

He shrugged, and a ghost of a smile reappeared. At least tiny parentheses creased the sides of his invitingly curved lips. "Actually, she didn't reveal a single secret. She didn't even call my ex-wife, who might have been able to provide a few embarrassing details."

This time it was Ellen who smiled sympathically. "Hostile split, huh?"

Reed shook his head. "Not really. We get along all right." This time Reed's smile was vibrant enough to make her tremble just a little, and she knew he'd forgotten whatever she'd said to cool his earlier enthusiasm. "Do you have a family, Ellen? The *Herald* article said you've just come to California."

It was a rather clumsy way to ask if she was married, but Ellen didn't mind. "I'm single now, but I have three grown children," she admitted. "They all live in Kansas and couldn't imagine why I wanted to leave the state. But I was sick and tired of snow, and sick and tired of living wherever my ex-husband had in mind, so I decided to head out for somewhere new. I was offered an entry-level job at Z & E with long-term career possibilities, so here I am."

To her surprise, Reed looked impressed. "I take it you're...not just filling in your spare time."

Ellen glowered at him, only partly in jest. "I may be starting late, Reed, but I'm planning to make up for all those years I spent wiping noses while my male peers were launching themselves in promising careers. Survey work may not seem very glamorous, but I have to earn my stripes in the field before I can expect to be promoted to a managerial position. Otherwise, no one would ever take me seriously.''

The look on his face made it clear that he was taking her seriously now. In fact, he seemed to be taking her a whole lot more seriously than he had a week ago.

''Ellen,'' he said quietly, ''I suspect that your supervisor knows he's very lucky to get a woman like you for a rookie's pay and will be quick to boost you up the ladder. If by chance he doesn't, a couple of years with a prestigious consulting firm like Z & E will give you what you need to get a good job elsewhere.''

Ellen should have felt flattered, and, in a way, she was. But still, there was something about Reed's professional interest that left her feeling flat...something she couldn't quite name. Again she noticed the quiet depths of his mahogany eyes and the beguiling curve of his lips. She was just beginning to imagine what it would be like to *feel* those lips on her own when she realized what was happening.

She wasn't thinking of Reed Capwell as a fellow professional. She was hankering for him as a man!

It was an unsettling thought, one she might have had to deal with on the spot if it hadn't been for the sudden arrival of a young man in blue jeans who bolted through the lobby door and called to the nearby security guard, ''Hey! There's a car out here with its windshield smashed to smithereens! You better come look!''

Ellen felt a lurch of panic as she remembered how close her own car—a spanking new Honda Accord—was parked to the building. It was the first car she'd ever picked out entirely on her own, and she'd even taken a Car Care for Women class before she'd left Kansas to make sure that she could do for the Accord what Howard had always done for all the cars she'd had before. She babied it as though it were a handicapped child, and the thought of it suffering anything more than the brush of a fallen leaf was more than she could bear.

"What kind of a car is it?" she blurted out, as though the young man had been speaking directly to her.

"It's a T-Bird. Real old. Turquoise, no less."

Ellen swallowed deeply before she turned back to Reed. But her relief was shortlived; as she watched, his complexion grayed and the luster in his eyes died. "I've got a turquoise T-Bird in that lot," she heard him mutter, not so much to her as to himself.

"Maybe it's not yours, Reed," Ellen suggested, suddenly ashamed of her selfishness. But she already knew that the chances of any public parking lot sporting two old turquoise T-Birds were practically nil.

Reed did not actually run to the parking lot, even so, she could barely keep up with his urgent, long-legged stride.

When they reached the car—ahead of both the young man and the guard—she didn't need to ask who owned it. Reed's countenance said it all. The car was old—it looked like a prop from an Elvis movie—but obviously cherished. Reed moaned softly and caressed the front bumper as though it were a wounded friend.

The exterior was okay, but the windshield was a mess. In fact, there was no windshield, just a splintered frame of glass around a huge, gaping hole. Inside, a dozen savage knife cuts lacerated the faded dash.

On the driver's seat teetered a cantaloupe-size, greenish-black rock that looked vaguely familiar to Ellen. She wondered if it triggered any memories for Reed.

REED RAISED ONE HAND in tepid greeting when the burgundy sedan pulled into the County parking lot. With one last troubled look at his T-Bird, he opened the sedan's passenger door and slipped inside.

The woman driving the car did not greet him. She did not smile. She didn't even wait for him to put his seat belt on before she swung back through the rows of cars toward the main thoroughfare.

Her blond hair was short, crisp and stylish. The pale green eyes that matched her ruffled blouse looked stern. Two fleshy arms gripped the steering wheel in an irritated gesture that was all too familiar to Reed.

As the sedan sailed past Sandi, who still kept watch over his injured car, Reed waved without enthusiasm.

Clara did the same. "I hope to God you've called somebody to tow that thing away for good," she said quietly, her voice a hoarse mixture of frustration and relief.

Reed shook his head, hoping they could avoid this argument. *God knows, we've both got each other's lines memorized,* he told himself. *No point in staging a rerun today.*

"Sandi found a body repair place that can fix it, Clara. Oldies But Goodies, or something like that."

Clara groaned. "Reed, the damn thing is dead. Why don't you bury it?"

They both knew she wasn't really talking about Nathan's T-Bird.

"I can't," Reed told her.

A thousand times they'd gone over this ground, each trying to make the other understand the way he or she had come to terms with Nathan's death. Reed had dealt with it by clinging to every memory of Nathan. Clara had coped by letting him go.

It was one of the reasons their marriage had not worked out. That and the fact that they had married for the wrong reasons.

Reed tried to remember just what he'd said to Ellen Andrews when she'd asked about his divorce this morning. All he could recall was that she had initially greeted him coolly, but had later warmed up considerably. They had been engaged in pleasant conversation before the kid had come charging in from the parking lot. Reed didn't remember a thing after that.

Had he said goodbye to Ellen? Probably not. Just his luck. Fate had handed him a second chance to get to know this very appealing woman; then snatched it away.

Reed knew how to get in touch with Ellen, but he wasn't at all sure that he should. He really didn't know her well enough to ask her out. Hell, she still called him "Mr. Capwell" half the time! There had to be some other way to "accidentally" further their acquaintance.

Clara interrupted his thoughts as she made a precise right turn onto the highway. "I saw the article about your business card."

"You and everybody else I know."

She almost smiled. "I thought you'd want to ask me what you were doing back then. I've always been your memory."

It was an odd way of putting it, but Reed knew what she meant. Clara was one of those people who could cheerfully remember the moment their son had cut his first tooth, the exact location of Jackie's last speeding ticket, the date she and Reed started escrow on their first house. They both knew the reason he hadn't asked her about his assistant planner years: he'd actually stopped thinking of her as his wife.

"Well, do you remember anything special about my first few years at the County?" If Clara came up with anything out of the ordinary, Reed would have a good excuse to call Ellen and pass on the information.

"Jackie started kindergarten two months after your first promotion," Clara informed him. "You were tickled pink to be moving over to Special Projects because all you'd done in Residential was work on Manzanita Meadows."

Reed studied her for a moment, trying to recall. Manzanita Meadows was a huge planned development—virtually a private town—that he'd inherited from his predecessor when he'd started working for the County. He'd told Ellen that, as a case planner, he'd normally handled twenty or thirty cases a year—which was true—but during the Manzanita Meadows years, he'd handled only Manzanita Meadows.

He tried to recall Ellen's description of the contents of the time capsule to decide if Manzanita Meadows might be a clue, but he couldn't remember anything but the curious blend of softness and strength in her gray eyes when she'd told him about her discoveries.

"Anything else?" he prodded Clara.

"Not that I know of. I suppose you might have some secret I never found out about."

Reed chuckled. "Not a chance. You could root up a secret I didn't even know I had!"

A year ago, bitterness would have poisoned the line, but now Clara responded with a smile. "It wasn't all bad, Reed," she said kindly.

He nodded. "It wasn't bad at all."

It hadn't been particularly good, either, but there was no point in bringing that up again. He'd always liked Clara and respected her, but he certainly had never fallen in love with her. She had deserved his affection, craved his desire, worked desperately, during the early years, to fill up the dark spaces in his heart. And he'd tried to let her in—really he had—but for some reason the miracle had never come to pass. Her bitterness had once been a source of great pain to both of them. But now they could act like the friends they really were.

After a comfortable moment of silence, Reed said, "I'm sorry." He was referring to his request, relayed through Sandi, for Clara to come fetch him on her day off. He was also sorry about lots of other things.

"It's okay, Reed." Her voice was gentle. "Sandi said Jackie was waiting for you at school. She's having trouble with her Camaro?"

He shrugged. "She says she is. I'll lay you five to one odds it'll start right up when I get there."

Clara glared at him sternly. "Has she been badgering you about another new car?"

"Well, I don't know if 'badgering' is exactly the right—"

"Dammit, Reed! Don't do it. Don't give in to her again."

He floundered. "If there's really a problem with it, Clara—"

"There isn't and you know it. If it were Nate who was having trouble, you'd pay for a tune-up and that would be the end of it."

It was true, so he didn't deny it. Fortunately, he didn't need to explain to Clara or to Nate, that he loved the boy no less than he loved Jackie. But Nate was a man, albeit a young one, and he'd always shown good sense. He was his own rudder. Jackie needed somebody to prop her up from time to time.

"I'm just going to look at the Camaro, Clara. You don't want her to have car trouble while she's going to get Sherry tonight, do you?"

Clara rolled her eyes. "If the car needs work, fix it, Reed. But Jackie doesn't need a new car. She needs a job and an apartment that she pays for on her own. Frankly, I sometimes think she'd be better off if you refused to give her another penny and she just had to fend for herself."

It wasn't the first time his ex-wife had voiced this sentiment. It wasn't the first time Reed had voiced his reply. "She wouldn't survive, Clara. You know it. Someday, maybe—"

"Not someday. *Never*. Not until you let her grow up. You've crippled the poor girl just the way you crippled me."

After that Reed fell silent. They'd gotten divorced so they could spare each other these daily arguments; there was no point in replaying all their old tapes, just as there was no point in wondering how Jackie might have turned out if her daddy had come home from the war and Reed had never tried to take over for his friend.

"Please junk that old car, Reed," Clara pleaded, her voice softer now. "For your own sake. Let him go."

In the rational, scientific part of his brain, Reed knew Clara was right. And he knew she'd truly loved her young husband when he'd marched off to war. If he'd come home, she would have been a good wife to Nathan for the next sixty years.

But he hadn't come home, through no fault of Clara's. There was absolutely nothing she could have done to save him.

But Reed had always wondered if there had been something *he* could have done for Nathan.

And something he could have done for Su Le.

BY TWELVE-FIFTEEN, when Ellen left the County offices with her list of landowners, Reed's T-Bird was no longer in the parking lot. All that remained was a pile of broken glass.

Ellen would have gladly sacrificed her lunch hour if Reed had needed her, but since he'd clearly forgotten her existence, she decided to carry out her own plans. Since the Westhope Historical Museum was only open on weekdays between ten and three, she'd planned to dart over there to chat with the curator, Edwin Thompson.

He was a frail-looking man, slightly stooped, wholly bald and poorly shaven. His trifocals were thick, and he wore a hearing aid over his left ear, but his sunshiny smile made him look as though he'd just started life yesterday.

"Is this your first time at the museum, young lady?" he asked Ellen brightly, making her feel as though she were seventeen.

"Yes, sir, I'm new to the area. They tell me over at the paper that you know everything there is to know about this place."

He laughed. It was a soft but somehow sorrowful sound. "The wife 'n' me helped set it up back in '53. She used to help out here before she passed on, God rest her soul. So it just seemed right for me to take over when I quit at the plant. I was foreman there for thirty-three years, you know."

Ellen didn't know—didn't even know what plant he was referring to—but she smiled her interest, anyway. "That's a long time. You must feel very proud of the contributions you made."

His shoulders straightened perceptibly. "Well, I just did my part. That's all anybody can really do, you know? We're all just part of the system. It's all the little fellers doin' their best that makes America great."

Ellen had never thought of it that way. Of course, she'd only been experimenting with her own political thoughts for a few years now, and she still occasionally found herself depending on Howard's beliefs for a quick frame of reference. She knew far more about his opinions than she did about her own.

"Mr. Thompson, I'm interested in seeing the collection of Sara Mae Rafferty's family clothes that were donated to the museum about twenty years ago. Would you know anything about that?"

His sun-leathered face creased into a joyful grin. "I surely would. I knew Sara Mae right well—her younger brother, Robby, was one of my best friends. And I can show you her collection right over here—'' he gestured toward the display case full of clothes rested against the north wall where a beautiful panorama of turn-of-the-century Westhope had been painted right on the wall ''—and even tell you somethin' about most of the clothes. I mean, I remember *seeing* them on some of Sara Mae's kin.''

He beamed so expectantly that Ellen didn't have the heart to tell him that all she wanted to know was the date the clothes had arrived. She listened attentively to his tales about each piece of clothing—some of it dating back to the nineteenth century—and tales of minor interest regarding numerous family members. She even asked a few questions to keep him going. He just looked so happy, so, well *useful,* that she couldn't bear to cut him off, even when he wandered on at length about monster earthquakes and killer floods over the years that had forced structural repairs to the turn-of-the-century Rafferty mansion.

It was a good half hour later when she asked, ''What a marvelous legacy Sara Mae gave to this museum! Do you happen to recall when the Raffertys donated these clothes?''

He looked startled, then stumped. ''Well, now, missy, you've asked me the one question I'm not sure I can answer right off. It was before my Lucy passed on, I'm sure of that, but it was after the kids were grown. I've got four sons and two daughters, you know. Lost one of my boys in the war.''

Ellen didn't ask which war. She murmured sympathetically, and thanked her lucky stars that so far none of her boys had ever had to face military action.

Losing a brother to the war machine had been more than enough.

After Ellen had told Edwin that she had three sons of her own—with her first grandchild due in June—and they'd compared notes on the trials of raising adolescents, she pressed gently, "Do you think there's any way you could find out what year Sara Mae's family turned over this collection? It's really important to me."

For a moment his smile faded, and Ellen was afraid that he'd realized that all of his proud explanations had been of little interest to her. Honesty forced her to tell him everything about the time capsule, adding generously, "Once I solve the mystery, I think it would be only proper to donate the contents of the time capsule to the Westhope Historical Museum."

That whispery smile fluttered back on his face. Ellen wasn't sure whether he'd seen through her act of pity, but even so she was sure that he appreciated her kindness.

"Mr. Thompson," she suggested, "might there be a record somewhere that tells what year these came in?"

Shamefaced, he shrugged. "Lucy used to keep records on all that sort of thing, but they, uh—" his watery blue eyes drifted toward a corner closet "—haven't been, uh, updated in a while."

Ellen's hopes collapsed. She recalled Reed Capwell's reaction when she'd suggested that he go through his mammoth files, and she was certain that the County offices were well organized indeed. Asking this dear old man to search through a closet full of musty boxes that may not have been touched in decades was just too much.

Ellen glanced at her watch and realized that she barely had time to wolf down a hamburger before her weekly one-thirty meeting back at Z & E with John and their project supervisor, Lars Lindroth. "Mr. Thompson, thank you so much for your time," she said briskly. "I've learned so much about the history of the area today. It's just been fascinating."

"My pleasure, missy. If I can think of when Sara Mae's kids turned over those clothes, I'll be sure to let you know."

Ellen handed him a business card—just in case. Sooner or later, he might remember when Sara Mae Rafferty's children donated her clothes.

Ellen was in such a rush to get to her Honda that she almost missed the exhibit of rocks just inside the front door. And she wouldn't have bothered to stop except that number four on her list of things to check out at the library was the time capsule's greenish-black rock. The fact that a similar type had been used to smash Reed's windshield had caused her to assume that it was a common stone in the area. But the detailed display—with ten or fifteen different kinds of local sedimentary rocks—showed nothing remotely similar.

Why, Ellen wondered, would somebody use a hard-to-find rock to smash in a car window? Wouldn't a kid or a wacko just grab the first thing at hand?

Of course he would, she answered her own question. Unless it was a premeditated attack and the rock was some kind of symbol.

It was a ludicrous notion, and Ellen shrugged it off before she reached the parking lot.

But she couldn't quite suppress her sudden shiver.

CHAPTER THREE

"NOW WE'LL MOVE ON to item number seven, tract four-five-nine-eight, case planner Ian Hawkson."

Reed, slouched in a poorly padded metal chair in the audience, straightened up at the sound of his underling's name. This was Ian's first presentation before the board of supervisors, and for all the false bluster Reed had seen the boy put on yesterday when they'd last discussed the report, he knew Ian was shaking in his boots.

It was unfortunate that Ian, with barely four months on the job, had been saddled with such a controversial project, but all the other planners' caseloads had been full when Ian had come on board. And though Reed had anticipated a certain amount of outcry over the proposed development, he hadn't expected a retired grandma to gather up letters of protest from everybody in the neighborhood when "her" birdwatching sanctuary had been slated for destruction.

The piece of land in question was the legitimate property of a builder who lived in Santa Barbara and had always intended to develop the land. Reed—and the planning commission—believed that low-density homes would have been appropriate for the property, but the developer's permit application sketched a plan for virtually yardless triplexes that would have changed the entire texture of the neighborhood and greatly increased the traffic on the inadequate adjacent roads. Today's presentation before the board was at the request of the developer who hoped that the supervisors would vote to overturn the planning commission's decision to deny his project.

Gladys Gordonson, wearing a prominent It's For The Birds pin on her ample bosom, would also have a chance to speak her mind. Reed had no doubt that her colorful campaign would find its way into this week's *Westhope Herald*. Shannon Waverly, notebook in hand, was sitting right in the front row.

The environmental impact report, completed by Zamazanic & Eagleton Consulting Engineers on behalf of Reed's department, had addressed the ornithological issue along with all the standard ones: botanical destruction, seismological dangers, sharp grades on which building would be difficult. Ian reiterated the findings in a slightly shaky tenor that made Reed suppress a smile as he thought of his own debut before the board. Of course, after two years in Vietnam, he'd hardly been a child, but there had still been a host of things about planning—and the business world—that had been entirely new to him.

Glancing at the four men and one woman who now sat on the board of supervisors, he tried to recall which ones had been there for the last twenty years. Certainly not Rose Terlich; women had just begun taking their place in the political arena back then. Paul Hernandez, only thirty-six, was a liberal environmentalist who was likely to support the bird group. The other three men were all in their sixties. Bald Emmett Mercer had been on the board so long that he acted as though he'd inherited it along with his father's fine-furniture business. Jefferson Baxter, on the other hand, had only served for eight years since he'd retired from real estate development, and rumor had it that he intended to use his supervisorial position as a stepping-stone to state office. Robert Robinson was a member of the "old guard," but a newcomer to the board. He'd been the baby-kissing mayor of Westhope for two decades before becoming a supervisor in the last election.

As Ian spoke—then sat down while the applicant got to say his piece—Reed mentally tallied the votes. Rose and Paul would support the commission's decision. The other three would overturn it. He knew it, they knew it, and the planning commission knew it. It made him wonder why they'd all bothered to gather here today.

When the floor was opened to the public, Gladys Gordonson made an impassioned plea on behalf of the endangered raptors that frequented the area. She made it quite obvious that she regarded the undeveloped meadow as a public park that "this outsider"—the man who owned it—had no right to destroy. It was neither a new argument nor a valid one. Gladys made reference to the Z & E section of the environmental impact report at least half a dozen times. And every time she stumbled over the laborious title, "Zamazanic & Eagleton," Reed's eyes drifted over to Lars Lindroth, Z & E's official representative this morning. He and Lars had been friends for years, and it occurred to Reed, that it would be entirely natural for him to mosey on over to say howdy to Lars after the meeting. While they were chatting, he could surely find a way to bring up Ellen's name.

Lars was a big, burly man, not fat so much as tall and muscular. His hair, what was left of it, was white. Tiny clumps of it clustered around his neck and ears. He had the kind of complexion that tended toward red even when he was calm. And most of the time, he was either laughing or bawling somebody out. He never stayed in a bad mood for very long.

"Can't say that was much of a surprise," Reed greeted his old friend after the final vote. The board had over-turned the commission three to two, just as he'd expected.

Lars shrugged good-naturedly. "Well, at least Baxter suggested that the applicant reduce the density. He usually wants to fill in every nook and cranny of land."

Reed had to agree. Over the years, he'd worked with Baxter a number of times before he'd given up real estate and gone into politics. His projects were sound, but he wasted no time on unnecessary environmental concerns or aesthetics. He built to code—no short-cuts—but no extra frills, either.

"Be grateful for small favors," Reed countered. "At least they've got to submit a modified plan so the traffic won't be so bad."

Lars glanced at Gladys Gordonson, who looked ready to burst into tears. "That won't help her any. Poor lady is convinced she owns that piece of land."

They made small talk for ten minutes or so, comparing notes on two upcoming projects that Lars was supervising. When Lars, in the course of the conversation, happened to mention a problem he was having with a member of his staff, Reed took advantage of the

moment to query, "I met a new Z & E gal not too long
ago. Ellen Andrews. Is she one of yours?" It was a safe
guess; most of the Z & E staff was overseen by Lars or
the fellow in charge of the engineering crew.

"Yep, I'm her supervisor. How'd you run into her,
Reed? Ellen's not working your turf. She's my survey
tech for that proposed hot springs resort site up at
Chumash Mountain."

There was no reason not to tell Lars the whole story.
"Oh, she dropped by when she was over here a week or
so ago. I guess she found my business card in some old
time capsule where she and her level man are staked
out."

Lars's gaze seemed to narrow. "Time capsule? What
the hell kind of hoax is that?"

Reed realized belatedly that there might be some
reason why Ellen hadn't shared her discovery with her
supervisor, and he hoped he hadn't spilled the beans.

"Gee, Lars, I don't know much about it," he backpedaled quickly. "Don't know much about Ellen, either. I was just surprised to see a woman her age doing
fieldwork."

Lars snorted. "You're not the only one. You should
have seen John Neff's eyes bug out when I told him he
was going to team with a gal old enough to be his
mother. I thought he'd have apoplexy."

Reed smiled. He could imagine. He might have reacted the same way at John's age. Hadn't Ellen said he
was the age of her boys?

"To tell you the truth, I tried to talk her out of it.
We've got plenty of drafting for her to do in the office—or even day work in the field. But she looked me
right in the eye and said, 'I didn't come two thousand

miles to be pampered,' and that was that. Girl's got guts. I can't fault her chutzpah."

Neither could Reed.

BY FRIDAY MORNING, when Ellen checked in at the office, she was seriously considering giving up on the time capsule. She'd spent a good deal of the past weekend going through the old newspapers at the county library in Bentbow—and the tiny branch in Westhope as well. She'd learned that Westhope had had a new throwaway newspaper every five years or so, and the library had kept consecutive editions of whatever seemed to be the leading rag at the time. Apparently her time capsule newspaper had never qualified as a major resource. The library had no record of it, and the librarian, a young woman in her twenties, could not identify any of the girls in the basketball picture.

Ellen was very nearly out of leads. One of her last hopes was Shannon Waverley, whom she planned to call this morning to get the name of the current girls' basketball coach. Maybe the coach could help her track down former coaches in the local league. Even the geological books she'd borrowed from the library had failed to reveal anything worthwhile about the greenish-black rock. Based on the pictures, it might be an igneous rock called diabase, but it seemed unlikely since the museum's exhibit indicated that most of the rocks in Bentbow County were sedimentary not igneous.

Back at her desk, Ellen discovered a phone message from Reed Capwell. She told herself that he'd surely called because he'd remembered something about his business card, and that was reason enough to be glad.

But a tiny voice inside her whispered, *Liar. This man makes your pulse quicken, and that's the real reason you're glad he called.*

It was an illogical response, and Ellen squelched it quickly. It took some doing to greet him prosaically, but she did it. "Mr. Capwell, this is Ellen Andrews returning your call."

There was a split-second pause, barely discernible and yet somehow troubling. "I told you to call me Reed," was his simple greeting. The faintest hue of disappointment shaded his masculine tone. "I only make developers call me Mr. Capwell."

Ellen's answering chuckle was a bit embarrassed. "I'm sorry, Reed," she told him, stressing his first name. "I didn't mean to sound unfriendly. I just wanted to avoid sounding pushy or personal."

Again there was a pause, almost a hesitation. It surprised her. The supervisor of residential permits wasn't likely to be a hesitant man. And the Reed Capwell *she'd* met hadn't sounded hesitant at all.

"Uh, Ellen, the reason I called you is probably more personal than, uh, professional. I wanted to apologize for running off so suddenly last week. I was a bit distracted about my car."

Ellen wasn't sure whether to be pleased or disappointed. He hardly owed her an apology; they hadn't been in conference. Still, it was nice to know that he'd remembered they had been speaking. And it was possible, wasn't it, that an apology wasn't the only reason for his call?

"I wasn't the least bit offended, Reed," she answered truthfully. "I was concerned about the damage. If it had been my car, I would have been hysterical."

No, that's not true, she realized in hindsight. *The old Ellen would have been hysterical. Howard's Ellen.* But the new Ellen, the self-made woman, would have found a way to cope with the disaster. She had insurance—insurance she'd carefully arranged for on her own. And she always carried enough cash to cover a cab if she found herself in a jam.

"I assure you that it's a rarity for such a thing to happen in the County parking lot," Reed declared. "In fact, I can't recall anything like that happening before. The most trouble we've ever had is a mobile home illegally parked overnight."

"Were you able to get your windshield fixed all right?"

"Yes, but it wasn't easy, considering the age of the T-Bird. And they couldn't fix the dash." He sounded heartsick. "My biggest concern was that my stepdaughter was having car trouble that morning and I was rushing off to rescue her. My ex-wife had to step into the breach. It all got rather complicated."

Ellen wasn't sure she wanted to talk about Reed's ex-wife. It was far safer to stick with the subject of the car. "Did the police have any idea what might have happened?"

"The cop I talked to figured it was just some obnoxious kid. Fortunately my insurance covered most of it."

Ellen wound the curl of phone cord around her finger as she asked, "Did you happen to notice that rock on your front seat? It was an unusual color. Sort of a greenish-black.''

She was greeted with silence.

''Have you ever seen a rock like that before?''

''Beats me,'' he said indifferently. ''A rock's a rock. It was the windshield I was worried about. And the dash.''

Ellen didn't want to press the issue, but she thought it might be important. After all, Reed hadn't seen the rock in the time capsule; she had.

''It looked just like the rock I found with your business card, Reed. I think it's an igneous variety called diabase. All the regional rocks displayed at the Westhope Museum are sedimentary.''

He chuckled softly. ''You must be pretty desperate if you're still looking for clues in Westhope.''

She bristled; it was just the kind of putdown Howard would have thrown at her. ''I'm looking for clues wherever I can find them, Reed. I sure didn't get any help when I went to the County.''

There was another silence, an uncomfortable one. Ellen knew she was still too quick to take offense when a man rejected her ideas, too quick to blame a stranger for sounding too much like Howard. But the years of Howard's insidious mental cruelty had taken their toll. Ellen's battered self-image was still in the process of healing.

She was about to apologize when Reed said softly, ''Actually, Ellen, I called to tell you I think I may have come up with something.''

She was dying to ask what he'd discovered, but she restrained herself. ''I'm sorry I snapped at you, Reed.

I'm just…a bit sensitive to criticism. I thought the rock clue might be a good one.''

"And it might be, for all I know," he conceded graciously. "But over the millions of years that the earth's crust has been changing, there have been dozens of tiny prehistoric volcanic eruptions in this area, Ellen, too small for anybody but a geologist to notice. Every now and then we've come across some mention of an eruptive block of some igneous material in an unlikely location. I could find you examples in probably half a dozen environmental impact reports in County files.''

"Oh," she said, deflated. Then, recalling a notion that had been troubling her, she asked, "But why do you think that the vandal picked your car, Reed? Why not mine or anybody else's?''

"Your guess is as good as mine," he admitted laconically. "It probably caught his eye. It's the sort of car that people tend to notice, especially now that all the new imports look the same. My T-Bird—'' pride dripped from every word ''—is really something special.''

"Is that why you drive it?''

It was a simple question, one which Ellen did not expect Reed to have any trouble answering.

To her surprise, his tone grew hoarse as he replied somewhat defensively, "It's a good car, and it's so old that my insurance fees are low.''

"It's a classic, Reed," Ellen said kindly, eager to move their conversation back to solid ground. She was no longer angry with Reed and actually glad that he'd rejected her rock theory. "I can almost hear the Beach Boys singing when I look at that old car.''

He laughed, and this time she shared his pleasure. "Jackie thinks her Camaro is a classic, and it's only five years old."

"John thinks I was born during the Civil War."

They shared the laughter of two people who are the same age and remember the same music and the same teenage idols. It was the first time since she'd come to California that Ellen felt just the right age—in her prime—instead of too old to be trying anything new.

It occurred to her that every time she talked to Reed Capwell she felt a little more drawn to him, a little more hopeful that he might be drawn to her. The notion made her feel warm and tingly, but a little bit scared. Even if Reed *had* called for more than an apology, her own situation made it unwise to start skipping down this primrose path. She'd been in California all of three weeks; she was barely settled in. She was still learning the names of the people with whom she worked, still learning to make decisions without seeing Howard's disapproving face. Feeling drawn to a beguiling stranger was hardly going to help her learn to stand on her own two feet.

Struggling for professional calm, she asked, "What did you find out, Reed? What did you call to tell me?"

"Well, a couple of days ago it struck me that my files might not be as overwhelming as I first indicated to you," he replied cheerfully. "Clara reminded me that during my first few years at the County, I was assigned to a 7,300-unit master-planned community called Manzanita Meadows. It was a never-ending octopus. I didn't work on any other projects until the last subdivision was approved. Chances are good that whoever I gave business cards to during that time was associated with some aspect of Manzanita Meadows.''

At once Ellen's heart swelled with hope. "So there's only one file to study, instead of the dozens you mentioned?"

"Well," he backpedaled a bit, "it means there's only one *project*. There must have been two dozen different tracts with separate merchant builders. So the files are still—"

"Endless," she finished for him.

For a moment, Reed was silent. Then he concurred, "Ellen, there are still a lot of files involved, but not nearly as many as I thought there were before." He sounded disappointed. "I thought this news would help you."

"Oh, Reed, I'm sure it'll help when I figure out what to do with that information," she assured him. After all, it was a clue—maybe—and it was certainly her first break since finding his business card. "Is there anywhere in the overall summary of the plan that I might find a list of contacts?"

"Sure. Several places. We keep a distribution list for all people who need to know what's going on at various stages of the application process: developers, police, fire safety people. And there's a billing record of consultants—"

"Consultants? Like me?"

"Well, like you when we need a topographical survey. Most of the time we need a biologist or a geologist or an engineer. Depending on the given project, the County hires a firm like Z & E to prepare the environmental impact report."

"Was Z & E the firm who wrote the EIR for Man-zanita Meadows?" Ellen asked, aware of a sudden quickening in her pulse.

There was a brief but meaningful pause before Reed said, "Yes. Yes, indeed! I normally wouldn't remember something like that, but Manzanita Meadows was such a huge piece of my life that it would be hard to forget. Lars was in charge of the project at your end, I remember that. Give me a little more time to jar my memory, and I might recall a few more pertinent facts."

"Reed, that's it!" Ellen suddenly squealed, earning a curious glance from Olga Rios, the young secretary at the front desk who always had a smile for John. "That's the link! Some of our people were up at Chumash Mountain twenty or thirty years ago when a previous owner was thinking about developing it. If one of those Z & E consultants was also assigned to work with you on Manzanita Meadows, he might have tucked your card into the time capsule and buried it when he spent the night at the cabin! It's the only place anybody doing fieldwork up there would stay!"

Reed chuckled softly. "I'll be damned. Ellen, you may be right. But there's a lot of ifs there, you know. Fortunately we don't have to rely on my memory to test your theory. I can have my secretary dig up a list of Z & E folks who worked on the project, and you can ask yours for a list of the Z & E staff that worked on the original Chumash Mountain survey." Surprising satisfaction colored his voice as he concluded, "Then we can compare notes over lunch. I'm supposed to pick up my daughter at the mechanic's, but I can call my ex-wife and ask her to pick up Jackie instead."

"Lunch?" Ellen repeated. Weeks had passed since she'd seen a human face—except for John's—during a meal. Any face would have been a blessing. But *Reed's* virile face would be something just sort of a miracle. "Do you mean today?"

"Of course I mean today. I'm too curious to wait another week till you're back in town. Aren't you?"

It wasn't until after Ellen called Shannon Waverly to see if the reporter had unearthed any clues that she remembered Reed's absolute indifference to the time capsule two weeks before. What had fired his interest now? Was it the thrill of the chase or the fact that, between the two of them, they'd finally stumbled on a possible clue?

Or was there some other reason why he seemed so eager to see her today? Might it be the same reason she was dying to see his face?

"I'VE BEEN WORKING HERE for thirty-seven years and I've never seen a man look so damn happy to see an environmental impact report," joked Commercial and Industrial Division supervisor Bill Hazlett as he joined Reed in the elevator and punched the button for the ground floor. As usual, Bill was munching on a donut and dropping crumbs on the floor. "Which appendix are you reading so feverishly?"

Reed grinned at his old boss as he closed the report. Ellen hadn't asked for it, but he was certain she'd want to read the sections written by whichever consultants turned up on both of their lists. Sandi, bless her heart, had compiled the County's list of Manzanita Meadows' Z & E consultants from the billings file in ten minutes flat.

He didn't see any point in explaining the details to his old boss. They were still on good terms, but not as close as they had once been. After all, they were headed in different directions. Reed was headed up; Bill was on his way down. "It's a long story, Bill. It has to do with a woman, a map and a rock."

Bill laughed out loud. "You'd think by your age you wouldn't still be excited about any one of them. I can still remember how hard your tail wagged when you first started working here, though. You didn't know a damn thing, Reed, but you were determined to be the best damn son of a bitch who ever called himself a planner."

"Are you saying I'm not?" Reed teased. It was an old game, one he'd long since tired of. But Bill had taught him the ropes years ago, and he felt a lingering loyalty to the older man. It troubled him that Bill had already mentally retired. Once, he'd been an excellent supervising planner, but now he was just filling up space.

"Seriously, Reed," said Bill, stroking his gray beard, "are you involved in something . . . unusual? Between that time capsule thing and your bunged-up car, we're beginning to worry about you."

Reed shook his head, eager to assure his old friend. "The smashed windshield was just bad luck. And though I could do without the publicity, the time capsule is proving to have some fringe benefits."

Bill grinned knowingly. "The rock or the map?"

Reed laughed as he walked out the elevator door. "If you've seen one map, you've seen them all," he called back to his friend. "And a rock by any other name is still a rock." He wasn't in the mood to air his private feelings about the woman.

At the moment, Ellen was only a casual acquaintance. He hoped that after this private rendezvous, she would become much more.

CAPWELL AND THE ANDREWS woman were meeting at noon, his contact said. She had not been enthusiastic about revealing what she knew, but when the supervisor—using the muffled, husky voice he always used for these calls—had proved that he knew where her precious girl spent every hour of the day and reminded her that he would not hesitate to carry out his threats, she'd been quick to cave in.

She didn't know much, she'd insisted. They were meeting for lunch. Neither knew anything of substance yet; all they hoped to find out was which names showed up on both lists—the County's and Z & E's.

"How can that hurt you?" she'd pleaded. "Even if they find out who left the time capsule, how can it possibly make any difference at this late date?"

The supervisor was comforted by the question. It meant she knew nothing at all about what had really happened, not even the part she'd once played. But it bothered him that he might have inadvertently given Capwell a clue by using the diabase to smash his car window. He'd been certain that Capwell would recognize the blatant warning—"Don't pursue the time capsule if you don't want to end up like the other one." After all, if the dead man had told him anything, Capwell would have realized the significance of the diabase at once. But apparently the rock hadn't meant a thing to him. The victim had been telling the truth about burying evidence, but apparently he'd lied about having time to tell Capwell what he'd discovered.

Unfortunately, Capwell was bright enough to put two and two together, anyway. Once he started asking hard questions about the evidence, sooner or later the right answers would come to him. The identity of the man who'd buried that old coffee can was not enough to endanger the supervisor. Things could only unravel if Capwell figured out *why* the poor sap had tucked that business card in with the rest of the information...then disappeared.

He could not allow Capwell to continue searching. He would arrange for a more dramatic demonstration to make his position crystal clear: Capwell and the woman would cease and desist searching for information at once.

Or they would cease and desist permanently.

CHAPTER FOUR

LA CHAPALA WAS A TYPICAL California Mexican restaurant, complete with black-velvet wall hangings of bullfighters and screaming panthers. A quiet, soothing fountain reigned in the central patio, and the lush surrounding greenery gave Ellen the feeling that she was in a tropical jungle . . . not a bad feeling for a blustery February day. There were no mariachis making the rounds at the moment, but Ellen had no trouble imagining the south-of-the-border trumpets and guitars.

The waitresses all wore traditional multicolored Mexican dresses, but the patrons sported everything from beach clothes to formal business attire. Ellen, wearing a well-worn ivory pullover sweater and clean khaki trousers, was more casually dressed than Reed. Today he wore a corduroy blazer, a button-down oxford shirt that needed a smidgen of extra pressing at the collar, and a dimpled smile that tugged at Ellen's senses from the moment she first joined him at the table he'd reserved. It grew wider as he shared the news that Sandi had found a copy of the Manzanita Meadows EIR—assembled, sure enough, by consultants from Z & E.

Their waitress was a pretty girl, no more than twenty, and Reed spoke to her with quiet respect. He ordered something called a "number seven" and suggested that Ellen do the same.

Her first instinct was to say, "That's fine for me, too." But she caught herself—Howard's face superimposed itself on Reed's—and insisted on glancing at the menu before she ordered one beef enchilada, refried beans and rice.

After a brief and somewhat awkward exchange of small talk, Ellen handed Reed the other two items she'd found in the time capsule—the newspaper article and the map. He studied them with care, then pronounced, "This subdivision map in the ad is a tract in Manzanita Meadows. Right about the middle of the development, as I recall. This red mark—" he shook his head "—probably doesn't mean anything, but if it does, it's probably pointing to an apartment complex next to these single-family detached homes for sale."

Ellen waited tensely. Surely that wasn't all!

"The geological map doesn't ring any bells right off hand, but I think it would be worthwhile to cross-check it with all the geological maps in this—" he handed her the report "—and if you don't find it in there, then ask Lars for the original survey map of Chumash Mountain."

"I already have that, Reed, for my own project. And I'm quite certain that this map doesn't cover any part of Bentbow National Forest." She'd spent a great deal of time checking maps of that area to no avail.

"Well, you can check the EIR. Maybe we'll get lucky." His grin warmed Ellen as he asked, "So, who worked at Chumash Mountain during our keystone years?"

The keystone years, as he dubbed them, were the years Reed had been assistant planner—1971 to 1974. Neither Ellen nor Reed was sure that the capsule had been buried then, but it seemed as good a place as any to start.

"I've got seven people. Well—probably only six. In 1972 one of the men had a bad fall and broke his leg up there before he could file a report."

"Jim Gregory," said Reed. "I'd forgotten all about that."

"You knew him?" Ellen's interest quickened.

"I still do. He works at the County now—in the Regional Plans section. A good steady guy but not given to flights of fancy. I can't see him burying a time capsule. Besides, I don't think I ever worked with him on a project. I don't even think we met until he'd left Z & E."

Ellen felt a moment's disappointment. She knew she should have been glad that they'd narrowed things down to six, but she had an uneasy feeling that Reed might eliminate everybody else, too.

"Here's the list," she said, handing him the paper. "See anybody you remember?"

As Reed reached for the file, his fingers brushed hers, and Ellen was surprised at the intensity of feeling triggered by the casual contact. Apparently Reed was, too, because his eyes swept up to meet hers as he took an audible breath. Just as quickly, he looked away. His fingers slipped away from hers as he leaned back with the file, but she had the strangest feeling that he really wanted to take her hand and just hold it for a while.

Did he really call me to apologize? she found herself asking again. *Did he ask me to lunch just to talk about the time capsule?*

She reminded herself that this was a quasi-business meeting, not a date, and she had no plans to get cozy with Reed Capwell. But when he smiled at her the way he was right now—ever so slightly, but smiling nonetheless—she couldn't come up with a very good reason why she should keep a safe distance. She'd worked so hard the last few weeks—the last few years! Didn't she have the right to a little fun?

Reed read over her list, murmuring absently to himself. She caught words like "Iverson," "Silverwood" and "rezoning brouhaha," none of which made sense to her. He mumbled half a dozen names, made some checks on the paper, then set it aside and pulled out a sheet from his pocket and startled mumbling again.

Impatient for his input, Ellen took advantage of the moment to study Reed openly, something she'd never really had a chance to do before. When he wasn't smiling, his dimples were barely visible, but his nicely curved lips—just full enough to be sensual—were as beguiling as ever. He still hadn't gotten his hair cut, but he had combed it recently. Only his temples were silver, Ellen noticed. The rest of his thick hair was not a true brown, but rather a rich chestnut with natural auburn highlights. She wondered if he might be the type of brown-haired man who grew a red beard. Then she wondered how his beard, or even his unshaven face, would feel against her hand. And she wondered—

"There are only three," he suddenly declared.

Ellen sat up abruptly, hoping her meandering thoughts didn't show on her face. "Three what?"

His eyes wrinkled along well-creased laugh lines as he explained, "Three suspects, of course. Three consultants who worked for Z & E and also worked with me on Manzanita Meadows.''

Before he could continue, their lunch arrived. After the waitress had departed, Reed explained what he had found.

''Our first candidate,'' he began in a charming parody of a game-show host, ''is a young man named Dale Castleman. He was the biology consultant on a major development that young Reed Capwell inherited from his predecessor. It took six months to complete the EIR, and there were half a dozen Z & E consultants involved.''

''And Dale's on my list? He worked out of the Chumash Mountain cabin?''

''He did. Dale was assigned to examine the effect of increased fishing, boating and trash on the lake up there as part of the original environmental impact analysis for the proposed hot springs resort.''

''And that would be in—''

''In 1973. Two years after he worked with me.''

Ellen grinned. For the first time since she'd started on this wild-goose chase, she was beginning to think they might be getting somewhere. ''Put him on the list, Reed.''

Reed grinned. ''Does look promising, doesn't it?'' He took a bite of his tostada, spilling about half of the mile-high lettuce on his plate. ''I don't suppose you know offhand if he still works for Z & E?''

Ellen shook her head. ''No idea. I don't know anybody who works for Z & E except for Lars, John and a terribly efficient secretary named Olga Rios, who giggles whenever John smiles at her. I've been introduced to a few others in passing, but I can't even recall their names, let alone their specialties." She shrugged in frustration. "What do you remember about Dale?"

"Not a lot, frankly. Round face, blond hair, very curly. He was pretty short, classic endomorph."

"Endomorph?" Ellen repeated, surprised at the technical term. "You mean he was fat and roly-poly?"

Reed gave her a mock scowl. "He was not fat. He was round. The proper anatomical term for this condition is—" He stopped, then ruefully laughed at himself. "Clara is always accusing me of being overly accurate, if there is such a thing. My apologies."

Ellen grinned, shoving aside her uneasy feeling that Reed still spent a great deal of time with his ex-wife even though he claimed that there was no love lost between them. "It's okay. Do you recall anything else about this endomorph? Like why he might have left a time capsule?"

Reed shook his head. "Nope. I don't remember anything about him at all. I haven't thought of him in over fifteen years, and if I hadn't noticed that the two names matched up, I probably never would have thought of him at all."

"Great," said Ellen, glad that she'd ordered something she could decorously consume with a fork. "Who's next?"

Reed hesitated, as though to heighten the drama. Or maybe, she wondered, because this was a name he didn't want to disclose?

"Sally Quinton. Hydrologist. Analyzed water feasibility for proposed Chumash Mountain site. Did the same thing for us on Manzanita Meadows. Found big problems at Chumash Mountain, nothing major at M.M."

Ellen watched his face for some sign of a change when he mentioned the woman, but she detected nothing. "Do you remember anything else about her?"

His answering grin was plainly an embarrassed one. "I remember that she looked terrific in a pair of jeans."

"Might you recall anything, uh, pertinent to the case?" Ellen paused for a moment, hoping her envy didn't show, before she added, "Or *is* that last observation pertinent?"

Reed gulped, looking truly embarrassed now. "No, it's not pertinent. I was married when I met Sally. Lots of the guys in the office drooled when she was around, but I wasn't one of them."

"Liar," teased Ellen.

Reed laughed out loud, then shoved his glasses back up his nose. "Okay, maybe I drooled a little bit. But only because things weren't all that great at home."

Ellen was surprised. "That was twenty years ago, Reed. Have you been divorced a long time?"

His smile dimmed so quickly that she wished she could have withdrawn the question, but it was too late. Reed pondered it for a moment or two before he answered, "Our youngest left for college last year. Clara wouldn't leave me until then."

It was an odd way to refer to a divorce. If he'd been so unhappy, Ellen wondered, why hadn't Reed left *her?*

Of course, Ellen had been unhappy for most of her married years but had lacked the courage to take any action. But somehow she didn't think that was the problem in Reed's case. She had the odd feeling that despite his marital strain, he wouldn't have left his wife under any circumstances.

"I take it you didn't want the divorce?" she said gently.

Reed shook his head. "No. It was her idea."

Ellen felt a moment's sorrow for this oh-so-appealing fellow, wondering how much he still grieved for his former wife. "I'm sorry, Reed. I know how hard it is to lose somebody you love."

Of course, in her case it had been the loss of her brother, not a lover, which had taught her the meaning of grief and driven her into the pseudo-safe haven of Howard's arms.

"Just for the record, Ellen, Clara doesn't top my list of losses. I didn't want the divorce, but not because I...well, worshipped her or anything. It just—" he paused for a moment, then finished softly "—it just didn't seem right."

"Because marriage should last forever?" she suggested, remembering how she'd grappled with that one before she'd walked out. But her marriage had been a mirage—not only to Ellen but to everyone. Her sons would have given her more support during the divorce if she'd revealed the sick mind games Howard had played on her. But she loved her children too much to shatter their image of their loving father.

"Not really. It's that..." Reed stopped, stared at her for a long moment, then said, "We're getting off the track here." Pointedly he glanced at his watch.

Ellen finished off her meal in silence, stung by his subtle rebuke. She didn't feel that she'd pushed the conversation into dangerous waters, yet suddenly he'd been treading water, afraid to swim.

"I've got a busy afternoon," Ellen told him stiffly. "You said there was a third name?" She felt like a coward, hiding behind her workday—a flexible schedule that could be altered at will—but she suddenly felt the need to climb back into the safety of her professional world where there were no distractions as beguiling as Reed. "Who else worked with you?"

"Steve Young." Reed scraped off the rest of his plate with an overly active fork as he said, "I remember Steve very well. We were—well, maybe not close friends, but quite friendly. He was a soil specialist. I think he and Sally were up at Chumash Mountain about the same time. At least, I have a memory of the two of them together." He grinned again, but this time his shining smile was wry. "Clara says I've got a terrible memory. I could be wrong."

Ellen didn't want to talk about Clara. "Maybe they were dating."

He shook his head. "No way. *That* I'd remember. Steve really had the hots for Sally. Most of the Z & E staff did. But she surprised the hell out of everybody and got married to somebody we'd never even heard of. That was about a year or so before she got pregnant and left the firm."

I'd like to see what pregnancy did for the way she looks in jeans, Ellen thought cattily, then mentally slapped herself. It wasn't like her to be jealous of another woman, especially one she'd never even met.

Abruptly she realized that it wasn't really Sally Quinton who'd aroused her jealousy; it was Clara Capwell, who'd once had the privilege of being married to Reed. The fact that she'd tossed away that privilege didn't seem to make much difference to Ellen's irrational feelings. Reed still felt something for the woman—any fool could see it in his face—and for some reason, that knowledge troubled Ellen quite a lot.

"I don't want you to get your hopes up too high," Reed commented.

Ellen blinked twice as she realized he was talking about the time capsule, not about her errant romantic thoughts.

"As I told you before, the County does a lot of work with Z & E, and Z & E is a huge operation. I would have been surprised if we *hadn't* run into a few Chumash Mountain people who worked with me on Manzanita Meadows. I'll track down these folks and get back to you tomorrow, but don't be disappointed if none of these leads pans out." Before Ellen could reply, he tacked on, "Shall we plan on dinner to discuss our findings? There's a nice little—"

Ellen shook her head. It was happening already; she could feel the power slipping from her hands. "No, Reed, thanks for the offer, but you've really done enough. Now that I've got the three names, I can take it from here."

A baffled look rippled across his appealing features. "Ellen, you don't know these folks from Adam. Don't you think it'd be easier for me to—"

Of course it would be easier, she wanted to snap. *That's why I always let Howard call up strangers for me; that's why I always let Howard do everything!*

If Reed knew the myriad brutal ways Howard had crippled her self-esteem and stripped her of her independence, he might understand. But her marital wounds were too deep to share with a stranger. Besides, she didn't owe Reed an explanation, not really.

Not yet. But he'd been terribly helpful and downright kind, and she didn't want to walk off with her coveted data and leave him feeling as though he'd been used.

"Reed," Ellen said truthfully, "the time capsule is my project, my puzzle. There is some information—like your involvement with these people—that only you can provide. But there's no reason why I can't do everything else myself."

He looked perplexed, but he didn't argue. Instead, he said quietly, "Okay, you make the calls. We can still discuss it over dinner, can't we?"

"Well, I don't know if—"

"I know it's your project, Ellen, but it's *my* business card, you know. That message must relate to me in some way. The person who buried it is most likely a friend or colleague of mine and a total stranger to you." He grinned beguilingly. "Besides, you're the one who aroused my curiosity."

This time his gaze was steady, and though there was no hint of flirtation in his straightforward tone, Ellen knew that his curiosity was not the only thing she'd aroused. Reed wanted to get to know her better; it was as simple as that. And she...well, in time, with careful consideration, she might want to get to know him, too. But not quite yet. Not until she got a better grip on herself in these strange surroundings. And not until she got a better grip on what kind of a man Reed was. In the few years that she'd been single, she'd learned that Howard-clones were everywhere.

"Reed," she said gently, fighting the urge to give in, "why don't you let me find out what I can about these people from the personnel files at Z & E? I'll try to track them down this weekend while I'm home, and if

I find out anything worthwhile, I'll call you when I'm back in the office next Friday.''

For a long, quiet moment, she had the feeling that he was not going to look away. His eyes were so warm, so patient, so unbearably kind, that it took every ounce of her willpower to keep from saying, ''Oh, what the heck, dinner tomorrow would be just wonderful! I'm so damn tired of staring at those four walls alone....''

But suddenly Reed glanced down, ostensibly at his pocket, as he pulled out a generous amount of change and tossed it on the table. ''Sure, Ellen. Whenever it's convenient. I guess we better get a move on. The clock is ticking.'' He did not sound annoyed, but he could not completely hide his disappointment.

It was a surprise to Ellen. She hadn't realized that she had the power to hurt a man...especially this one. As she followed him briskly to the front of the building, he tossed the cashier the bill and a credit card.

''Reed, please let me—''

''No.'' Now his tone lacked patience. ''*I* asked *you* out to lunch. You shouldn't have to pay for it.''

''You were doing me a favor, Reed. You brought me the infor—''

''You don't have to pay for that either,'' he countered, and this time his tone *was* brusque. She knew he wasn't just talking about the meal.

Ellen felt positively glum as she waited for the cashier to process Reed's credit card, then followed him out to the parking lot. His brilliant turquoise T-Bird—complete with a new front windshield and an afghan draped over the badly scarred dash—was parked a row or two beyond her own Accord, so she had no logical way to say goodbye before they reached her car.

"I can't see why your daughter doesn't love that car, Reed," she said, trying to break the awkward silence. "You've certainly given it loving care. Did you buy it when you were young and keep it all these years?"

He shook his head but didn't look at her. "I didn't buy it. It was...sort of a gift. I got it just before I married Clara."

Ellen couldn't think of a suitable reply. It was time to say goodbye; she knew that the safest thing would be just to say, "Thanks for lunch, and thanks for the information." But then he would drive off thinking that he'd made a fool of himself trying to date a woman who had no interest in him. And nothing could be further from the truth.

Abruptly Ellen stopped. Startled, Reed stopped, too. Instinctively he turned to face her, read the apologetic confusion in her gray eyes.

"I'm not sure I'm ready to date anybody right now, Reed," she blurted before she could stop herself. "Even casually." She licked her lips, then honestly confessed, "But if I were, I'd be inclined to start with you."

His eyes widened. He looked surprised and pleased and a little dismayed. The silence took on all shades of meaning before he managed to come up with a reply.

"I didn't mean to push, Ellen." His tone was strained. "I didn't think dinner was all that big a deal." He shoved his glasses back up on his nose...slowly, as though to gain some time. "I wasn't expecting... well, anything else but food and conversation."

Ellen felt her neck color with chagrin. The poor man was only trying to be friendly! "I'm juggling a lot of feelings right now, Reed," she admitted. "At times I feel like the world's most capable woman, and other times I feel like a little girl who's just gone off to school. I'm used to relating to men in a certain way that I now know doesn't work for me. I'm just not sure I've got a firm-enough grip on my dreams to...well, to risk learning another way to play the game.''

Reed stared at the ground, but said nothing.

He'll never ask me out again, Ellen realized sadly. *I've blown this one hundred percent.*

And then he slipped both hands in his pockets and faced her squarely. ''I'll let you pick up the tab next time if it would help,'' he suggested with a ghost of a grin. He made it sound like a supreme sacrifice, and she wondered, seriously, if for Reed it might well be.

An answering smile lit Ellen's lips. Reed's grin broadened, and suddenly everything was all right between them again. For just a moment they stood there, close enough to touch but not touching, letting the quiet rays of newly shared warmth encircle the two of them.

When the mood was broken by two chattering women strolling by, Reed reached into his wallet and dug out a business card and a pen. He wrote ''home'' and a phone number on the back before he handed it to Ellen. ''Keep this handy in case you need a friend,'' he said softly ''If it ever shows up in a time capsule, I'll know who's responsible. It's an unlisted number, and I don't give it out to just anybody.''

Ellen thanked him for the card and tucked it into her purse as they walked the last few feet to her car. She was almost ready to tell him she'd changed her mind about Saturday night—what could be the harm in one dinner?—when he asked abruptly, ''Is *this* your car?''

Ellen didn't like the disapproving tone of his voice. She'd picked out this highly rated Honda Accord with inordinate care. She was not about to listen to a single word of male criticism.

"You've got a flat tire," Reed observed, gesturing toward the left rear wheel. "When was the last time you checked the air?"

"Two weeks ago," Ellen declared with more force than was absolutely necessary. She could prove it; she kept a complete maintainence log in the glove compartment. The first few times she'd checked the tires she knew she'd let out too much air in her fumbling, but she was certain she'd gotten the hang of it now.

"Have you run over any glass today? Nails in some construction yard?"

Ellen glared at him, the brief moment of warmth they'd shared evaporating as she recognized the old chauvinistic song and dance of which Howard was a master. How had she failed to perceive that Reed Capwell was cut out of the same cloth? Generosity, she'd learned the hard way, was often a secret method of control. It was one of the many ways that Howard had used in public to cloak his sick need for total domination.

"No," she insisted. "I have done nothing stupid. And the tires are still on warranty. This car is only eight months old."

Reed gave her a sympathetic, if patronizing, smile. He didn't say, "There, there, don't worry your pretty little head about it," but she could see it in his eyes. He took off his blazer and laid it on the hood, then started to roll up his shirt sleeves. Still, he moved so quickly that it wasn't until he said, "Pop the trunk latch, will you?" that Ellen realized what he was about to do.

"No," she snapped. She didn't mean to sound obnoxious; she knew she wasn't talking to Howard, but to Reed. Yet at the moment, she could have interchanged the two. It would never have occurred to Howard that she might be capable of changing her own tire, or that, if she lacked the skill, she'd like to take this dry, sunny afternoon with help at hand as an opportunity to learn how to do it for future use. Nowadays she lived alone; she regularly traveled deserted unpaved mountain roads, day and night. She couldn't risk being a helpless female even if the idea had appealed to her. In the long run, she was more concerned with her safety than her pride.

"I'm going to do it myself," Ellen said.

Reed grinned maddeningly.

She wanted to slap his face.

"Don't be silly. You've got to go back to work. It'll take you hours; I can have you on your way in five minutes."

"I don't care if it takes me all day," she told him stoutly, hoping to God she could figure out how to do it at all. "I'm going to do it myself."

Reed's lips pursed. His earlier warmth had fled. "Ellen, you don't strike me as the raving feminist type. You don't have to prove anything to me, and you sure as hell won't be in my debt. This can be an exhausting, messy job and—"

"It's *my* exhaustion and *my* mess," she persisted. "I own this car. It's my responsibility. I'm going to do it myself."

For a moment their eyes locked. Reed looked frustrated and perplexed; Ellen felt helpless and angry. Why did men always do everything for women and then complain because women had no idea how to do those things themselves? *Damn you, Howard, for teaching me to be a coward!* Ellen cursed to herself. *Damn you for denying me the right to learn how to take care of myself.*

A hundred times she'd asked him to teach her how to fix things—a flat tire, a blown fuse, a sliding glass door that was jammed. No matter how simple the task, Howard had told her it was too hard for her, laughed at any tentative efforts she had made, and then regaled his sons and friends with an exaggerated and humiliating version of the incident. Eventually she'd stopped trying, stopped believing she could do anything by herself. By the end, she'd even forgotten how to ask. Listening to Reed, Ellen felt as though she'd taken an uncomfortable step back in time. And she secretly wondered if she might be taking on an impossible task.

Reed must have sensed Ellen's irresolution, because he reached past her and tripped the latch inside.

"This will just take a minute," he said.

Ellen grabbed his arm. Tears pooled in her eyes, but she fought them back. She *had* to do this one simple task by herself, even though this was the last man on earth she wanted to offend.

"Please, Reed, don't make me fight you," she burst out in anguish. "Don't make me be rude. To you this is just a tire that needs to be changed. To me, it's . . . a lot of things too complicated to explain right now."

Her eyes met his again. They were still moist, glistening with pain.

Clearly baffled, Reed straightened, but he did not step away. He was so close that she could smell his leathery after-shave; so close that one of his knees pressed against her thigh. It suddenly occurred to Ellen that she'd like to press a whole lot more of herself against him. She wouldn't mind at all if he just took her in his arms and kissed her, then promised to make all the troubles go away.

"I just want to help," he said softly, brushing the back of one hand across her cheek. It was the first time he'd ever touched her with unmistakable tenderness. Why did he have to pick the wrong time to do something that felt so incredibly right? "So much of your life must be difficult right now, Ellen," he whispered. "I just want to fix this one problem for you."

She felt herself melt at the gentle touch, the true concern. She couldn't stay angry. She couldn't keep all her feelings bottled up inside.

"If you really want to help me, Reed, let me do it myself," she pleaded. Although his fingers had left her face, she could still feel the magic of his hand. She longed to pull his fingers back and press them against her trembling cheek. "For twenty-five years I lived in cotton batting. I thought it was a cozy nest. It turned out to be a prison."

Ellen hoped Reed would understand that she'd confessed something very private, something that very few people knew.

"My husband did everything for me, Reed," she tried to explain. "He liked me barefoot and pregnant. He used my fears to chain me. Sometimes he even manufactured them." There was so much more she could have told him, but the mere *memory* of Howard's cruelty was hard for her to bear. She wasn't ready to talk about it to anyone.

Reed's gaze was still on Ellen's, his body warm and close. She waited for him to slip his arms around her, admitted to herself that she'd be deeply disappointed if he didn't. She took a deep breath and held it...until Reed stepped back.

"I'm sorry, Ellen," he said huskily. "I'm not sure I understand—I mean, I'm *certain* I don't understand—but I...I sure don't want to get in your way."

She knew, by the tone of his voice, that he really *didn't* understand. He probably was used to relating to women just the way Howard did, and Howard had never understood, either.

"Maybe we could do it together," he suggested, clearly straining to come up with a compromise. "I could...explain the procedure to you as I go."

Ellen longed to agree, but she knew it would be too easy to let him do it all.

"Please understand that I have to do it by myself," she insisted softly. Fear of those nights driving on Chumash Mountain pushed her on. "I have to *know* I can do it by myself. In the rain. On a slippery hillside. In a thunderstorm after dark."

Reed shuddered, as though the idea of her coping with such a trial alone was more than he could bear. At last he said briskly, "Okay. I'll just stand and watch. If you have any questions—"

"I can't do it with you hanging over my shoulder," Ellen told him, desperately wishing he wouldn't make this any harder. Already she could imagine the way

Howard would ridicule her. He would have found a way to make her fail. "It'll make me too nervous."

A fresh flash of irritation washed across Reed's rugged features. He grabbed his jacket from the hood of the car as he brusquely declared, "I'm going to go inside for another cup of coffee, Ellen. But until I'm sure you've got a safe vehicle, that's *absolutely* as far away as I'm going to go."

This time Ellen didn't fight him. She'd won the most important round, and she had to admit that it *would* be comforting to know she could still ask him for help if she fell flat on her face. He wasn't Howard; Howard would not have backed off. She felt a gust of chagrin that she'd been so hard on Reed. She didn't know him very well. It wasn't fair to assume he'd be as barbaric as her ex-husband.

"I'll come in and tell you when it's done," she promised, hoping that his anger would abate.

"And you won't be too stubborn to ask for help if you're in over your head, will you, Ellen?" he asked pointedly.

"Of course not." Her smile was tense. The earlier warmth between them seemed to have vanished. As he turned abruptly and marched inside, she felt wilted, frightened and utterly alone.

Damn you, Howard! she cursed as she opened the trunk. But she couldn't bring herself to curse Reed.

REED NURSED HIS COFFEE for twenty minutes before he snuck back toward the front window of La Chapala to peer out at the parking lot. When he pulled back the red-and-green curtains by the cash register, he saw Ellen on her knees by her Honda, turning the bolts, but he wasn't sure if she was still battling to remove the flat tire or fastening the spare back on. Then he realized that it had to be the spare, because it was a smaller tire—one of those new three-fourths jobs. To his surprise, she was twisting each knob just a little, going from one bolt to the opposite one rather than moving in a simple clockwise pattern. Apparently she knew enough to balance the stress.

Despite his earlier frustration, Reed felt a curious pride in her achievement. He couldn't imagine why this small victory was so important to Ellen, but if it made *her* happy, it made *him* happy. He did not understand why she'd fought him so hard over changing the damn tire, but he had gotten the heart of her message: if he wanted to get to know her any better, he'd have to try to be less paternal. It went against his grain to stand around twiddling his thumbs while a woman did a man's work, but if that's what it took to convince Ellen that he respected her, he'd have to learn to do just that.

When she picked up the flat tire and hoisted it into the trunk, Reed hurried back to his table to wait until she came in to get him.

Ellen was disheveled but glowing when she marched back into the restaurant. Her eyes met his with a striking air of confidence that had been lacking before, and Reed had to admit that the fire he read there made her even more appealing.

"You can go back to work now, Reed," she proudly proclaimed. "Everything's under control."

He grinned at her. "Congratuations."

She took his extended hand. "Thank you, kind sir."

She tried to pull away, but he held on for just a moment. Suddenly they weren't shaking hands anymore; their fingers were embracing. It felt good to touch her this way; it felt inexplicably right. Maybe he didn't understand everything that was going on in her life right now, just as he had never understood Clara. But he knew that he already felt something for Ellen Andrews that he had never felt for his ex-wife.

His fledgling emotions encompassed all the reasons a man should want a woman—respect, common interests, tender warmth and quickening libido. No sense of guilt and obligation ladened his growing feeling for this enchanting female. No third party, reaching out from the dead to shake him, colored the quietly building desire pressing him toward her now.

He grinned at her without restraint and felt a sensual somersault inside him as her slowly growing smile mirrored his own.

"Can I see you tomorrow night?" Reed asked. He hadn't meant to be so blunt. She'd already said no, and he'd vowed not to push it. But everything seemed to have changed since he'd let Ellen fix the tire by herself. They'd had their first fight and made up. Now she was glowing again.

He couldn't believe it when her smile faded and her fingers slipped from his eager hand. It was all he could do not to grab it again, force her not to let go.

"Reed," she protested softly, "I told you I'd have to think about that."

"You've had twenty minutes," he pointed out reasonably. "When you came in here it looked like you'd made up your mind."

A moment ago we were together, heading down the same path, he longed to remind her. *I knew it and so did you. So why are you pulling back again, telling me no when you want to say yes?*

Ellen ran a nervous hand through her dark tresses. Suddenly Reed ached to do the same.

"Reed, I just need to sort through some things. There are so many kinds of tires I haven't yet learned to change."

A man of Reed's scientific precision found such a vague metaphor a bit hard to follow, but he got the point. More or less.

"I stayed out of the way this time," he pointed out cheerfully. "I can stay out of the way again."

Her exaggerated grimace made him laugh. "Okay, so you had to push me out of the way," he admitted. "But I *did* leave eventually." He paused a minute, then met her eyes again. He waited until she faced him head on, waited until he felt that pulse of magic throb between them again. "Think about it, okay?" he urged, his tone soft, low, beguiling.

Reed's own urgency surprised him. Never had he pressed a woman this hard for a date. "I'll call you tomorrow. If you still say no, I won't press you." He gave her a cautious smile as he gestured toward the door. "At least not for a week or so."

To his surprise, Ellen's eyes lit up with a new kind of pleasure that he had not glimpsed in them before. A slow but vibrant smile—a rainbow of joy and hope—ribboned her lovely face as she leaned toward him ever so slightly. She'd told him to back off, and yet he suspected—no, he was certain—that she was greatly relieved that he hadn't yet given up the struggle.

Never taking his eyes from hers, Reed let one hand ever so cautiously brace the small of her back, ostensibly to steer her through the crowded restaurant. But he didn't remove his hand once they got outside, and Ellen offered no protest.

Together they walked back out to her car, a quiet pulse of magic matching their unrushed strides. Reed was feeling exceptionally warm, and, unless his imagination was working overtime, Ellen was just slightly trembling.

He longed to take advantage of the moment to kiss her, but he decided it would be risky to push her any further right now. They were both running late, and she had, by her silence, more or less acquiesced to his wishes. What more could a man ask for?

He would give her the night to think about it. Tomorrow, say nine or so, he'd call her with specific plans for the evening. He'd make a few hours of his company sound so beguiling that there was no way she could refuse.

When they reached her car, Reed reluctantly relinquished his hold on Ellen to inspect her handiwork on the tire. He wanted to make sure the bolts were securely tightened before she drove off. Fortunately, she'd done a perfectly respectable job and he was able to tell her so. She beamed as he said goodbye and offered no protest when he promised to call her in the morning.

He felt radiant as he circled her car on the way to his own, but his joy transformed to panic the instant he spotted her other rear tire. Like the one she'd just changed, it was flat as a pancake, and this time Reed didn't need to ask how a brand new tire had inexplicably lost so much air.

There was an unmistakable slash in the sidewall.

Reed had never gotten a close-up look at the tire Ellen had already changed, but he was willing to bet dollars to donuts that the slash in it would be an exact replica.

CHAPTER FIVE

"I'M CALLING THE POLICE," Reed declared, his voice taking on a hard tone that Ellen hadn't heard even when he'd found his beloved T-Bird vandalized.

The words chilled her almost as much as the sight of the knife slash in the second rear tire. She'd assumed the cut in the first tire was the result of the wheel bumping against something sharp. Reed's alarm made it clear that someone had deliberately tried to leave her with two flat tires. Or, at least, some oddball had wanted to leave *somebody* in the parking lot with two flat tires.

"It could just be a random thing, Reed," she suggested rather feebly, knowing she was lying to herself. "I haven't been in California long enough to make friends, let alone enemies."

Impatiently he shook his head. "I don't think the message is for you. Look at the knife cut. Same style as my dashboard. Somebody knew you were having lunch with me, Ellen, and he wanted to give me a message. And he was none too subtle about it, either."

Ellen felt a tiny shiver, but she suppressed it at once. "Reed, I can see that the cuts might be similar, but on the other hand, they could just be... coincidental. I don't understand why anybody would care one way or the other about us having lunch together."

"I'm not sure anybody does. I think somebody wants me to start worrying a great deal, and whoever it is knows me well enough to know that I'm going to worry about your safety a great deal more than I'm going to worry about my own. It's possible that this has nothing to do with you, Ellen. You could just be a...a pawn."

Ellen wasn't quite sure how to answer. "Reed, I don't know why anybody would try to get you through me. We barely know each other."

He stared at her then, stared until she had to look away. "Obviously whoever did this is more perceptive than you are," he said coolly.

Ellen swallowed hard. "All I meant was...maybe there's some other reason. Something that has to do with the two of us exchanging information."

Reed studied Ellen morosely. "The time capsule, you mean? We're accidentally digging up something that somebody wants buried?"

Ellen shrugged. "It's possible, isn't it?"

He kicked the flat tire without much force. "Possible, but not very likely. I didn't even mention it to the police officer who took the report on my car because it seemed so farfetched." His eyes met hers uneasily. "I can think of some other possible explanations."

The tone in his voice gave Ellen a shiver. She didn't think that anger was what moved him this time. It sounded like fear.

"Reed, what are you—"

"I'm going to call the police. We can discuss it with them. And you better call Lars and tell him you're going to miss that meeting. Then we'll have to get you some new tires and—"

"Reed!" Ellen interjected. "For heaven's sake, I'm not an infant! You don't need to tell me what to do."

He kicked the tire again, with true venom this time. "Dammit, Ellen, I can't just stand here knowing somebody's threatened you and not do anything! I'm not used to standing aside, wringing my hands while a woman I care about is in danger! Is that so hard for you to understand?"

Ellen had just thought of another explanation— Reed's recent interest in her might have stirred up some jealous woman from his past—but something about the intensity of his eyes stilled her tongue. A tiny voice within her warned that Reed's urgency was out of proportion to the situation. And yet she was certain that Reed Capwell was not a man who was easily alarmed. He knew something—or had guessed something—that Ellen didn't know.

She was certain that he was not yet ready to tell her; maybe he hadn't even figured it out himself. The only thing she was sure of was that he was profoundly troubled by what had happened, and his need to take action was greater than her need to do everything herself.

"I saw a bank of phones in the restaurant, Reed. Would you mind calling the police while I explain the situation to Lars? And you're absolutely right about the tires. I'll have to replace them at once. If you can spare an hour or so to take me to a tire store, I'll be forever in your debt."

Reed took a deep breath. For a moment he reached out as though to touch her face, but his hand fell to her shoulder instead. He squeezed it gently.

"Ellen...I'm going to figure out what happened. I'm going to take care of it."

Ellen felt a sudden brush of mist in her eyes. She wasn't sure whether she should feel grateful for Reed's concern, irritated by his presumption, or—considering the possibilities he tacitly suggested—just plain terrified.

THEY MADE THEIR CALLS quickly, then waited a good half hour for a police cruiser to arrive. A young man and woman, both in uniform, took down Ellen's statement, but failed to look impressed when Reed mentioned his own vandalized car the preceding week.

"Did you file a report of the damage, sir?" the male officer asked.

"Yes, but at the time it just seemed like random violence. It wasn't until later that Ellen reminded me that the rock that was used is the same kind she found in a time capsule she's been investigating—"

"She's been investigating a *time capsule?*" the woman asked, skepticism frosting her tone.

"She found my business card in a time capsule. It's how we met. There is no other link between us. For both cars to be sabotaged—"

"Sir, excuse me, but this is urban southern California. You don't need a conspiracy to explain two acquaintances getting their cars vandalized within the same month."

Reed's fists tightened as he tried to maintain control. "The knife slashes are the same MO."

The two officers exchanged amused grins. "I suppose you have an extensive background in detective work, Mr. Capwell? Or do you just watch *Murder, She Wrote* re-runs all the time?" the man asked with a wink.

At this point Ellen interceded. "Officers, I know this sounds odd, but Mr. Capwell may have a point. It could just be a coincidence, but there might be a correlation. The rock used on his windshield—"

"I thought it was a knife used on the dash," the female officer jibed.

Ellen sighed deeply and explained her whole story from beginning to end. Reed resisted the urge to jump ahead and fill in details; he'd already trampled on her feelings enough today. Besides, it was pitifully obvious that neither of the officers were taking the time capsule theory seriously. They took a few notes, suppressed grins as they said "yes, ma'am" half a dozen times, then promised to let Ellen know if they tracked down any vandals. By the time they left, Reed was quite certain that the only person who was likely to track down the perpetrator of this crime was Reed Capwell.

BY THE TIME ELLEN reached the *Westhope Herald* office, it was almost six o'clock, and she was afraid Shannon Waverly had gone for the day. But Shannon was just locking the door when Ellen bounced out of her car, uncertain whether to say hello or retreat until Shannon spotted her and waved enthusiastically.

"Ellen! Any news on the time capsule?" the other woman greeted her warmly.

"Well, I guess so. I meant to get here earlier, but I had . . . well, I had an afternoon you wouldn't believe. Right now I feel lucky to be moving along under my own steam."

Genuine concern shadowed the other woman's face. "Well, that doesn't sound too good. I take it you

weren't able to get much information from Reed Capwell at lunch?''

"Well, actually, Shannon, I did. It's just that...well,
it seems so long ago."

"Lunch seems so long ago?" Shannon looked genuinely curious now.

"It's a long story." It had taken most of the afternoon to drive to a tire store, make a purchase, and put
the new tires on Ellen's car. Reed had been helpful, but
he'd given advice only when she asked for it, and this
time he'd cheerfully shared the task of changing her
tires. He'd also offered to take her out to dinner, since
it was getting so late, but she'd told him that she had
other plans. He'd looked surprised, but he hadn't pursued the subject, and Ellen had decided that it would
be better not to explain herself to him. She'd also decided that it would be wise not to see him on Saturday
night—not until she got a better grip on her mixed
feelings—and he hadn't fought her when she'd told him
that news, either.

Apparently Ellen's weariness must have shown on
her face, because Shannon said, "I'm not going anywhere. You want to go next door for a hamburger while
you fill me in?"

It was not until that moment that Ellen realized how
badly she wanted to share her feelings with a friend.
Not that Reed wasn't a friend, but he was also a challenge, a question mark, a very *masculine* sort of friend
whose friendship was fraught with potential compli-
cations. Shannon, on the other hand, was a compas-
sionate woman whose casual cheeriness involved no
strings.

"I'd be delighted, Shannon. I've got an aerobics class at seven, but I can squeeze in a hamburger before then."

They stepped inside the burger place and ordered burgers and coffee, both conscientiously opting to forgo the fries.

Without much prodding, Ellen told Shannon about the cross-referenced names, the cars and Reed's concern that she might be in danger. She didn't say anything else about Reed, but Shannon seemed to read between the lines.

"Sounds to me like Reed Capwell might have a special interest in your safety, Ellen."

She tried to hide her embarrassed smile. Actually, Reed had an excessive interest in her safety, and she wasn't sure whether to be flattered or frightened by his intensity. If only she hadn't been so drawn to him, she could have made more rational decisions where the man was concerned. She knew she'd offended him half a dozen times today, which was especially unfortunate since he'd done so much for her. Still, he was . . . well, he was pushing. He seemed ready for a deep relationship; Ellen was not. What made it hard was that she wanted him anyway and couldn't seem to keep from letting him know it. No wonder he found it so hard to back off! She was surely giving him a very confusing mixed message.

"Reed Capwell strikes me as the sort of man who feels uneasy if he's not in charge of everything, Shannon," she told her new friend, not really answering the question. "I was married to one for twenty-five years. I can spot the type a mile away."

Shannon sighed. "I think I got stuck with the opposite. Mine never took responsibility for anything. By the time I gave up on him, I knew he was dead weight. The only good thing he ever did for me was father my daughter. Now *she's* a jewel. Doesn't take after him in the least."

"You mentioned that she used to play basketball, Shannon. She must be about the age of my boys."

"Twenty-five," Shannon said brightly. "She's in medical school. I'm afraid marriage is not on her immediate horizon. I hope she'll find the right sort of man after residency, but that's a long way down the road." Before Ellen could answer, Shannon said, "Speaking of the right sort of man, I was talking to dear old Edwin Thompson at the museum yesterday, and I want you to know that he's doing his best to find out what you wanted. He's been searching through the old closets at the museum."

"Oh, I didn't want him to do that!" Ellen protested. "I'm sure it's like looking for a needle in a haystack."

"Actually, Ellen, he has very little to do with his time, and he feels very important helping you out. He sort of feels like you've deputized him. I don't think he'll uncover anything earth-shattering, but I think you've given him a new lease on life."

"Well, that's good to hear. He seemed so...well, so lonely."

"He is. His wife was a real sweet old gal, and I don't think he's ever really gotten over her loss. You know, Ellen, after you left last week I got to thinking about the timing of that newspaper. There's an obituary on the back, you know? I wonder if the page was torn out because of that. I checked out the family."

"And?"

She shrugged. "Nothing conclusive yet. And nobody in town has a twenty-year-old roster of girls' basketball teams or coaches, either. But I did find somebody who recognizes one of the girls on the team. At least, she recognizes the family traits."

"Family traits? What do you mean?"

"Well, one of the girls is a Ruskin. They all have those round faces and bucktooth grins like their mother, Irma. But she had a whole passel of kids—five or six of them were girls—and we're not sure which one's in the picture. I tracked down Irma's oldest son, and he confirmed that the girl in the picture is one of his sisters, but even he doesn't know which one. They all played basketball, and they all looked alike. Julie says it's not her, and Marylou's on vacation. The others have moved away, but Julie's going to send them copies of the photo and get back to me on the date."

"Shannon, that's great!" Ellen replied. "If we can narrow down the date, Reed may be able to pinpoint some critical aspect of the Manzanita Meadows approval process or actual development. I was planning to contact the people on our joint list this weekend, but I never got back to the office so I didn't get their addresses from my boss. Besides, I'm so exhausted after today that I may just spend the weekend in bed."

As soon as the words were out of her mouth, Ellen thought of Reed. There was no reason for it, not really. He'd only asked her out to dinner; he hadn't asked to spend the night between her sheets.

But he wanted to. She knew it. And even though she'd told him that she didn't want to see him Saturday night, she knew that she wanted that, too.

REED SPENT THE EVENING watching his favorite John Wayne movie, *She Wore a Yellow Ribbon,* with his gray tabby, Catnip, curled up on his lap. He loved the action of the old westerns. The Old West cavalry was another lifetime: it seemed like fiction. Modern war was real.

During the movie, he managed to keep his worst fears at bay, but once it was over, he found himself reliving his afternoon with Ellen . . . and reliving another afternoon twenty years ago.

I suppose you have an extensive background in detective work, Mr. Capwell? the young officer had razzed him.

Reed hadn't answered, unwilling to discuss his past with a stranger unless it was absolutely necessary. How could he explain that he knew all he ever needed to know about revenge and unheeded warnings? Twenty years had passed, and he still remembered every moment as though it were yesterday.

Captain Harrison had approved the mission with reservations. The other officers involved had insisted that it was worth the risk. Somebody—they weren't sure who—was leaking information to the North Vietnamese. Military intelligence had to send someone in to ferret out the traitor.

Su Le was a beautiful, brilliant, experienced spy. Reed had met her during a previous mission. They had fallen in love almost immediately, though they'd both fought it for a while. Su Le didn't want to leave her homeland; Reed had no intention of staying in Vietnam. Her grandmother had been appalled at the potential "mixing of blood" and had vigorously opposed their plans for marriage. Gradually, Reed had won the regal old lady over. She'd come to realize that by the time the U.S. left South Vietnam, Su Le would be ready to leave her country, too, and so would her family. Reed promised to find a way to bring her grandmother and her sister—the only members of Su Le's family to survive the war—back to the United States with him.

Reed had never loved a woman the way he'd loved Su Le. In all his life, nothing had ever felt so right. And then Nathan—Nathan, who had buoyed his spirits, shared his boots and risked his life to rescue Reed on two occasions—was sent underground to cover Su Le. Captain Harrison had refused to grant the assignment to Reed because he felt that since Reed was personally involved with Su Le, he wouldn't be objective.

Su Le's grandmother did not know everything her granddaughter did, but she knew that Su Le worked bravely for the freedom of her country. Once she begged Reed to protect Su Le. He assured her that Su Le would be safe.

In hindsight, he realized that the greatest irony was that he really had believed it. He believed that Nathan would be safe, too. With the confidence of youth, Reed had been utterly unable to imagine, for an instant, that anything tragic could really happen to *him*. In the time-honored belief of young soldiers, it was the other guy, and the other guy's buddies, who were going to die.

The mission was a success. Su Le located the traitor; Nathan captured him and brought him back to Saigon. They were both safe. It was over.

But the traitor's family swore revenge, and two months later, both Nathan and Su Le were dead.

In that lull before the storm, Reed had been uneasy, but he had taken no precautions. Neither his best friend nor his woman had had the sense to be afraid, and he had not wished to offend or alarm them by pressing his own concerns for their safety.

A thousand times he'd asked himself why he hadn't ignored their protests and found a way to protect them, anyway. A thousand times he'd vowed to do it differently if fate ever gave him another chance.

Now fate had sent him Ellen Andrews, and Ellen was in trouble. She didn't know it yet, or maybe she didn't want to know it yet. But Reed knew.

And he could not forget.

He went to sleep telling himself that he couldn't force her to protect herself, couldn't force the police to protect her, either. But he couldn't seem to convince his unconscious, because he woke in the wee small hours drenched with sweat, as old nightmares cloaked his mind.

He did not try to go back to sleep. He knew from past experience that it would be hours before he could push the memory of Su Le—calling his name as they tortured her—from his haunted heart.

Twenty years from now, he didn't want to have the same dreams about Ellen.

CHAPTER SIX

ELLEN SPENT MOST of Saturday trying to settle into her apartment. She'd tucked away her clothes, filled her bookcases and arranged pots and pans in the kitchen within four hours of her arrival last month, but except for setting up her three favorite pictures of her boys in the living room, she'd done nothing to make the place feel like home. She hadn't even unpacked the reading lamp she'd bought from Mercer Furniture; she was still using the unopened box as an end table.

Maybe it will never feel like home, she told herself glumly, recalling the odd sense of disquiet she'd felt when she'd opened the door last night...as though she'd barged into some stranger's living room. Nothing had seemed quite the way she'd left it. *Maybe I can only feel at home with Howard.*

Of course, that was a ridiculous notion; she hadn't felt at home with Howard for a long time. She'd just felt stupid, ridiculed, trapped...and protected from the world. Nobody had ever slashed her tires when she'd been married.

Diligently she pushed away the memory and the nudge of fear. It was a coincidence, an obnoxious prank. Reed was excessive in his worry.

As she finished potting the five new plants she'd purchased that morning, she tried to remember why she'd told Reed that she couldn't see him tonight, especially since she planned to spend the evening looking for clues in the environmental impact report. At the time, it had seemed imperative to assert herself. Now it seemed a bit ridiculous. She'd been lonely ever since she'd moved to Bentbow, and her only opportunities to meet new people were the brief weekends she spent in town.

And Reed Capwell was the only one she'd met that she was eager to see again.

Well, that wasn't true exactly. She had enjoyed her dinner with Shannon, and the people at the gym were certainly pleasant. The owner was a woman about her age who claimed she'd once been overweight, and seemed to understand why, after three pregnancies, Ellen had to work so hard at maintaining her figure. June had applauded Ellen's determination to keep on an exercise schedule despite her unorthodox and arduous job.

But it was easy to be friendly to the women, and even the men, she met under normal circumstances. Reed was different. He touched something deep within her— something she couldn't quite name—and she knew that whatever it was she felt for him was not going to go away just because she kept trying to vanquish the feeling.

Ellen was just about to hang her favorite picture on the wall—an underwater color shot of a baby seal— when the doorbell rang.

Instinctively she glanced at her watch. It was almost seven; the very hour Reed had originally asked to pick her up. Was it possible that she hadn't made herself clear? She wasn't sure whether she was more thrilled or irritated at the possibility that he'd ignored her wishes.

Brushing some loose strands of hair out of her eyes, she moved quickly to the living room and peeked out through the curtains. A familiar turquoise T-Bird squatted in the street.

To her surprise, she felt a curious mixture of impatience and delight. She'd *told* the damn man she didn't want to see him this weekend, and she was hardly dressed to greet anybody. But still, the mere thought of his presence was enough to whisk away the effect of the long solitary hours she'd spent in the apartment all day.

Not bothering to tackle her appearance—under the circumstances, it was hopeless—she opened the door and squinted though the setting-sun glare.

Reed didn't looked dressed for a night on the town. In fact, he looked more casual than she'd ever seen him ... and, for some reason, more appealing. Well-worn jeans, slightly ripped at one knee, hugged his long legs. A faded red T-shirt, adorned with a rhinoceros and the logo pun, Planners Have Poor Site, showed off the sturdy muscles of his chest. He wore high-top athletic shoes that might have started life as white but were now a determined shade of street-dirt gray.

"Uh, hello, Ellen," he said softly. A sheepish grin played across his face, deepening his dimples. "I know you asked me not to bother you this weekend, but I—" his brown eyes flitted up to meet hers, then glanced away "—I've got something I really need to tell you. I hope I didn't come at a bad time."

A sudden rush of warmth took Ellen by surprise, and before she could conceal her delight, she was smiling at Reed.

"It's a great time," she told him openly. "I've been working all day and I need a break. Have you eaten?"

He looked surprised. "Well, uh, not recently. I had a can of soup at one o'clock."

Ellen opened the door a bit wider and ushered him into the room. "I'm too tired to cook or go anywhere, but you're welcome to one of my frozen microwave meals, or we can order something in."

Reed still looked astounded. "I'd be happy to call a—" He stopped, studied her more intently, then said, "Whatever you'd prefer."

I'd prefer a hello hug to all this fencing, she felt a sudden urge to tell him. But such capitulation was not on her dance card for the evening. Slipping both hands in her own jeans' pockets, she said simply, "I've got chicken fettuccini, lasagna, and some kind of Salisbury steak. They're all really quite tasty, and low calorie, too."

He shrugged his shoulders. "Your choice."

"I won't think you're bossy for picking your own meal, Reed," she told him straightforwardly. "I just don't want you to make *my* selection for me."

He grinned again, and this time it was a real grin, an open greeting to a genuine friend. "I hate Salisbury steak," he admitted cheerfully, "but I'd kill for fettuccini."

Ellen laughed. "It's yours. I think I've got two of them, anyway."

He followed her into the tiny kitchen as though he belonged there, making mildly flattering remarks about her apartment while she pulled out the frozen dinners and set the microwave to thaw. He followed her back into the living room and held up her baby seal picture against the wall so she could figure out the best place to hammer the nail. She noticed with pleasure that he did not offer to do the hammering for her.

"How long have you been here?" he asked, glancing at the other four pictures leaning against the couch and the lamp box. "I can't tell whether you just moved in or went on a buying spree at Mercer Furniture."

Ellen plopped down beside the pictures and smiled up at him. "I only bought the lamp at Mercer's. The rest of this stuff is mine. I saw a couch there I'd really like to get when I can afford it, but the price is . . . well, beyond my means."

Reed grinned. "No problem. You tell me which one it is, and I'll get you a discount."

Ellen stared at him. "Legally?"

"Of course, legally! Emmett Mercer is on Bentbow County's Board of Supervisors. I've known him for years. He used to do the furnishing of the model houses in the Manzanita Meadows tract, and every other tract around here."

"So why does he give you a discount? Or should I call it a kickback?"

Reed shook his head. "It's nothing special he does for me. Mercer runs his furniture business like a used-car lot. Only outsiders pay the full amount. Anybody who's lived here for a while knows that Supervisor Mercer loves to dicker. You tell him you're interested but the price is too high. He says no dice. You come back a week later. He says maybe they're having a sale soon. You ask him to let you know. He calls you in a few days and slaps a sale price on the couch just before you show up. He mentions somebody else who came to look at it and is due back at five. You look anxious, you agree." He laughed. "Twenty percent off, I guarantee it. Just point me in the right direction."

"Thanks for the tip." Ellen returned his gracious smile. "I don't know when I'll have the chance to get back to Mercer's. I've only been here for three weeks, and I've spent most of that time up at Chumash Mountain. At this point I think I feel more at home in the old miner's cabin we get to bunk in."

"You and John?"

Ellen rolled her eyes as Reed sat down beside her, keeping a discreet distance between his knees and hers. "Actually, it's only a technicality. John's only unrolled his sleeping bag three times since we've been working up there. Apparently he's on close terms with a forest ranger who's assigned to an outpost about five miles away. He has to hike through pretty rough terrain to reach her, but he doesn't seem to mind."

"A forest ranger?" Reed repeated skeptically.

"Yes, a forest ranger. A *female* forest ranger." She grinned. "Didn't you know they made that kind?"

Reed met her eyes with some sobriety. "I'm not really that far back in the dark ages, Ellen," he informed her. "You ought to know that planning's such a new field that it's free of a lot of the good old boy traditions, and we've got almost as many women in the profession as men. I defy you to find one in my section who doesn't think I treat her appropriately."

"I believe you," she assured him. "But then again, I doubt that your case planners find themselves in many situations where their safety is ever questioned. Planning isn't a field that makes many physical demands. All it takes is a good mind and proper training."

"And diplomacy," Reed tacked on. "Don't forget that."

Ellen chuckled, relaxing in the warm glow of having a friendly face before her. "Have you had a hard week, Reed?" she asked more sympathetically.

Again he rolled his eyes. "Honestly, sometimes I think I'm living in the middle of a cartoon. I started off on Monday arguing with a woman who insisted that her fourteen minipigs could not be classified as 'commercial swine' because she'd die sooner than eat one. And on Wednesday, some other loony-tune found it necessary to expand my vocabulary with a list of creative obscenities because I suggested that across the street from a toddler's playground might not be the best locale for his new belly dancing bar. 'It's a free country,' he said. When I asked him if he had any children, he hung up on me."

Ellen fought a growing need to take his hand, to squeeze it in a quiet gesture of comfort...or at least camaraderie. But she was glad she'd restrained the impulse when he said more sternly, "But the worst of all was worrying about you."

She met his eyes at once. "Small children need your protection, Reed. I am an adult."

Suddenly he took her hands—both of them—in a gesture that was far more urgent than romantic. "Even adults need protection sometimes, Ellen. Even adults get hurt. Sometimes they even die."

She couldn't stifle a sudden shiver. For a moment she wondered if he might be off balance. Weren't they always warning women about letting casual acquaintances into the house?

But at once Reed released her, rubbing his temples, then his eyes.

Damn you, Howard! she secretly berated her ex. *You taught me to be afraid of everything. If I can't trust Reed Capwell, my instincts aren't worth a damn.*

Deliberately Ellen reached for Reed's free hand. "Reed, I'm sorry if you've been worried about me. But I'm a careful person, and the police don't think there's any reason for me to be on guard. Please take it easy. You worry too much."

"Now," he said tersely. To her surprise, he stood up abruptly, staring at the picture she'd just hung, jamming both hands uneasily into the back pockets of his jeans.

For the first time Ellen realized that there was more to Reed's concern for her. He wasn't just a compulsive worrier, or even a raving chauvinist. There was a *reason* he was so afraid for her. Whatever that reason was, it wouldn't hurt for her to have a little more patience with him.

He's not Howard, she had to keep telling herself. *I've got to let him be himself.*

And that's when she knew that she didn't want Reed to give up on her, didn't want to reject this fragile yearning that he incited within her. She'd been alone so long—not just the two years since the divorce had been final, but for so many years before that, when she'd gone through the motions of acting happily married even when she was desperately lonely for a man to share her true soul with . . . though she didn't even realize it herself.

"Reed," she said softly, "I told you yesterday that I had . . . reasons for being so prickly about male help."

He nodded slowly. "You mentioned something about your ex-husband. I admit to being curious, Ellen, but I didn't want to push."

Ellen took a deep breath, then edged a little closer. "Reed, he was...is...a very unbalanced man. When I was young, I thought he just wanted to protect me when he'd tell me not to talk to strangers and always to lock the doors."

She could see that Reed considered such behavior reasonable; so had she. Bravely she plunged on. "Then he started to think of other reasons why I shouldn't go anywhere on my own. If I wanted to go shopping in another city, he'd read me an article in the paper about the number of accidents on that particular road. Every time I mentioned going back to school, he'd remind me that some poor girl had been raped and killed in the college parking lot...or another college parking lot, maybe in some huge city a thousand miles away. When I wanted to apply for a part-time job, he told me the car wasn't reliable, and every time I'd ask if it had been fixed, he'd mention some other part that had just gone bad."

When she stopped to collect herself, Reed didn't interfere, so she went on. "He didn't just hound me about safety. When I tried to run the scouts' cookie sale, he reminded me that my math was terrible, and we'd be liable for any errors. When I volunteered to write the school newsletter, he ridiculed my spelling and said the other mothers would all laugh at me. When I wanted to start going to a gym, he said I was so clumsy I'd probably break something and end up a cripple." Fighting the pain of the memories, she broke off and stared bleakly at Reed. "It's not any one thing. It's the

way he *trapped* me. He filled me with fear, and he
dished out orders as though I were a child! And I . . . I
let him do it, Reed. For twenty-five years. Sometimes
I fought back; sometimes I didn't even try. He was just
too strong for me . . . for the person I was back then. But
all the time, I *knew* that the real Ellen was being sti-
fled. I hated Howard for burying me, and I hated myself for letting it happen." *And I'll hate myself even
more if I ever let it happen again.*

Reed met her eyes with a depth of compassion that
surprised her. Gently, he said, "I'm sorry, Ellen. I
should have been more sensitive. You tried to explain
why you were resisting my help."

Waves of warmth lapped at the remaining dregs of
bitterness. "Reed, I know I go overboard at times,"
she apologized, greatly relieved that he'd understood.
"But the trouble is, I'm still learning how to be myself. For so many years I've just said yes to everything
a man told me to do that I guess for a while I need to
say 'no' to everything. I know that's not right, either,
and I hope the time will come when I find a balance.
But right now I'm still, well, swinging back and forth
on the pendulum."

Before he could answer, the microwave beeped a request for attention. Ellen could have ignored it, but
suddenly the atmosphere seemed too intense, so she
excused herself and escaped to the kitchen. After re-
setting the oven for another few minutes of cooking,
she started pulling out plates, placemats and silver-
ware. She didn't ask Reed what he wanted to drink.
Except for half a quart of milk that she hoped would
get her through breakfast, all she had was water.

"Can I help?" he asked belatedly, looking like a little boy who'd forgotten to wash his hands when he'd been called to supper.

Ellen smiled gently. "You can do the dishes, Reed. There ought to be two of them."

This time his smile was slow, inviting, and it stirred a breath of hope in Ellen's chest. It stirred another kind of feeling much lower, a feeling she'd almost forgotten could move her. With Howard, sex had been more an obligation than a pleasure. Not that he'd ever pressed her, particularly; he'd just assumed that if he went through the motions that made him feel good, it would be okay for her. "Okay" was the right word for it; even in the early years, it had never been more than that. One of the vows Ellen had made to herself on the day she'd moved out was that if and when she ever took another lover, she would *demand* equal pleasure, or she'd toss the man right out of her bed.

The sudden memory of that private declaration wafted through her mind now, startling her with its timing. She was looking at Reed—no, she was smiling at Reed—and he was grinning with a barely muted confession of his own desire. It wasn't something she'd expected to happen this evening—and she suddenly realized, with an almost sharp pang of regret, that she wasn't at all ready for the next logical step. She wasn't even sure she was prepared to start dating this man on the most casual basis; she most certainly wasn't prepared to start sleeping with him.

Abruptly she turned away, grabbed the two paper trays of fettuccini out of the microwave five seconds before the timer ran out, and quickly arranged them on the plates. Part of her was appalled that she was actually willing to serve a guest a frozen supper, and part of her was thrilled that she'd triumphed over old habits.

But the friendly repartee they'd shared earlier seemed to vanish over dinner. The tiny table in the living room—the only table in the house—seemed barren without flowers, and Ellen couldn't stifle a nagging feeling that she'd like Reed to know that she could cook.

"You said you had something to tell me," she told him bluntly, uncomfortable with the stilted silence.

He deliberately took another bite of fettuccine, chewed it for a while, then swallowed hard. "It's not the sort of thing I can just spill out over dinner," he finally told her.

"I should have made a salad," Ellen answered. It was a ludicrous reply, a non sequiteur, but for some reason it put Reed at ease.

He gave her another sheepish grin and confessed, "We're both nervous as hell, Ellen. Why don't we just admit it and get it over with."

Ellen licked her lips, then bit the lower one. She tried to ignore his bluntness, tried to pretend that everything was okay. Instead, she blurted out, "Okay, I'm nervous. I'm in a new apartment, a new job, a new city with a man I barely know and keep finding myself wanting to get to know better. I'm tired and sweaty and I look like hell and I feel like a lousy hostess feeding you a frozen dinner after twenty-five years entertaining guests as a gourmet cook."

Reed stared at her, his expression sober but attentive. He didn't say a word as Ellen babbled on, "It bothers me that you showed up when I told you not to,

Reed, and it bothers me that I'm so glad you're here. I don't know what you came to tell me, and that also makes me nervous. But nothing makes me shakier than wondering what's going to happen when you get around to kissing me, because I keep telling myself that I ought to keep my distance but I really don't want to.''

Reed stared at her. Then he leaned forward and slipped one hand around her neck. Gently he tugged; she didn't fight him. His lips claimed hers an instant later.

A tornado of surprise twisted Ellen's soul. Her whole system seemed to go on red alert: desire, hope, fear and joy all danced together. Reed might as well have tossed her upside down. When she landed again, he was still across the table, watching her closely. His warm fingers still braced her neck.

She was having trouble breathing. She gave up trying to feign poise.

"We'll get better at it with some more practice," Reed said prosaically, but there was nothing prosaic about the sudden huskiness in his voice.

Ellen nodded in agreement—she could do nothing else—then felt a great, chilly emptiness when he let her go.

In silence, Reed ate a few mouthfuls; Ellen just pushed her noodles around with her fork. To her surprise, the next words out of Reed's mouth formed a question.

"You are, uh, legally divorced?"

Ellen was both touched and surprised by the question. Most men would not have asked. Most would not have cared.

"Absolutely. Are you?"

He nodded. "I told you that. I told you right from the start."

Ellen tried to smile, but she was too busy regaining her equilibrium. She was forty-four years old, for Pete's sake! A simple kiss should hardly knock her flat.

But it wasn't a simple kiss. She knew it and Reed knew it, too. They both lived in a world far removed from casual dating and Saturday night sex. Ellen would be willing to bet that Reed hadn't kissed more than two or three women since he'd been divorced, and if he'd done more than that, it was only because he'd truly cared for them.

Abruptly Reed stood up and cleared the table. Ellen considered stopping him—she'd only been kidding about having him do the dishes, after all—but suddenly it seemed that almost anything was better than sitting here staring at each other.

It was starting to get cool, so Ellen took advantage of the moment to grab a sweatshirt, comb her hair and start a fire. By the time Reed rejoined her on the carpet ten minutes later, the flames were beginning to crackle and her tension was beginning to thaw.

He didn't touch her right away, but he lounged close enough that her shoulder brushed his chest. She could feel his heat, feel those strong muscles, feel the tension in him as he waited, surely, for her to turn to him.

"Did you really have something to tell me, Reed, or was that just an excuse to come over here tonight?" she asked him.

He leaned forward, so close that his lips almost brushed her nape. "I have something to tell you," he responded slowly, "but even if I hadn't, I suspect I would have come."

Ellen didn't answer. She wasn't even sure that she could speak.

Reed kissed her neck—gently, a mere nerve-jangling peck—before he told her, "Ellen, I don't date much. I'm not thrilled about living alone, but most of the time women just complicate things. They're so—" he struggled for the word "—fussy. They worry about how they look. They worry about how *I* look. They worry about how it looks to everybody else if we go here or there or *don't* go. And when we end up alone in front of a fire, neither one of us has much to say."

Ellen turned to face him. Firelight warmed the rough contours of his face. The smell of wood smoke warmed her heart.

"I sense something different in you. Maybe it's because you chose to be a survey tech when you could have stayed safely bottled up in a temperature-controlled building. Maybe it's because you seem so strong and yet so scared."

Her eyes flared, and Reed pulled back.

"Dammit, I don't know how to say this right, Ellen. Please don't get mad at me for being myself. I'm trying to tell you that I wasn't, well, *looking* when you first showed up in my office, so maybe I didn't know you were special right away." He cupped her jaw with one warm hand. His thumb grazed her ear. "But I know it now, Ellen. I want you near me. Please don't keep sending me away."

Somewhat tremulously, Ellen rested her soft cheek against his half-shaven one; she closed her eyes as his thumb outlined her mouth. She was surprised by the sudden wash of need that swept her, the desire to curl up in his arms.

Is it really Reed's affection I'm aching for, she wondered, *or just the security he offers?*

She didn't want to push him away, but she didn't dare let him come any closer. Not until she had a better grip on herself. Not until she knew what she wanted . . . and how she was going to feel after he went home. Reed really cared for her. It wouldn't be right to let him think she was ready to plunge into a relationship when she was still feeling so unsettled.

"Tell me what you came to tell me," she ordered in a low voice. "I really need to know."

He moaned softly, so softly she would never have caught the sound or its meaning if she hadn't been in tune with his breathing and the pulse of his heart. The hand cradling her head tightened; his lips brushed her throat.

She knew he didn't want to talk; he wanted to make love. So did Ellen, but not enough to go against her instincts. It was too soon. There were too many feelings competing in her heart; she couldn't ignore them to succumb to her body's demands.

She smothered a sigh and forced herself to pull back. *Not yet, Reed, not yet,* she longed to tell him. Instead, she sat up, cross-legged, and warmly took his hand.

He took a deep breath and faced her warily. "I'm sorry, Ellen. I'm out of practice. I seem to keep reading you wrong."

She shook her head, feeling foolish. "You're reading me exactly right, Reed. Half of me, that is. It's the other half—the one that's all mixed up and squirrelly—that you're having trouble figuring out." She leaned forward and kissed his chin—the merest brush, a gesture more than a touch. "I'm having trouble, too."

His grip on her hand grew more steady, but he readjusted his position, sprawled legs and all, as though to match her platonic posture. For a long moment he just stared at the fire. Then, abruptly, he stated, "I was in Vietnam."

"I'm listening," was her quiet reply.

Reed shifted uncomfortably. He squeezed her hand. A log fell over and one spark flew high. "Ellen, I was in military intelligence. Some of our projects were successful. Some I would rather forget." His sad brown eyes met hers. "But I have no guarantee that everyone from that time in my life has forgotten me."

Ellen felt a chill slither down her spine. She tightened her grip on his hand. "Have you ever been threatened before?"

He shook his head. "Not since I left 'Nam. But I was dealing with people who have generations of memories. It's possible that a friend or relative of someone I helped remove from a pivotal position has just now managed to get to the States or to track me down. Or he may have had some other reason for waiting this long to retaliate."

Ellen thought for a moment, then realized that she was weighing Reed's facts the way she'd always weighed Howard's—as though he, a man, must somehow have divine insight. Rather abruptly, she said, "I can't see what Vietnam has to do with me."

"We're close. Anybody who wanted to punish me or warn me off might try to hurt you."

Ellen shook her head. She could almost hear Howard's voice. "Reed, nobody knows that I...that I matter much to you. Even if there is a crazy person out there who deliberately messed up both of our cars, it can't have anything to do with Vietnam. It might— maybe—be related to the time capsule, but I still think there's a good chance it was just a coincidence."

"It wasn't a coincidence!" His voice grew tight. "I dealt with this kind of stuff in the war, Ellen. A rock through a windshield is random violence. Cuts with a knife are a trademark. And your tires were slashed the same way."

Sudden fear made her angry. "What's your point?"

"My point is, you're in danger. You need protection until the police catch whoever slashed those tires."

Ellen dropped his hand and stood up abruptly. "You promised not to coddle me, Reed. Can't you keep your word for even half an hour?"

"I never promised not to be concerned for your safety," he countered swiftly, also rising to his feet. "I only promised not to try to bulldoze my way into your life."

"Same thing."

Reed put both hands on Ellen's shoulders and turned her around. There was a look in his eyes she'd never seen before. "It is *not* the same thing! I didn't try to steamroll my best friend in 'Nam. I never told him what to do! He said he could take care of himself, and I believed him. And he was a trained operative! So was—" she was certain he was going to drop a second name, but he seemed to cut himself off abruptly before he finished "—so was I."

Suddenly he was shaking. Ellen was shaking, too.

"Ask me where he is now, Ellen! Ask me what all my courteous restraint did for *him!*"

"Reed—" It was a whisper, a croaked apology. The anguish in his voice was killing her.

"He's dead, dammit! He's been dead for twenty years! I'd give up my right arm and my left one too if I could bring him back, but there's not a damn thing I can do! If I'd stuck my neck out then, risked his anger the way I'm risking yours, it might have made a difference." His face was turning red. "Now you tell me to back off. You tell me to go to hell. I don't care. There's trouble out there. I can smell it. And I'd rather have you refuse to ever let me see your sweet face again than have some cretin hurt you. Throw me out if you want to, but promise me you won't take any chances! I just can't go through it again."

And just that simply, Ellen saw a whole new picture of Reed Capwell. Under his placid, sunny exterior, he was a man of great depth. He knew pain. He knew fear. And the forces that drove him to warn her of danger were nothing like the forces that had driven Howard. She could refuse to submit to his fear. But she could not reject his tenderness. There had never been any possibility of personal freedom while she'd lived with Howard. With Reed, she might have to compromise, but at least there was hope.

As her eyes met his, she could see the great frustration there, the lingering pain, the longing to hold her close and keep her safe. Ellen knew she could not meet all of his needs without denying her own, but she knew that the two of them could find at least one small patch of common ground.

He was still gripping her shoulders, so she couldn't easily touch his face. But she had no difficulty sliding both arms around his waist in a gesture of comfort...and probably much more.

The angry desperation that had seized his mouth softened as he felt her soothing fingers; his grip on her shoulders eased. Then his arms slipped around her back.

"Oh, Ellen," he said softly. "I don't want to scare you. I just can't bear for anything to happen to you. I can't go back to such hell."

That's when she kissed him, with no hesitation and no restraint. There didn't seem to be any other way to tell him how sorry she was about his friend...how sorry that the death still haunted him after twenty years. She told herself that her fierce embrace was only sympathy, and for the first few moments, it was probably true.

But at some point that comforting kiss got away from her. She lost track of all the angry words and tentative touches that had foreshadowed this moment. She was surrounded by Reed's arms, Reed's essence, Reed's manly scent, and all she could think of was *him*.

Urgently he pulled her closer; her arms tightened around his back. His T-shirt seemed to ride up as her fingers found a warm patch of skin. A twin to his earlier moan floated from his throat to her ear, and Ellen felt the quickness in his body as she pressed herself against him.

In an instant, she understood three things. He was aroused; she was aroused; and if somebody didn't put on the brakes in a second, they would both end up in her bed. Part of her rejoiced at the thought, but part of her felt like a tumbleweed in a twister. It was that helpless feeling she'd left Howard to escape, and she'd vowed never to let her feelings about a man rule her again.

Gently Ellen broke off the kiss. She braced her hands on his waist, then, when he didn't seem to read her message, moved them up to press lightly against his chest.

She knew the exact instant that Reed understood. His body froze. His breathing seemed to stop. For a long, tense moment he did not release her, but she knew he'd stepped away in his heart.

Then his arms fell to his sides. Soberly his eyes met hers. "I'm going to set a world record for apologies this evening, Ellen. Maybe you should just wear a sign when you want me to touch you and take it off when you want me to stop."

Ellen felt ridiculous. She didn't know what to say. But she couldn't have Reed blaming himself for something that wasn't his fault.

"I want you. I'm just not ready," she blurted out.

He stared at her in some confusion. "Did you think I was going to kiss you twice and then throw you down on the floor?"

She colored. "No, I don't mean 'not ready' like that. I mean—not ready. Not prepared."

They were still about six inches apart, and Ellen's nipples were sensually taut. It was terribly hard to keep Reed at a distance, hard not to press herself back against his chest. "Prepared?" he repeated cautiously. Then his eyes lit up. "I had a vasectomy thirteen years ago if that's what—"

"It's not," she corrected him, watching the brief flare of hope die. "I had my tubes tied, too; that's not the problem."

This time he did step back. In fact, he turned to go. "Ellen, before I have time to stick my foot back in my mouth again, I think I better leave. Thanks for dinner and—"

He stopped in midsentence as Ellen grasped his hand. She laced her fingers with his and held him fast.

Reed's beautiful eyes tried to read hers and clearly failed. "Don't play games with me, Ellen. If you'll just tell me straight out what you want from me, maybe I can deliver it. Maybe not. But at least I won't keep stumbling over your feelings as I crash around like a bull in a china shop."

Suddenly Ellen wished she'd just taken him to bed. It would have been so much easier. It might have felt so right. Now she was likely to lose him altogether, and the thought made her physically ill. And two hours ago she'd been telling herself that she'd be better off if she never saw him again.

"I want you to hold me," she heard herself confess. "I want you to kiss me and tell me you won't rush me but you won't give up on me, either. I want you to stay for a long, long while, but I want you to promise me that we won't make love tonight." She felt ridiculous, but to her amazement, Reed only looked relieved.

"You're telling me," he said slowly, "that I really am moving in the right direction . . . I'm just moving too fast?"

She nodded. She licked her lips.

He took a step closer. "Do you . . . really think you could care for me? In time, I mean?"

Ellen's grip on his fingers tightened. "Reed, I already care for you. I've been thinking about you ever since we met."

A slow, happy grin splayed across his face, and he tapped their joined hands against his thigh in an almost boyish display of pleasure. "You want to go to a movie?" he asked.

"Tonight?"

He nodded. "I think a date in a public place might be wise."

Ellen grinned. She'd been true to herself and she hadn't lost him! "If I can have popcorn, you can pick the show."

"Deal." He kissed her again, but this time it was a gentle, friendly kiss, and nothing more.

He tried to give her the same kind of kiss three hours later when he brought her home. By then Ellen was feeling so warm, so happy, so full of the joy of his touch, that she kissed him back in a way that let him know he made her sizzle.

It was a long kiss, so hot it scorched her...so hot she knew at once she'd made a mistake. She wasn't at all sure she had the strength to tell him to go.

To her surprise, it was Reed who broke off the kiss, even though he trembled with the effort.

"I made you a promise, Ellen Andrews, and I intend to keep it," he told her huskily, refusing to step foot inside. Slowly he dropped his arms from her waist, leaving her feeling bereft and painfully aware of what she was giving up. He took a deep breath, closed his eyes and opened them again, as though to gain control.

Ellen did the same.

"Reed . . ." she whispered, not at all sure what to do next.

But Reed did. He gave her a dimpled grin, kissed her chastely on the cheek, then raised one eyebrow rakishly as he vowed, "I should also warn you that my promise expires at midnight."

THE SUPERVISOR DIDN'T like his contact's last report. He didn't like it a bit. Capwell was already getting the picture, but the Andrews woman had gone straight from replacing her tires to Shannon Waverly and spilled out everything! Now it would look odd if Waverly didn't put the story in the paper, but if she did, everybody would take a keener interest in that old coffee can, and some of the very people whose interest he did not wish to arouse would be far more likely to pay attention. Separately, nobody knew what had really happened; after all this time, surely none of them cared. But if that Andrews woman stirred up the hive, the bees might start buzzing. And after that lunchtime tête-à-tête comparing notes with Capwell, chances were good that she was well on her way to tracking down the queen bee and some key drones.

It didn't help any that the supervisor had had no luck at all finding the evidence Ellen Andrews must have hidden. He hadn't had any trouble checking her desk at Z & E; he'd just tossed Olga Rios a cheery smile when the secretary had glanced up to make sure he was someone she knew. Breaking in to the apartment had been a little harder, but no one had seen him slip in through the unlocked window. He hadn't found a thing in her papers there—just letters from her sons and some notes on her current Chumash Mountain project. The supervisor knew he'd have to go check the cabin eventually, but he hated to make the long trip, and he'd have no excuse for being up there if anybody recognized him. Besides, Ellen and John were there during the week, and when they left on Thursday night, Ellen probably took the coffee can with her. Any way he looked at it, stealing the evidence was not going to be easy. In any event, by now it might be too late for such a theft to do much good.

All in all, it would probably be easier just to kill the woman now and be done with it. At the rate she was going, the supervisor didn't think she'd leave him with any other choice.

CHAPTER SEVEN

IT WAS A LONG and difficult week in the mountains. Ellen tried to respond to all of John's suggestions regarding the survey—including the ones that she was certain he'd make only to a rank beginner—but she found it difficult to suppress her irritation with his patronizing observations. She also found it difficult to wait for the weekend when she was going to see Reed.

Her first weekend with him had included some very strange ways of getting to know a man. A business lunch had turned into a police report and tire-shopping trip; a nondate had turned out to be a deep and tender encounter; the next afternoon had transformed itself into a beautiful matinee at a local theatre group's production of *Oklahoma* before Ellen had rushed off to the gym. All in all, Reed Capwell had simply painted her life with sunshine.

She still knew that it was entirely too soon to be getting involved with a man, but somehow common sense was not enough to keep her from feeling joyous as she remembered his smile. More dramatic was her memory of the way she felt when he'd kissed her goodnight, fighting, she was certain, every ounce of the banked passion that she was fighting herself.

By Thursday night, when she returned to Bentbow, Ellen was dying to see Reed, but it seemed a bit premature to call him the instant she arrived. The only message on her answering machine was from Shannon Waverly, who wanted her to know that Julie Ruskin had heard from two of her sisters, one of whom recognized another girl in the photocopied picture as a good friend of her youngest sister, Marylou, who was still out of town.

On Friday morning, after a brief call to Shannon to set up a lunch date, Ellen decided that it was time to act on the information she'd received from Reed last week. She had two things on her list to do. The first was to talk to the staff geologist, Lucy Silverman, about the properties of diabase, where it was likely to be found, and why there was no mention of it in the Manzanita Meadows EIR. She also wanted Lucy to look at the geological map she'd found in the time capsule, which appeared to be a copy of the official geological map in the report she'd scrutinized. Then she planned to ask her supervisor to help her track down his three former employees. Personnel would certainly object to Ellen's looking at private files that were none of her business.

"Hi, Lars," she greeted the red-faced man at the office, hoping he was in a good mood. "How goes it down here in civilization?"

"Everything's going to hell in a hand-basket, but other than that everything's just fine," he answered gruffly, his broad red face hinting at a smile. "How's life in the mountains?"

Ellen grinned as enthusiastically as she was able. Not for a moment did she intend to let Lars know how tired she was, let alone how boring and lonely she found her evenings on Chumash Mountain, both with and without John.

"It's refreshing, Lars. I'm enjoying the challenge."

"Good." He turned back to his desk before she could question him about the personnel files. Still, she had to persevere—she was no longer asking out of idle curiosity. Something odd, maybe even dangerous, was going on, and she intended to get to the bottom of it.

"Lars, I need to ask a favor. Actually, I just need your permission to... well, to get some information from personnel."

He raised his shaggy white eyebrows. "Personnel? You want to check your file?"

"No, I want to check the files of three people who used to work here. I need phone numbers or addresses for Steve Young, Dale Castleman and Sally Quinton."

Lars laid down the pencil in his hand and stared at her blankly. "You want the phone numbers and addresses of three people who worked here fifteen, twenty years ago? How on earth do you even know these people? John hasn't even been here long enough to know them."

Ellen took a deep breath. "I don't know them. I just think they might have some information that I need."

Lars rubbed his flat chin. "I'm waiting."

She swallowed hard, then gave her boss a quick rundown on the time capsule mystery before she explained, "Reed Capwell and I compared a list of the original Chumash Mountain survey Z & E staff with the Z & E consultants he worked with as an assistant planner. Those three names ended up on both lists. I think one of them must have buried the time capsule. It's the only logical explanation."

Lars glared at her. "Look, Ellen, I didn't mind you playing Ellen Andrews, P.I., on your own time, but keep it out of the office, okay? I *know* Steve and Sally and Dale. They're good people, all of them, and they still live in the area, or near enough. Your time capsule's been in the news; if one of them had buried it, you would have heard by now. I don't like the idea of handing out private information so a stranger can hound folks about something that has nothing to do with them. It doesn't seem kosher, somehow."

Ellen could see his point, but she couldn't let go, either. Not with the memory of those slashed sidewalls and Reed's carved-up dash and smashed windshield.

"Lars," she revealed reluctantly, "there's a chance that it isn't just an ordinary time capsule. There's a chance that it's connected somehow with some trouble Reed and I have been having. The police don't seem to think so. I don't think they care much one way or another. But Reed cares a lot about his old T-Bird, and I care a lot about my new Accord."

Lars cocked his shiny head to one side and squinted. "What's your car have to do with this? Or Reed's, for that matter?"

She hated to tell him; he was likely to fuss as much as Reed had. But it was too late to back out now.

"Reed's car window was shattered by a rock two weeks ago. It's an odd rock, rare in the area, and a virtual twin to a rock I found in the time capsule. There were knife slashes in the dashboard, as well."

Lars's eyes narrowed, but he made no comment.

"When I called last Friday after lunch to say I had a flat tire, it was a bit more serious than that. Both of my rear sidewalls were slashed. Reed thinks they could easily have been cut by the same person with the same knife."

Now Lars looked genuinely alarmed. "Surely you don't think anybody who ever worked for Z & E did something like that? Reed knows those three people! Not for a minute—"

"No, Lars, I don't think any of *them* did it! Neither does Reed! But all this trouble came about after I found the time capsule, and I imagine that one of them might remember something from their time at Chumash Mountain that might give us a clue as to what is happening."

He shook his head. "I suspect that you've just had two unsavory incidents that prove we live too damn close to L.A. They probably don't have anything to do with each other, and nothing to do with the time capsule at all."

"I'd agree with you, Lars, except for the rock. It's a type that just doesn't belong here. A vandal doesn't track down an oddball rock to smash the nearest car."

Now his eyes grew grave. "Ellen, what's this rock look like?"

"It's diabase. Greenish-black. Igneous."

"Igneous?" he repeated. "Why, there hasn't been volcanic action in this part of California for at least 40,000 years."

"I know. Lucy Silverman said it would take a massive excavation of earth to bring something like that to the surface—a landslide caused by a flood, an earthquake or a volcano, or something of that nature. Reed says that renegade chunks of diabase periodically show up in oddball places, but nothing like that is even mentioned in the Manzanita Meadows EIR or indi-

cated in the geological map I found in the time capsule." She didn't add that she'd even considered the
possibility that the cryptic reference to "fault" on the
back of Reed's card referred to an earthquake rather
than somebody's guilt, but the EIR had only mentioned earthquake concerns in passing—and dismissed them—in the standard query of any southern
California EIR Lucy said there was no scientific record of any unusual seismic activity in the Manzanita
Meadows area, or Chumash Mountain, for that matter.

"It sounds like this rock was brought in from somewhere else as part of a collection," Lars said.

"Possibly. Probably. But where it comes from
doesn't matter so much as why it was used to vandal-
ize Reed's car. It's hard to believe that the similarity
between the two rocks is coincidental."

Lars stood up slowly. "I don't like this, Ellen. I don't
like the idea of one of my employees being harassed.
Especially a young woman without family in town."

Ellen wasn't sure whether to be angry or touched. A
young woman without family in town! She was going
to be a grandmother, for Pete's sake! But she was a
good twenty years younger than her supervisor, and in
his eyes, she was sure she did seem rather young. When
Reed smiled at her, she felt sixteen again.

"I'll arrange for you to get the information you
need, Ellen. But I don't want you to take any chances.
Don't do anything dangerous on your own."

"Thank you, Lars. I'll be careful," she promised.

She strode off with all the confidence she could
muster, but she found it hard to conceal the fresh alarm
that Lars had awakened within her. She'd tried to tell

herself that Reed was overly sensitive about safety because of his background in the war. She didn't know a thing about her blustery boss's past, but she knew that, to a lesser extent, he shared Reed's concern.

Ellen was concerned, too. But she refused to be frightened. Howard would have expected her to be scared; he would have fussed and hounded and coddled her until she was terrified.

But Howard was gone, and she was on her own in California. She couldn't afford to be uneasy. She had to be brave and strong.

Some things were easier said than done.

UNDER NORMAL circumstances, Reed would have just placed a call to a woman he was interested in dating and let the chips fall where there might. Yes, no, maybe some other time . . . it never mattered much to him.

But Ellen was different. Ellen mattered too much altogether. And Ellen was so terribly touchy about male-dominant roles that he was afraid to do anything that might seem too aggressive. He'd hoped she'd call him on Thursday night to take the decision out of his hands, but when she hadn't done so by four o'clock on Friday, he decided he'd have to call her. She was only free on the weekends; he couldn't bear to let this one slip away.

And yet his rational, analytical mind told him that pursuing Ellen might not be a wise thing for him to do. She'd made it clear that she wasn't ready to get involved with any man; she still hadn't shed all the baggage of her divorce. By his very nature, he was protective of those who mattered to him. Ellen claimed that a "care giver" was the one kind of man she absolutely did not want.

But she wanted him anyway; he'd felt it in her hands, seen it in her eyes. If he just gave her time . . .

"Hello, Ellen, this is Reed Capwell," he greeted her rather formally when he got her on the phone. He didn't want to sound overly cool, but on the other hand, he didn't want to reveal how eager he was to see her if she was going to tell him that she'd changed her mind again.

"Hi, Reed, I'm glad you called," she said, her tone rather businesslike. "I wanted to tell you that Lars gave me the phone numbers and addresses of our three links. I've set up appointments to see Steve and Dale tomorrow. Sally Quinton has moved to San Diego and has an unlisted number. I'm going to try to track her down on Sunday."

Reed wasn't quite sure what to say. He was glad Ellen was making progress in solving her mystery, and glad nothing terrible had happened to her this week. But he'd hoped that she might be glad to hear from him for some other reason. If she was, she was keeping it to herself.

"That's great, Ellen. Did Steve or Dale give you any information?"

"No, but to tell you the truth, I didn't tell them very much. I want to show them the contents of the time capsule and see if it jars their memories. Neither one admitted burying it, but it's possible that they'll know something about the stuff inside, anyway. At least, that's my theory."

It was a great theory. The only thing wrong with it was that it didn't have anything to do with him. In another moment, she was likely to hang up and tell him she'd drop him a memo about the outcome some time next week.

Feeling a bit silly, Reed asked, "Would you like some company? I know both of them, you know. I know you can ask questions as well as I can, but since the cotter-pin of this search might lie in the work I did with one of those guys, there might be something that would come to light if we chewed it over together."

There was a silence. Then Ellen said, "That's a good idea, Reed. If you don't have anything else to do to-morrow—"

"Not a thing, Ellen." And then, because he wanted a real relationship with this woman, he added, "To tell you the truth, I was hoping to spend tomorrow with you. I've . . . missed you this week, Ellen."

To his surprise she hesitantly confessed, "I've missed you, too, Reed."

He exhaled slowly. "I sure didn't get that impression when I said hello."

Tension radiated through the telephone wire. After a shaky silence, she said slowly, "I didn't want to sound . . . overanxious, Reed. I was afraid by now you might have decided that I may not be worth the trouble. This thing between us is . . . well, an uphill struggle in some ways."

"Ellen," he said softly, "this thing between us is *inevitable*."

When he heard her take a deep breath, he desperately wished she were close enough to touch. This was one time he was certain she would not refuse his kiss.

BY THE TIME ELLEN reached her Friday night aerobics class, she was almost too tired to move. She wished she'd just gone home and taken a bath...or better yet, gone home to Reed.

It was getting harder and harder to fight him. Worse yet, she couldn't really think of a good reason to keep doing it. He was trying so hard to accommodate her needs. And the bottom line was, he was succeeding.

Tomorrow would be the perfect time to reach out to Reed, to celebrate the way he made her tingle, to luxuriate in the power of making him tingle in return. The old Ellen would have been too shy to make love with a man she'd only known three weeks. Could the new Ellen reach out for what she wanted and shed her fears?

The class took more out of her than usual, but Ellen still doggedly did her weight-room exercises afterward. By the time she was halfway done, she was so limp that she knew she wasn't putting out her best. Apparently the vigorous shop owner knew it, too.

"A bit of energy, now, Ellen!" June urged her as she sweated away on the leg press. "You want those quads to be super-strong."

Ellen tried not to glare at her. "I hike all day. You'd think that would make them strong enough."

"Hiking strengthens the calves and to some extent the hams, but doesn't do much for the quads," June told her. "You need balanced leg muscles for superior strength."

Ellen tried to push harder. "How much strength do I need? All I want to do is feel reasonably fit and keep the flab off my hips. I really do the weights just to tone my arms."

"Your greatest strength doesn't come from the arms," June corrected her, "though of course you should work on every muscle in your body. A woman's true power lies in her legs."

By the time Ellen got off the leg press, she didn't feel the least bit powerful. She felt too weak to crawl.

As she drove slowly home to her empty apartment, she felt the vulnerability of her true physical strength. If Reed was right—if somebody was trying to warn her—what good would a pair of strong legs do her?

She shivered as she thought of her slashed tires. Pulling into her dark apartment garage, she suddenly wondered if a man who used a knife so ruthlessly on a tire would wield it with equal abandon on a woman's throat.

REED KNOCKED on Ellen's door at 8:45 a.m. and found her, to his delight, wearing a dress. It was a casual knit creation that fit snugly around her waist, then flowed enticingly below her knees. The royal blue was a perfect complement to her lovely gray eyes.

"Good morning," he said, delighted by the smile that broke across her face when she saw him. "Do we have to go back to ground zero this weekend, or can I kiss you hello?"

His greeting seemed to set her back for an instant. Then she pulled open the door and motioned him to come inside. "I think a ritual of greeting would be acceptable," she teased.

Reed slipped both arms around Ellen and gently kissed her. With more vigor than he'd expected, she kissed him back. The embarrassed look in her eyes told him that she hadn't intended to be so bold.

For a moment Ellen rested in his arms, her face just millimeters from Reed's chest. He could feel his own heart pounding—or maybe it was hers—and he knew that a simple hello kiss was not nearly enough to meet her week-long hunger...or his, either.

"Ellen," he said softly. At once, she glanced up, the hunger in her eyes unmasked, and he kissed her again.

This time she didn't even try to pretend she didn't want him; her whole body eagerly pressed against his as Reed's tongue danced with her own. His hands pressed against her lower back, then sensually eased down past her spine. Cupping her hips, he brought her close against him, reveling at her tiny whimper.

"Ellen," he breathed again. The single word was an aching plea.

She nuzzled his throat with the top of her head. "It's been a long week," she whispered.

He didn't answer; he just kissed her again.

It was a long kiss, too long for a man and a woman who were about to spend the day interviewing other people. Reed would happily have chucked the morning's plans and locked the door, but Ellen eventually broke free of his embrace.

"I guess we better get going," she declared unsteadily.

It was not the declaration he had hoped for. He almost said "please," but managed to refrain. He kissed her again, more cautiously this time, and her answering kiss was friendly but made no promises.

"It's...almost nine o'clock, Reed," she announced, her voice trembling slightly. "I really think we should go."

He was gratified by the unsteadiness of her voice and her slightly breathless air. Her eyes met his uncertainly, then closed as she leaned up for one more kiss. It was a deep kiss, more like the first, and this time it was Ellen's tongue that begged to play with his. But after a minute, she broke off this kiss, too, then leaned against his chest.

"You know how I feel, Reed," she warmed him by confessing. "But I...I think we should take care of business first. We have...we have all day to be together."

He rather hoped she meant "We have all night," but he didn't press her. He kissed her on the cheek, then reluctantly stepped back, waiting for Ellen to lock the door. Reed took her hand as they started toward the street, and to his delight she gripped his warmly. But when they reached the sidewalk, she turned sharply to the left.

The T-Bird was to her right.

"Where are you going?" he asked.

"To my garage, of course." Her eyes were daring him to contradict her. "This is my expedition. I invited you along, remember?"

Recalling all the fuss they'd gone through over the tires, Reed was tempted to say, "What the heck, we'll take your car." And he didn't mind riding with her, not really. But they were on his terrain, not hers, and she was already making a long weekly commute. Cautiously he answered, "Sure, I remember, and you can drive if you like. I just thought that since you're new to L.A. and just came back from Chumash Mountain, you might appreciate letting somebody else drive.

If we were in Kansas, I'd sure be eager to relinquish the wheel.''

To his relief, he seemed to have struck the right note. Ellen said, "I guess that does make sense. My Honda is just wonderful, but I'm getting my fill of driving up and down that mountain.''

"I can imagine. I'm not even sure how to get there.''

As he opened the door for Ellen, she spelled out just what the trip involved. By the time they reached the freeway, she was sharing highlights of her last letter from her oldest son and Reed was bringing her up to date on Nate's new girlfriend in Arizona.

They reached Dale's house in less than fifty minutes. He lived in a fairly posh older area. Every home seemed to be framed by large, ancient trees, and no two houses were alike.

The sense of peace, however, was just an illusion, at least it was at Dale's home. As Reed ushered Ellen up the sidewalk, he could hear two angry voices, one male, one female. The male voice was Dale's.

At the door, Ellen touched his hand and asked softly, "Should we ring the bell, Reed? I hate to interfere during a family squabble.''

Reed wasn't quite sure what to do. If he'd been dropping by unannounced, he certainly would have left and come back later. But Dale was expecting them. Besides, it seemed to Reed that sometimes it was just as well that a fight was interrupted. Back in the days when he and Clara had quarreled so often, Reed had often wished for the phone to ring or somebody—even a door-to-door salesman—to drop by.

"Let's play it by ear," he suggested, unable to resist nuzzling Ellen's hair as he rang the bell. "We might be doing Dale a favor. Just pretend you didn't hear a thing."

Ellen was grinning at him when the door swung open a moment later.

Dale was wearing a red Friends of the Earth T-shirt and well-worn jeans. Except for the scowl on his face and the extra twenty pounds he carried, he still looked much like an overgrown, curly-haired choirboy. He stared at Ellen as though she were an agent for the IRS.

Before she could speak Reed said enthusiastically, "Hi, Dale. Good to see you again."

Dale's eyes flitted uncertainly to Reed's, registering the familiar face as he acknowledged Reed's outstretched hand with a cursory shake. "Yeah. Hi," he said noncommittally, then glanced back inside before opening the door another inch.

"Dale, this is my friend Ellen Andrews. She's doing survey work on Chumash Mountain for Z & E, living in the cabin just like you did."

"Right. She called," he replied, as though Ellen were not even there. He glanced back into the house once more, then said, "Uh, I guess you guys should come in."

It wasn't the most gracious invitation Reed had ever heard, but he knew this would be their only chance.

"What a lovely home you have, Dale," Ellen commented warmly as she stepped inside, ignoring the fact that her host was treating her like Typhoid Mary. "That's a magnificent picture of the Grand Canyon."

"My wife picked it out," Dale replied sourly, glancing again toward the back of the house.

Reed decided not to wait for an invitation to sit down. He remembered that Dale was not long on niceties, but he couldn't recall him being rude. Of course, his surliness might just be the result of his fight with his wife, or whoever the woman was. Still, there might have been another reason for his odd behavior. Was it possible that Chumash Mountain was a sore spot with him?

"So where do you work these days?" Reed asked, hoping to ease the situation before they launched into any serious discussions.

"Uh, City of Orangewood. It's not bad. You still at the County?"

Reed nodded. "I'm a supervising planner now. Otherwise not much has changed."

"How's Clara?" It was the first truly personal comment Dale had made, and though it was an awkward one to field, it still gave Reed hope that their visit might not be in vain.

"Uh, she's fine. She's . . . living her own life now."

Dale's eyes widened. "You two broke up? I would have sworn—" he broke off as his glance darted back again. A door slammed, possibly from the wind, possibly not. "Marriage," grumbled Dale. "It's like riding a Ferris wheel. One day you're up and having a ball, the next you're lying on your back kicked in the teeth."

Ellen glanced at Reed. There was a personal kind of intimacy in her glance that had not been there a week ago. He felt a flush of warmth, of comfort, of coming home. He sensed she was silently acknowledging the fact that it was a lot easier talking to Dale with Reed's help; at least he'd been on good terms with the biologist once upon a time. Still, Dale wasn't making it easy for either of them.

Suddenly Dale hunched forward and looked at Ellen intently. "On the phone you said you needed to show me some stuff. What is it?"

At once Ellen opened the file folder and handed him the newspaper page, the map and Reed's card, flipping it over so he could read the back. "I found these in a coffee can by the cabin along with a greenish-black rock. Do **any** of these things mean anything to you?"

He took the newspaper and skimmed the articles, then turned over to the development. "It's one of George Haversham's tracts in Manzanita Meadows," he said to Reed. "I wouldn't think you'd need me to tell you that."

Reed shrugged. "That's the only thing we've figured out so far."

Dale raised his hands in a questioning gesture. "What difference does it make? So you found some trash at the cabin. Big deal."

"It's not trash, Dale," Ellen corrected him. "It was neatly folded and buried for some reason. Since I dug it up and mentioned it to Reed, both of our cars have been vandalized and the perpetrator used the same kind of rock as we found in the can. It's an unusual rock in Bentbow County. Do you recall ever seeing any greenish-black diabase in the Chumash Mountain area?"

Dale shook his head. "I don't even know what it is. I'm into plants and animals, not rocks."

Another door slammed in the back of the house. Dale winced. The phone rang. Someone picked it up on the first ring and almost immediately slammed it down.

"Look, Reed and uh, Ellen, I wish I could help you, but I really don't know a thing." He stood up, his body language clearly saying that the conversation was over.

"I wish I could spend more time chatting, but I've got, uh, things to do today."

Ellen opened her mouth as though to argue, but Reed put his arm around her firmly and steered her toward the door. "Thanks a lot for your time, Dale. It was good to see you again."

"Sure, Reed. Yeah, it was good."

Dale practically pushed them out the door and closed it firmly behind them. Ellen leaned against his chest and whispered, "He's hiding something!"

"Yes, but I don't think it's got anything to do with the time capsule."

Before Ellen could answer, a strident female voice boomed out from the living room, "Did you finally get rid of them? How dare you walk out on me when I'm telling you what a louse you are! And I suppose you're going to tell me you've never laid eyes on that woman before in your life! Just like you'd never laid eyes on that waitress at the Chez Louie last night!"

Reed took a deep breath and ushered Ellen toward the car. He wondered what happened between a man and woman who started out where he and Ellen were now—just starting to fall in love—and ended up where Dale and his woman were headed. It was a sobering thought.

"I don't envy Dale," he told Ellen. "I sure hope Steve's having better luck with his wife."

As it turned out, Steve had been widowed and remarried since Reed had seen him last. When Reed expressed sympathy, Steve's kind brown eyes admitted that he still felt some pain, but his broad smile assured his old friend that he'd found a new lifemate who filled him with happiness.

Reed was beginning to wonder if *he* had just found a new lifemate as well. Oh, it was much too soon to tell. But on the other hand, he wasn't a kid; he knew what he wanted. And he'd been all but blind to women for a number of years. Ellen was pretty, but she didn't have the kind of looks that bowled a man over. There was something else in Ellen—something shy, something brave—that spoke to Reed in a way no woman had spoken to him in a very long time. It reminded him, in a way, of the way he'd once been drawn to Su Le.

"I'm surprised you didn't track down Sally Quinton when you found yourself single," Reed quipped to get the conversation started in the direction of Chumash Mountain. "As I recall, you thought she was hotter than a kiln."

Steve laughed. "Oh, yeah, she was hot. But she was also married the last time I saw her, and as I recall, Peter would have shot any man who looked at her cross-eyed. He was ready to go gunning for me just because we stayed up at the cabin together for a while. I never met a more suspicious husband."

Reed leaned forward and teased, "Did he have any reason to be jealous, Steve?"

Steve laughed. "Don't I wish! Sally was so damned businesslike when we were up there. They were only engaged then—hadn't been for very long, either—but she made it clear to me that she'd decided Peter was it for life and that was that."

Ellen made no comment on the discussion, but Reed was beginning to wish he'd come to see Steve alone. He and Steve had had one of those male-bonding, jovial relationships where every other word is a joke, and a lot of those jokes had centered around Sally Quinton's body. Neither one of them had ever seriously pursued her, but now, with Ellen sitting beside him, he felt slightly uncomfortable, just the same.

Subtly, he reached out an arm around her and let his fingertips fall on her shoulder. In high school, it would have been a bold gambit—to see how much touching he could get away with—but today he made the move deliberately to assure Ellen that he had not forgotten she was there. He felt her tighten as he touched her, then relax after his fingertips gently stroked her once or twice.

Reed wished *he* could relax. He was churned up, edgy, and he had been all day. There were too many things on his mind to concentrate on meeting old friends and unearthing clues. He still was uneasy about the damage to Ellen's car and the damage to his own. Somebody was warning him off. If it *was* the time capsule that was causing the trouble, should they be pursuing it at all? And if it wasn't the time capsule, was it fair to let Ellen get close to him—worse yet, to let their relationship become known?

In another life, he would have turned to Nathan for advice. Nathan would have offered quiet support, even if he hadn't known what to do. But Nathan was gone, and the other men he'd served with had drifted away. He didn't even get Christmas cards from most of them anymore.

He'd never gotten one from Captain Harrison, either, but he knew his old C.O. would never forget him. Their last parting was permanently etched in Reed's memory. They'd all been in uniform, clean, pressed and shiny, on the day they'd said goodbye. The captain was not a man for sentiment, but he'd barked at his men: "What has happened here is over, but in some ways it will never end. We are bound by blood. Just as we have kept each other alive in this corner of hell, we will keep each other alive anytime, anywhere, if we need each other again."

Reed had known then, as he knew now, that he could always call Captain Harrison for advice. He knew where he was stationed, because he'd read an article about him recently—he was a colonel now. It wouldn't be difficult to get a message through to him. Still, Reed couldn't quite bring himself to call his old CO. The man's job was to deal with matters of national security, literally life and death. Slashed tires—even *Ellen's* slashed tires—just didn't seem worth troubling him.

Yet.

Reed let Ellen do the talking as she handed Steve her file folder and told him what she'd told Dale. Steve gave the file a great deal more attention than Dale had; he even pondered the note on the back of Reed's card awhile. And he told them everything he could remember about his stay at Chumash Mountain—the weather, the potential project, his daily activities—but none of it seemed germane.

"I wish I could help you guys," Steve concluded regretfully. "The mystery itself is rather intriguing, and I've gotta admit I don't like the idea of anybody trashing that old T-Bird. It was a classic even when I knew it."

"It was born a classic," Reed said proudly.

"As I recall, didn't you buy it from a friend?" Steve asked.

Reed found the simple question hard to answer. "I...
inherited it from one. We fought together in 'Nam. We
shared everything. He didn't come back, so...I got the
car."

He didn't add that he'd also gotten Nathan's wife.
He wasn't sure why he'd said as much as he had; even
back when he'd known Steve well, he'd never confided a word about Nathan. Now—as he glanced ten-
derly at Ellen—Reed realized that it wasn't Steve he was
telling at all. He wanted Ellen to know who he was,
who he was inside, but he'd never found it easy to bring
Nathan casually into a conversation.

Ellen did not turn around to face him—that would
have been too obvious—but to his surprise she turned
her shoulder just slightly in his direction, brushing his
chest with a level of unspoken intimacy. It was such a
subtle motion that Reed almost missed her silent attempt to soothe him, but when the file in her hand—
and then the hand itself—gently brushed his knee, he
had no doubts about her quiet message.

And no doubt what was going to happen when they
returned to Bentbow for the night.

CHAPTER EIGHT

WHEN THEY GOT on the freeway, Reed took Ellen's hand in a gesture that was both sweet and curiously electrifying. It felt so right to her that she just squeezed his fingers; she didn't try to talk.

A good twenty minutes passed before she said softly, "I'm going to drive down to Sally Quinton's last address in San Diego tomorrow. You want to come along?"

Reed warmed her with a dimpled smile. "I'd be delighted. It's a long drive, though, and you can't spend the night and get back to Bentbow at dawn, so we better get an early start."

Ellen waited for him to suggest that they could get an early start faster if they spent the night together, but he didn't. She was both relieved and disapppointed. She didn't think she was quite ready to spend the night with him, but she was, paradoxically, ready for him to ask.

She was even ready to be persuaded.

"Do you have any plans for the evening?" he questioned softly, as though he were reading her mind. "I don't mean to overstay my welcome, but since you fed me last Saturday, I think it'd be fair for me to do the same for you. I've even got something that isn't frozen."

Ellen smiled. "Going to put me to shame, are you?"

Reed chuckled with her. "Hardly. I only know how to make three things: steak, pork chops and barbecued chicken. Throw in a salad or frozen vegetables and you've pretty much got the whole picture."

"Which is it tonight?"

"Take your pick, but the pork chops are already thawing."

"Gee, Reed, I feel like pork chops tonight," Ellen teased him.

"That's terrific. I just happen to have some in my refridge."

She was sharing his grin when he pulled up on the right side of the driveway of a tastefully landscaped California ranch-style tract home. The left side was already occupied by a gold Camaro.

"A bit modern for you, isn't it, Reed?" Ellen asked.

Reed rolled his eyes. "It's not mine. Jackie must have dropped by. I usually see her when it's her turn for her little girl, but she had Sherry last weekend."

"She doesn't have custody of her daughter?" Ellen asked, rather surprised. Granted, the world was beginning to acknowledge that some fathers were better custodial parents for one reason or another, but it was still not very common.

"No. Well, actually, Sherry isn't even Jackie's daughter. She just thinks of her that way. She's her ex-husband's little girl. Jackie just got so attached to her that he consented to let her continue the relationship after their divorce. I think it's sort of a relief for him not to have to entertain a toddler for a whole weekend."

Reed didn't get a chance to say much else before a blond girl in her early twenties floated out of the house, waving at Reed as she met his car in the driveway. She was pretty, in a frail and delicate sort of way. She bore no resemblance whatsoever to Reed.

"Hi, Daddy! I've got great news!"

Reed got out of the car, hugged his daughter, then gestured to Ellen as Ellen hopped out of the car, too.

"Honey, this is my friend Ellen Andrews. Ellen, my daughter Jackie."

There was an intimacy in their warmth that filled Ellen with a curious rush of tearfulness. Suddenly she realized that she was very far away from her own boys and missed them terribly.

"It's nice to meet you, Jackie," she valiantly declared. "Your dad has told me a lot about you."

Jackie smiled, clearly a bit taken aback. It was obvious that she'd never heard of Ellen.

"It's, uh, nice to meet you, too, Mrs. Andrews," she said pleasantly.

"Please call me Ellen."

"Ellen," the girl repeated uncertainly, tossing her father a bewildered glance.

"Ellen's trying to solve a mystery, Jackie," Reed informed her, as though the mystery alone could explain Ellen's presence. "She found a time capsule with my business card in it up on Chumash Mountain."

This time, Jackie nodded with more confidence. "Yeah, Mom said something about that. Kind of weird, huh?"

Ellen nodded, following Reed's lead as he ushered them into the house.

"Well, it's an adventure," Reed said. Then, just as she was getting uneasy about Reed's true feelings, he added, "And a blessing, Jack, because otherwise I never would have met Ellen."

He put his arm around Ellen in the subtlest of gestures, but the message was clear to Ellen and clear to his daughter, too.

Right on cue, Jackie answered, "Well, I guess you've got somebody out there to thank for burying it, huh, Daddy?"

Reed winked at her. "You bet."

As soon as they were seated in the living room and a purring gray tabby had claimed Reed's lap, he asked his daughter, "You said you had good news?"

"Yes, Daddy, the greatest!" Pride swept over her lovely features. "I did what you said. *I got a job!*"

Ellen hadn't forgotten how hard it was to get a job as a teenager, but Jackie acted as though this were her first, and she wasn't a teenager. She had to be at least Barry's age. And Barry—her youngest—was halfway through college.

"Honey, that's terrific!" Reed enthused, before he even asked about the position, which turned out to be a swing shift at a convenience store. Obviously getting a job was not an easy task for his daughter, and he applauded her victory.

After they discussed the details for several minutes—with Reed reminding Jackie that *keeping* a job required scrupulous adherence to the boss's decree—Jackie said quietly, "I'm still having trouble with the Camaro, Daddy. You said you might buy me a new car if I helped pay for it. I figure with my new job, I can pay you a hundred dollars a month. I picked out a Toyota Camry today—three years old, great condition, good price—and I was hoping we could go get it tomorrow.''

Reed looked taken aback. ''Tomorrow? Honey, Ellen and I are going to San Diego tomorrow. Besides, I think we need some time to see—''

''Daddy, I'll be working at *night*.'' Her tone was not quite petulant, but certainly pleading. ''It's not in all that great a section of town, and I want to make sure I have reliable transportation. You promised me. . . .''

At that point, Ellen stopped listening. It was a family discussion, the kind she herself had had a thousand times with her sons. Parenting was always hard; sometimes it was downright impossible. In the end, Reed told Jackie that he'd call her back later in the evening.

''We've been gone all day and we're hungry, honey. Let me fix dinner for Ellen and give it some thought.''

''Okay, but I've got a date at seven-thirty. He's real nice, Daddy. He's a teller at your bank.''

After that, Jackie politely told Ellen how glad she was to meet her, wished them both a great evening, and disappeared with only a glimmer of a grin. It was obvious that she adored her father, and equally obvious that she thought it was amusing that he had a woman friend with whom he wanted to spend time alone.

Ellen wondered how amused her own sons would be if they knew that their mother was actually contemplating making love to a man who was not their dad.

REED LET ELLEN HELP him with dinner, and he had to admit that it felt good to have her at his side. When they weren't fighting over who was in charge, their motions together seemed quite natural. He wondered how natural their interaction would be after dinner.

After last weekend, when she'd started and stopped so many times, he was leery about letting their touching grow intimate. And yet—he could not deny it—he wanted more from Ellen than holding hands.

"What are you going to do about Jackie?" Ellen asked him once they were settled down to eat. "Is her Camaro really in bad shape?"

Reed shrugged uncomfortably, his last conversation with Clara weighing heavily on his mind. She didn't want him to help Jackie pay for anything, especially a new car. But she *did* want Jackie to get a job. "It needs some work, but it's sure not hopeless. On the other hand, she is offering to pay for this car, and that's a first for her. It sounds as though she's picked out a sensible vehicle, too. I hate to spike that sort of enterprise."

Ellen studied him a moment, then braved a suggestion. "Maybe you should have her sign a contract with you, the way she would at a bank, guaranteeing a regular monthly payment. It doesn't matter how much it is, Reed; you could make it low. What's important is that she sticks by her agreements."

"Madam, can I assume you've been down this road before?" he asked, raising his eyebrows playfully.

Ellen laughed. "Three times, Reed. And the rocks in the road never did get smoothed out. But I'm glad to say that all my boys have turned out well. Not that there weren't some difficult times here and there, but—" maternal pride glowed in her eyes "—they're all wonderful kids."

"Good. You're lucky." He studied her for a moment, then asked, "Are they on good terms with their father?"

She nodded. "Yes. Their relationship with him is different than it is with me, but actually, they get along pretty well with both of us."

"If one of them asked for money to buy a car, would you say yes?"

Ellen smiled. "Reed, I barely had enough money to buy my own car. About all I can offer my kids at the moment is emotional support. If they need to borrow money, they have to go to their father."

Reed pondered that a moment. "Ellen, I hope you'll understand what I'm about to say. It has nothing to do with you, but everything to do with Jackie. I promised to call her back by seven-thirty, but before I do, I'm going to have to excuse myself for a moment to call Clara."

He watched her closely, hoping she wouldn't remind him of the obvious: it was bad form to take time out from a date to call your ex-wife. Her lips did seem to stiffen just a tad, but all she said was, "If you've got an extension in some other room, I'll do the dishes while you make the call."

To Reed's surprise, she leaned forward and kissed him gently—no, teasingly would be a better word— then started to clear the table.

Only the stiffness in the set of her shoulders gave her discomfort away.

"CLARA LIKED THE IDEA of a signed contract," Reed told Ellen when he brought her some hot cider about half an hour later, "and she was thrilled that Jackie had bestirred herself to get a job. So I followed your advice. I told Jackie I'd loan her the money with the understanding that she pay me back at the rate of one hundred dollars a month. If she's more than a month overdue at any time, I told her I'd repossess it, like any bank would."

"Did you mean it?" Ellen asked.

Reed thought about it. "I think so. I mean, if she's really trying and something goes wrong, maybe not. But if she gives me the same old song and dance, I will, Ellen. I swear it. She's too old to be happy—I mean, truly happy—acting like a child and counting on her daddy to bail her out of her scrapes. If Nathan were alive—"

He broke off suddenly, so suddenly that Ellen knew he'd said something he hadn't intended to say.

Gently she probed, "I thought Nathan was in school in Arizona." Had he used the past tense when he'd mentioned his son and she'd just failed to hear it? Or was the reality too painful to tell people?

"Nate—my boy—is fine, Ellen. He is in Arizona. He was named for Jackie's biological father. Clara's first husband."

"She named *your* son for her *ex*-husband?" Ellen asked, bewildered and irate on Reed's behalf.

"No, no. We named him together. Nathan didn't leave her; he…died. He was a special friend of mine."

Ellen took a deep breath as the impact of his words hit her. He wasn't talking about just any friend; he was talking about his friend in Vietnam! He'd never mentioned his name, but surely he could not feel such pain for more than one person. How had he ended up marrying his best friend's widow? Surely he hadn't double-crossed Nathan; that just didn't seem like the Reed she knew. Besides, he and Clara would never have named their son for a man she'd been unfaithful to.

Ellen had a dozen questions to ask, but she knew that this was a difficult subject for Reed. When he was ready, he would tell her more. It was not her place to push.

"I'm sorry, Reed," she said softly. "I didn't realize that Clara had been married before. I thought it was a first marriage for both of you." As an afterthought, she added, "I'm surprised to learn that Jackie is your stepdaughter. You seem so protective of her, as if you can't think of her as anything but your little girl."

"She *is* my little girl, Ellen. Blood makes no difference; family love is based on other things. Jackie only remembers Nathan because we keep his memory alive. She hasn't seen him since she was a toddler. In her heart, I've always been her daddy."

Ellen reached out for Reed's hand, warming to his touch. "It's so hard sometimes to let them go," she admitted. "I thought I'd finally let all of mine leave the nest, but Matthew broke his leg about five years ago, and when they called me, in my mind I saw him as a toddler, lying on the ground. I drove to the hospital like a madwoman, and when I got there, I was so astonished to see this muscular twenty-two-year-old coming toward me on crutches that I didn't even recognize him!"

Reed chuckled warmly. "Is Matthew your youngest?"

"No, actually he's my middle son. But in some ways I can tell him things I can't tell the others. He was sick a lot as a child and I spent more time, well, coddling him. I love them all in different ways, but Matthew... well, it's different."

Reed took a deep breath. "I know what you mean. I'm as proud as punch of Nate, but he's always been so much more independent than Jackie that I never felt...oh, I don't know...needed. Nate and I hardly ever quarrel, but I don't think we're quite as close because his life is...well, it's *his* life, and it would be pretty much the same even if Clara and I weren't part of it. But Jackie—well, she just wouldn't be Jackie without us."

Ellen pondered that comment for a moment, then suggested, "Maybe you kind of like that, Reed. Being needed so much."

His silence made her wonder if she'd gone too far. But after a few tense heartbeats, he answered, "I think you're right. On the other hand, I wouldn't be much of a father if I didn't give a damn about what Jackie needs. I know she needs to toughen up, but I don't think turning my back on her would really be in her best interests, either. I think my love—and Clara's— provides the greatest stability in her life."

"I guess it's an issue of balance, Reed. Being a parent is never easy. The best you can do is the best you can do."

There was another silence—a comfortable one—before he said, "I guess that holds true in all relationships, Ellen. You learn as you go, and you hope that the other person cares for you enough to forgive an occasional blunder."

She considered the ramifications of his comment before she answered, "Reed, I care for you enough to forgive quite a few blunders." She didn't try to restrain the warmth from her tone. "I hope you care for me enough to do the same."

"Ellen Andrews," he said softly, his voice curiously low, "I care for you enough to forgive us both for anything we've done and anything we might yet do." Ellen's whole body tingled; she could feel the heat in her face as he whispered, "Perhaps you'd like to come a little closer and we could ... consider some new sins we might have to forgive each other for."

Reed didn't touch her, but he lounged nearby on the carpet, and his eyes showed his eagerness to take her in his arms. As the cinnamon cider warmed her inside and out, Ellen could feel Reed's long legs brushing her bent knees. She could sense his desire, calling to a need deep inside her. She knew she still wasn't ready for what he had in mind, but she couldn't bring herself to say, "Reed, just hold me for a while, but don't expect anything more." When he reached out and touched her waist, the intensity of her sensual response took her completely by surprise. Her response to Howard's lovemaking had always been prosaic. But when Reed touched her, even casually, Ellen felt like a shooting star plummeting from the sky. She couldn't stop herself from moving toward him.

"So how do you like California?" he asked, his voice too low and husky to match the casual words.

"The weather's good and the people are friendly," Ellen replied, setting her cider on the tiled rectangle in front of the fire before he could see that her hand was shaking. "I guess I can't complain."

Reed's hand splayed out across her back and rubbed her gently, but he made no effort to pull her closer. He seemed oblivious to his effect on her. "I've never been to Kansas. Drove through one corner of Nebraska once, though."

"Pretty much the same unless you happen to live in one state or the other. Then they're different as night and day."

They shared a chuckle. Somewhere in the laughter Ellen found herself a great deal closer to Reed, and she realized that his arm was all the way around her now. She knew what he wanted, and she wanted it, too. She wasn't fighting Reed, but she was fighting a sense of panic that was hard to mask.

Still, when she looked at Reed, so gentle, so warm, it was hard to recall any good reason to keep him at a distance. Maybe it was time to stop putting up fences. Maybe it was time to stop expecting the worst from men.

Reed took off his glasses and lay them on the rug. He pulled Ellen closer, until her face was just inches from his own. When he kissed the corner of her mouth, she felt shivery, light-headed, in a deliciously dizzy way. She knew he was giving her plenty of time to back off or escape altogether, but she couldn't seem to find the energy to slip away. The panic didn't ease, but the clutch of desire pushed it out of the way.

Suddenly Reed's eyes grew solemn. The hand on her back stopped moving. "I missed you this week, Ellen." He'd told her he missed her before, of course, but that had been casual conversation. Now his voice throbbed with a different kind of urgency. "I wanted to just call and check in. I wanted to meet you for lunch or take you out to dinner, or read the morning paper with you over the breakfast table."

Ellen confessed huskily, "I missed you, too."

Reed looked touched but uncertain, and she couldn't blame him. She'd given him nothing but mixed messages since they'd first met, and she knew she was giving him a kaleidoscope of answers now. She was saying "yes," she was saying "no," she was saying "maybe... if you give me one more kiss...."

Now she leaned forward, admitting, "I thought about you all week. I didn't know just what I'd say to you when I saw you, but I was counting the days."

He licked his lips and studied hers. "Tell me, Ellen," he said softly. "Just tell me what you want. Maybe I'm just rusty, but I'm just having one devil of a time trying to figure you out. I don't want to be clumsy, but—"

This time words were redundant; she silenced him with a kiss. It was a simple kiss, a cautious one, but it was a welcoming invitation nonetheless, and Reed took it as one.

He kissed her back, gingerly, but the soft motion stirred something deep within her.

"Ellen," he whispered, and this time the word was an intimate caress.

She leaned into his embrace as he wrapped his other arm around her and pulled her down beneath him. Her hands cradled his face as she kissed him again, more deeply this time. Even now he was careful, banking the fires she sensed stirring within him. But then he kissed her again, with urgency this time, and she heard him muffle a low groan.

Ellen clutched him more tightly. Reed dropped his head to kiss her throat, deeply and fully. She hadn't expected him to touch her in quite that way, and the sweet heat of his tongue shook her to the core. She was losing control, losing desire for control, losing consciousness of anything but the man in her arms.

"Oh, Reed," she gasped.

His arms slipped around her sides as his thumbs stretched up the sides of her breasts, almost, but not quite, reaching her tautening nipples. Her moan of hunger surprised Ellen as much as it jolted Reed. He kissed her throat again as his hands brushed softly over the soft knit of her bodice. She pressed against him and moaned again. It felt so good, so incredibly good, to be in this man's arms, to feel his majestic hands fondling her aroused breasts. She remembered now what desire really felt like; she knew how good it would feel to tug off her clothes and join with this man.

Then Reed murmured, "Don't ever wonder how I feel about you, Ellen. I haven't touched a woman since my divorce. I wanted to wait until I felt this happy, this full, this certain." His eyes were beautiful, warm with more tenderness than Ellen had guessed a man could feel. He laid one hand on her face and whispered, "Don't be afraid to tell me what you want. I want tonight to be just right for you."

It was in that moment—that achingly beautiful moment—that Ellen realized she wanted the night to be just right for her, too. But she had not given a moment's thought to what would be right for Reed.

She was appalled at her own selfishness. This kind, sexy, sensitive man had opened himself to her, trusted her with his deepest feelings. Incredibly, he was falling in love with her, embarking on a long, sweet journey. Ellen wanted to go with him, but she knew she was no where near ready to travel that far. Though it hurt to admit it, she wanted him tonight mainly to reclaim what Howard had stolen from her: her right to sexual satisfaction and her faith in herself. She longed to feel cherished by somebody.

Someday she knew she might fall in love with Reed. Someday she hoped she'd deserve him. But rising affection, potent sensual need and her own bewildered emptiness were no excuse for making love with him when she knew that he'd take the surrender of her body as proof that she'd also surrendered her heart. Reed deserved better. He was a wonderful man and he had the right to a woman who could give him all of herself. A woman whose courage was greater than her fear.

Reed's hands slipped down to Ellen's waist, over her hips, then edged up under her skirt. The fire within her sizzled. She knew she had another three seconds before the flames would singe her self-control.

"Reed," she whispered with a gasp, "please don't misunderstand this, but—"

His scorching hands froze. "Dammit, Ellen, not again!"

She didn't need to say another word. The mood was shattered.

Reed sat up abruptly, leaving her on the floor with her skirt askew. "I didn't push you!" he growled, grabbing his glasses and jamming them back on his face. "I gave you every damn chance in the world to say no. Why didn't you just say it instead of... well, dammit, leading me on?"

"Reed, it's not that simple!"

"Ellen, we're adults, not children. I can live without sex, but once I let down the barriers, it's—" he glared at her as he stood up shakily "—it's damn hard to pull back so fast."

She felt ridiculous . . . and physically frustrated, too. Every fiber of her body ached for him. How could she explain to Reed why she'd spoiled something so special. "I know it's hard, Reed. It's hard for me, too."

He glared down at her in surprise. "Then why did you do it? Why did you spoil it . . . again?" He didn't sound accusatory so much as genuinely puzzled.

She sat up cross-legged and gripped his foot, the only part of him she could reach. "Reed, I'm so drawn to you. Emotionally. Physically. Mentally. It's such a compelling thing that it scares me."

He took a deep breath. "Ellen, the way I feel about you scares me, too. But I trust you. I'm ready to—" He broke off suddenly, as though he'd read her mind.

"Reed," she said uncertainly, "I'm very fond of you. With a little more time, I'm sure that—"

He waved a hand, uninterested in her clumsy protests. "Save it, Ellen. You can't feel what you don't feel. I'd rather you be honest with me." His straightforward words couldn't hide the hurt in his low tone.

Stomach churning, Ellen reached out for him with both hands. She waited an eternity before he finally took them gingerly in his. "I feel so much for you, Reed," she confessed. "But I'm still—" she tried to steady her voice "—still so much more scared than certain. Once I yield to you completely, I'm not sure I'll still be . . . well, *me*. This new me. I haven't had enough time to grow strong. It would be the easiest thing in the world to just surrender my independence to a loving take-charge kind of man like you."

He stared at her from what seemed like a great distance. Slowly he released her pleading hands. "Would that really be so awful, Ellen? Surely you understand that I care for you deeply. I would never let anything happen to you."

She shook her head. "I'm afraid you would let me disappear into old helpless Ellen. A sweet shadow of her man. Not a woman in her own right. And that's who I want to be."

He thrust both hands in his pockets and closed his eyes. Slowly, he shook his head and met her gaze once more. "Ellen, I'm not trying to make you over. I'm just trying to love you as you are. From where I stand, it seems like you're making that a whole lot harder than it has to be."

"I'm so sorry, Reed." Ellen was near tears by now. "I think maybe you're so sure of who you are that all you have to worry about is whether or not I'm the right woman for you. But I've got a lot more to juggle. Whether or not you're the right man for me has a lot to do with whether or not I'm the right *me* for me."

She'd hoped to make things better with this explanation—the best one she'd yet come up with—but Reed's expression darkened as she spoke.

"You're not just talking about sex, are you?" he said sadly. "You're still not sure if you want to be my... special friend."

The ache in his voice wounded Ellen, and she found herself rising quickly to slip both arms around him. "Oh, Reed, I am sure. I just..." She couldn't quite find a way to finish the sentence, which was just as well, because Reed glumly finished it for her.

"You're just not sure you want to take the risk."

THE PHONE WAS RINGING when Ellen walked in the door, so she dropped her purse and hurried into the kitchen. Out of the corner of her eye she noticed some scraps of paper on the floor by the fireplace, and she wondered why she hadn't noticed the fallen trash during her morning housecleaning. But all such mundane thoughts vanished from her mind the instant she heard Reed's deep voice on the phone.

"Find out anything important?" he asked, after he'd told her about Jackie's new car and she'd explained how she'd tracked down Sally at her current address after two false leads in San Diego. "Sally is an astute observer. If anything out of the ordinary had happened up there, she would have noticed it."

"Sorry, Reed, but she didn't notice much except for all the guys salivating over her." She managed to chuckle; having met Sally, she was less jealous. "You must be more subtle than most, Reed. She didn't notice your lolling tongue."

"Ellen!" he protested. "I never—"

"Never mind." She laughed again, and he joined her. Ellen was in a terrific mood. All day she'd felt confident and happy. The old Ellen never would have tracked down a stranger and driven alone to the Mexican border. The old Ellen would have been afraid to do anything so daring alone. The old Ellen wouldn't have spent the day longing to feel Reed's hands on her body and aching to see his face.

She'd had plenty of time today to sort out what had happened the night before. She had panicked. She had hurt Reed badly. And she'd learned that he meant so much to her that she could never bear to hurt him again.

Now she said lightly, "The poor thing is struggling with her weight now and says her husband is much more secure these days. Truly, Reed, she's a delightful person. Unfortunately, she doesn't recall anything odd about her work up on Chumash Mountain. But she did say that it was such a long time ago that it might take her a while to remember everything she did back then. She promised to call one of us if anything else came back to her in the next few days."

"One of us?" he asked with exaggerated hopefulness.

"Stick it in your ear, Capwell!" Ellen razzed him. "I'm the one who went to see her. She'll probably call me."

"Nobody can reach you. You're always gallivanting about in the mountains. She'll have to call me," he concluded smugly.

Ellen let him have the last word. It felt so good to talk to Reed, so good to know she'd carried out her mission by herself, so good to discover that they'd talked for ten minutes without a single mention of her safety. She was tingling at the mere sound of his voice. His laughter filled her with joy. She dreaded another week in the mountains in her chosen professional simply because it meant another week without the sight of his beloved face. Despite her confusion, her caution, her fear, the truth was impossible to ignore any longer.

Ellen was falling in love with him.

Suddenly she was tired of debating with herself. She knew what she wanted: an evening curled up in Reed's arms. An evening that didn't end with an awkward expression of adolescent confusion while he incited the slumbering sensual hunger within her. An evening of giving and receiving a new kind of love that had never been part of her life before.

"Have you had dinner, Reed?" she asked, her voice taking on a different, throatier tone. "Would you like to come over?" After a second's pause, she said truthfully, "I'd really like to see you tonight."

It had been a long time since Ellen had flirted openly with a man, and she wasn't at all sure she remembered how to do it, but Reed seemed to have no trouble following her lead.

"I'd like to see you, too, Ellen." His voice deepened as he said her name, and she realized that he'd been holding back, desperately trying to keep her from hearing the depth of longing in his earlier words. "But it's too late to worry about cooking. How about if I pick up something—Chinese, maybe?—on my way over there."

"Sounds good to me."

"Should I pick up something for dessert?"

"Some fortune cookies, maybe. I have a feeling you're going to feel very lucky tonight."

Her comment seemed to take Reed by surprise, and Ellen herself had to admit that it was a remarkably blunt statement. She was surprised she'd made it. At once she backtracked, "What I mean, Reed, is that..."

When her voice trailed off, he said softly, "Ellen, I care for you very much."

For a long moment she said nothing. Then she yielded to the heat. "Reed," she answered, feeling deliciously quivery inside, "feed the cat before you leave the house. I don't think you'll be going home tonight."

"Yes, ma'am," he answered, both shock and delight in his wry tone. "I'll be there in thirty minutes."

Ellen hung up the phone with a delirious grin on her face, feeling as though she were seventeen. She was gripped by a topsy-turvy sensation of joy and desire and embarrassment. Had she really just asked Reed to spend the night? Yes. *She had invited him to make love to her.* And she very much wanted to make love with him.

It was time. It felt right. Their earlier misunderstandings had been but a glitch in the process of getting acquainted; even after last night everything was finally going to be all right.

She closed her eyes and savored the joy. Reed Capwell. He was the man she wanted, maybe the man she'd wanted all her life. And—incredibly—he wanted her, too.

She decided to take a lightning-quick shower and change into something casual and just the tiniest bit provocative before Reed arrived. And—the thought occurred to her as she darted through the living room— she had to take a moment to pick up those scraps of paper near the fireplace on the floor.

She couldn't have gone more than three steps before her eyes focused on the carpet and she realized what she saw. The scraps of paper were color photos torn to shreds. Beyond them, heaped and broken, lay the shattered glass and twisted frames that just that morning had held the pictures of her beloved boys.

CHAPTER NINE

REED WAS WHISTLING as he came up the walk, feeling ridiculously happy and proud. Tonight, Ellen was going to give herself to him at last. His patience had finally been rewarded; his great longing for this special woman would be fulfilled. Once she made love with him, Reed was certain she would not try to pull away again.

He juggled the boxes of Chinese food as he rang the doorbell, then nearly dropped them when the door burst open and Ellen fell into his arms.

At first he thought she was greeting him with passion, which was flattering but a bit out of character for the calm and logical female he knew. But in an instant he realized that she was sobbing.

"Ellen? My God, Ellen, what's wrong?" Reed asked, dropping the boxes with a thud as he wrapped his arms around her.

"He cut up my kids!" she whispered, her teeth chattering despite the tepid air.

"He *what?* Your boys are—"

"They're okay! I called them in Kansas. But he tore up their pictures and left them on the floor. I was so afraid! I couldn't reach Matthew at first. He didn't answer the phone, but I found him at his girlfriend's. Reed, I was terrified! I can't think!"

He tightened his grip on her and pulled her in the door. "Wait here just a second. I have to check the apartment."

"Reed, I checked. Somebody's searched my things, but there's nobody here. I—"

"Let me check." It was a small apartment, and he covered the ground quickly. Nobody in the messed up closets, the tub or behind any doors. A bit of mud in the bedroom; the sliding glass door had been jimmied but was now tightly closed.

After his quick check, Reed found Ellen leaning against the front door, as though she were preparing to flee. He took her back in his arms and rubbed her back, but her knotted muscles refused to give at all. She trembled and wept as she clutched him.

He felt so helpless, so angry—with the intruder and with himself. He had known she was in trouble, even though Ellen herself and the police had denied it. He had known and done nothing, because he'd wanted her too much to risk her wrath. It was a mistake he would not make again.

"It's so hard to be brave and strong all the time, Reed," she whispered through her tears. It was the first time she'd ever admitted these feelings. "So hard to pretend I don't need anybody. Sometimes I just want a friend, you know? And sometimes I wish I had a man in the house just to kill the fear. But then I remember—"

She broke off and started to cry again.

Reed drew her closer, kissed her cheek, her forehead, her dark, wavy hair. He rocked her softly, murmuring all the words he'd longed for days to tell her, words she was finally willing to hear. "I won't let anyone hurt you, Ellen," he promised. "I swear to you, I won't let it happen again."

He was talking about Su Le, not the pictures, but Ellen didn't ask any questions. He held her as tightly as he dared while her sobs grew softer. Mentally, he was already dialing Colonel Harrison, glad that he'd tucked the number in his wallet after he'd taken the time to track it down.

Reed did not release Ellen as he asked, "Did you call the police?"

"Yes, but when I told them there was no intruder on the premises, they didn't seem too concerned, even though I told them about our trouble the last two weeks. They said they'd send somebody over to talk to me, but I haven't seen anybody yet." Her eyes filled once more with tears. "I called you first, Reed, but you'd already left."

She didn't make it sound like an accusation, but still he felt as though he'd let her down.

"I was just getting our dinner, Ellen," he explained, recalling the boxes on the front step. "I came as soon as—"

"I know, I know." She pressed her face against his chest, but she didn't start crying again, which he took to be a good sign. She had actually calmed down considerably when the doorbell rang.

It was a plainclothes policeman who introduced himself as Detective Newman and quickly flashed his badge. He did not look pleased when Reed asked him to take it out again so he could study it.

Once he was satisfied that the badge was legitimate, Reed invited him in. "I'm glad we have a trained investigator on the case at last, Detective. Your uniformed officers don't seem to take this kind of thing seriously.''

The man studied him dubiously. ''Our office received a call from a Ms. Ellen Andrews. You would be...?''

''Reed Capwell. I'm a friend. I was on the way over here when she found the pictures. And I was with her when she called your officers last week when her tires were slashed.''

Newman nodded. ''How convenient. Do you spend a lot of time together?''

To Reed's chagrin, Ellen chose this moment to jump into the conversation. He'd been trying to spare her—she was still fighting tears—but she seemed impelled to take over the reins.

''I spend four days a week working up on Chumash Mountain,'' she explained a bit shakily. ''I first went to see Reed when I found a time capsule up there with his business card in it. Some...odd things have been happening since then.''

The detective shot Reed a suspicious glance. ''Since you met this man?''

''Well—'' Ellen glanced at Reed uneasily ''—you could put it that way. But what I meant was that the trouble started after I found the time capsule and made its contents public. I went to the newspaper—''

''About the time capsule, or the tires?''

''The time capsule.'' Now Ellen looked confused. ''I did tell the reporter about the tires Friday night, but that was...well, a personal discussion. I don't think she put it in the paper last week, but I didn't check.'' Now she turned to Reed. ''Did you see that edition? I didn't ask Shannon to keep the tire trouble a secret; it didn't even occur to me. But if you're right, Reed—"

"Right about what?" the detective cut in.

"I think Ellen may have come across some information that somebody doesn't want revealed. I think it's pretty obvious that somebody has been giving us clear warnings about something."

"Us?"

Reed explained about his car while the detective took down notes. Then he asked some more questions, mainly of Ellen, dating back to the discovery of the time capsule itself. Unlike the first officers they'd talked to, this one seemed to take the situation seriously. Still, he could not offer much in the way of real help. He said he didn't have any officers to spare as bodyguards; he told Ellen to get new locks for the windows and bolt her door.

Then to Reed's astonishment, Detective Newman said, "So, tell me, Ms. Andrews, if I get the picture here. You find this time capsule with Mr. Capwell's business card. You think he buried the stuff. He says he didn't, but ever since then you've had nothing but trouble. He keeps calling you and he claims that his old car got bunged up, too."

Reed was shocked at the implications of the detective's summary, and he wasn't sure whether to be mad as hell or glad that the cops had finally put somebody suspicious on the job.

He took heart when Ellen said, "I *saw* his car, Detective Newman. The windshield was destroyed and so was the dash. The damage to my car was actually quite light in comparison." Then she tacked on, "Detective, Reed loves that car as though it were one of his children. It's not old and crummy, it's—" her eyes met his as she verbally danced around any mention of Nathan "—it's a family heirloom. An antique. If he had any reason to frighten me—which is absurd—he'd find some other way than damaging that beloved car."

"They couldn't fix the dash," Reed growled, his tone revealing the extent of the wound. "They told me to just cover it up."

Detective Newman winced at the classic car's fate. For the first time, he seemed to realize how deeply he'd insulted Reed. Now he said, "Mr. Capwell, I don't mean to sound accusatory. But the lady's the one with a problem tonight, not you, and it's my job to examine every possibility. Surely you can see that from my point of view, the time capsule isn't the only new thing in Ms. Andrews' life. The big change is *you*."

It was an observation that haunted Reed throughout the rest of the policeman's stay and continued to trouble him long after he and Ellen had picked at the Chinese food and tried to consider her options. When she excused herself to go take some aspirin, he used the kitchen phone to make the call he should have made two weeks ago. It was time to get some answers . . . or at least figure out what questions to ask.

"COLONEL HARRISON, this is Reed Capwell," he declared when he finally got his former commanding officer on the line. "I served under you at—"

"—Saigon. My God, Capwell, surely you didn't think I'd forget?"

The harsh tone could not hide the genuine warmth in the man. Reed remembered it clearly; it was the reason he felt free to call Harrison after all this time. There were some things that men went through together that were not forgettable; time made no difference, nor did subsequent pains or joys.

"No, sir, I did not. But it has been a while, and I just—"

"Yesterday." With that one word, Harrison dismissed the past twenty years. "You call just to chat, Capwell, or you want to reenlist?"

Actually, Reed had expected to spend a little longer reheating their dormant relationship before he launched into his rather bizarre situation.

"Sir, I called to ask if there's been any...activity recently that might relate to any of my operations overseas."

That's all he said, but the colonel got the whole picture instantly.

"How bad is it?" he asked. "Are you injured?"

"No, sir, not yet. Just vandalism and some underhanded threats against a friend of mine who hasn't a clue as to how to defend herself. The worst of it is, she won't even let me protect her."

The colonel growled as Reed gave him a recap of what had happened, then asked, "What makes you think it's related to Vietnam?"

"I don't, really. It's just that I can't think of any other explanation for what's been going on. It's not random, Colonel. It's a very specific campaign against me and a woman I hold dear. Anybody who knows anything about me would realize that there's no better way to get to me."

"True enough," said the colonel. "Have you been close to this woman long enough for it to be public knowledge, or would he have to have specific information?"

Reed thought about that. "Fairly specific. I've only known her a week or two."

"That's not nearly long enough for an old vendetta. I mean, I'm not discounting the possibility that somebody might come after you after all this time, Capwell, but if he did, he'd plan it long and carefully. He would have been planning for twenty years. And I don't think a brand new lover would factor into those plans. I think he'd go after your children."

The words were a knife thrust to the gut. Reed saw Jackie almost daily, but he decided that a quick call to Nate in Arizona would be a good idea. "He went after Ellen's kids, at least symbolically."

"Sounds like your new lady might have brought trouble with her, Capwell. How much do you know about her past?"

Reed thought about that for a moment. "Not a whole helluva lot, come to think of it. All I'm sure of is that she's pretty determined to make a break from it and start over fresh."

Colonel Harrison exhaled slowly. "I think you're wise to keep looking over your shoulder, Capwell, but I have a feeling you're looking in the wrong direction. Either this female brought trouble with her, or one of you has stirred up a hornet's nest pretty damn recently. I'd sit down with her and go over the last couple of weeks and see what you've been involved in either deliberately or accidentally. Maybe one of you— or both—saw something you shouldn't have, or pressed some buttons you didn't mean to press."

Reed was silent for a moment. "I can't speak for Ellen, but the only strange thing that's happened to me lately is learning that somebody buried my business card in a twenty-year-old time capsule that nobody wants to claim." Once Reed had laid out his handful of facts and suspicions, Harrison said softly, "I'd check out everybody involved with the original development of Manzanita Meadows, Capwell, and see who's anxious to hide his secrets. Most things are buried because somebody doesn't want them to see the light of day."

BY THE TIME ELLEN returned to the kitchen, her fear had abated and fatigue had taken its place. At the moment, a romantic liaison was the last thing on her mind, and she was embarrassed by the memory of her provocative invitation for Reed to spend the night with her. Still, she didn't really want him to leave. She was afraid to be alone, and she hated the feeling. Ellen feared that she might never be able to stand on her own two feet again if she gave in to the fear tonight.

Reed stood up when she walked into the room, his eyes dark and troubled. "Ellen," he said tightly, in a voice that crackled with angst . . . or command.

Before she could answer, the phone rang.

"Let me get it," Reed said. "It might be him."

Part of her wanted to say, *I can handle him myself,* but part of her felt sickened by the notion. Before she could offer any protest, Reed snatched the receiver from the cradle.

"Hello," he snapped into the phone.

Ellen waited tensely while he exchanged two or three lines, then said, "It's your ex-husband. One of your sons told him what happened. Should I tell him to get lost?"

About the last thing Ellen wanted to do at the moment was listen to Howard fuss at her, but she couldn't bring herself to let Reed run interference for her. Besides, whichever one of the boys had called him was probably quite upset, and setting the record straight seemed to be the least she could do as a mother.

Ellen took the phone from Reed. "Hello, Howard," she said as calmly as she was able.

"Ellen, what the hell is going on out there? Who is that jerk and why is he in your apartment at this hour? I told you a thousand times not to go off on your own! I told you you'd regret it! I told you you'd be crawling back to me on your knees someday! Now can you get to a plane yourself or do I have to come out there and get you?"

For hours Ellen had been battling fear, but now her adrenaline rushed to the surface in unmasked anger. "Howard, I am fine. Unless you called to discuss one of our children with me, we have nothing to talk about."

"Ellen, Matthew says you could have been killed! He's scared to death somebody will come back tonight and murder you in your bed! Now, I'm telling you, get out of that place and hop on a plane. If you can't get a flight tonight, stay with a friend."

"Howard, listen to me closely. I am not returning to Kansas. I most certainly am not returning to *you!*" It took all her self-control not to shriek the words. "Now, if you want to do something useful, keep a close eye on the boys for the next few days. I will take care of myself, thank you."

She heard Howard pounding something near the phone. "Dammit, Ellen, I will not have this! I've given you plenty of time to get over this . . . midlife crisis! I even let you carry out the divorce! But surely now even you can see that—"

"Howard," she said bluntly, "I'm hanging up."

She did so, feeling vaguely proud of herself, despite the concerns that still fluttered around her. She had stood up to the man! She'd rather face the picture-cutter than kneel down to Howard again.

She turned to Reed, expecting him to cheer her courage, and discovered that he'd left the room. It didn't take too long to find him; he was breaking a broom to block her sliding glass door. She hurried to him, about to report her victory, when he said bluntly, "That'll hold for tonight. Now, I want you to pack a bag so we can go."

"Go?"

"To my place." It was not a suggestion; his tight lips might as well have issued a military command. "Guest room or my bed, your choice, Ellen. That's not the issue here."

Ellen felt a fresh rise of anger, and this time it wasn't directed at Howard. "The issue here is whether or not I want to—"

"You won't need your regular Chumash Mountain supplies because you're not going back until we get this straightened out," he plowed on dogmatically, oblivious to her protest. "I'll call Lars in the morning and explain to him why you can't be allowed to go up there alone. I'm also going to tell Shannon Waverly to put an article in the *Herald* stating you've come to a dead end and are not searching for any more clues to the time capsule.''

"Reed, you have—"

She got no further before the phone rang again. Reed grabbed for the extension by her bed, but Ellen, who was closer, beat him to the punch.

"Ellen, how dare you hang up on me!" Howard shouted in her ear. "This is no time for theatrics or your female tricks! There's a pervert on the loose out there and you—"

"Goodbye, Howard," she said bluntly, hanging up the phone again.

Reed took a deep breath. He looked furious now. "If he calls again, let me handle him. Better yet, let's get out of here. He doesn't have my number."

"What difference does it make?" Ellen snapped. "You two sound identical tonight. The only difference is that I can hang up on him."

Reed glared at her. "This isn't the time for one of your lectures on independence, Ellen. Someone may be trying to kill you! This is no time to discuss female pride!"

"When is a good time, Reed?" she demanded hotly. "When I'm safe and cozy and there's nothing to fear? It's easy to be brave then. It's easy to pretend that I'm a strong person. But if I'm going to toss away my dignity the minute some little problem comes up—"

"This is no little problem!" Each word bit like a knife. "Dammit, Ellen, *we are at war!*"

"Who's at war?" she barked back, feeling as though she were back in Kansas, reliving her last married fight. How could she have believed her future lay with Reed?

"You and Howard? Come on! Somebody broke in here, and I'm scared. I admit it. But I'm not hysterical anymore! You braced the glass door and I'll bolt the front one when you leave. Detective Newman said I'd be okay." She wrapped the words around her like a shield of armor, but Reed pierced that comfort instantly.

"There's nothing else Detective Newman *can* say. He doesn't have the manpower to protect you. He can't provide you with security, so of course he doesn't want you to worry. He's willing to take his chances. I'm not. You're too damn special to me."

And you're special to me, too, Reed, Ellen longed to tell him, the surprising rush of tenderness diluting her anger. When his eyes darkened with concern, she felt a curious tearfulness that was hard to ignore. She remembered only too well the feel of his lips on hers the night before, the desire and hope that had urged her to invite him over just hours before. Desperately she wished she could turn back the clock, but it was too late for that, and she knew it.

"If I'm special to you, Reed, why don't you stop trying to bully me? Have a little faith in my ability to protect myself, to take reasonable precau—"

"I had faith in Nathan, and Nathan's dead!" he shouted. "Now I'm not taking any chances. Pack a bag, dammit, and let's get out of here!"

"Reed, we are not in Vietnam. We are not dealing with some undercover enemy."

"You don't know that. I called Colonel Harrison to check that possibility, but—"

"You called the *Army* about this?"

"I just called an old friend. For heaven's sake, Ellen, I've got to examine every angle. With your safety at stake, I can't leave any stone unturned."

"Reed, you talk as though I'm a child. I can take care of my own safety!"

"Fine. Terrific. So why did you call me? Why did you throw yourself in my arms? Why did you cry for an hour after I got here?"

"I was upset!" Ellen's voice grew shrill. "I was scared and I needed a friend! Not a bulldozer, not a chauvinist, and not a Howard-clone!"

On that note, the phone rang again. Ellen snatched it, but Reed seized her wrist and physically tugged it out of her hand.

She heard him issue a few short orders, then bark, "Unless there's an emergency with one of the boys, I'm warning you, don't call here again."

He slammed down the phone, then took it off the hook and laid it by the bed. "I took care of him," he said almost smugly.

"I could have done it," Ellen snapped. "All you've done is add fuel to the fire, convinced him I can't handle this situation on my own."

"Well, maybe you can't," Reed answered. "Maybe you shouldn't. Maybe—"

"Maybe," Ellen countered crisply, "you should go home."

Reed glared at her. His lips tightened so much they almost looked like Howard's. "I care for you, dammit, and I won't stand by while you're terrorized or hurt!"

Ellen stared at him defiantly. "So you plan to haul me off to your place whether I like it or not?"

His eyes were unyielding. "You can come with me, or I can stay here."

"Why don't you just ship me off to Kansas?" she taunted him.

Reed didn't budge. "That's fine, too. But I will not leave you alone tonight unless you have somebody else to protect you."

For a long moment, she did not speak. Fury laced with some new emotion, a sobering kind of pain, etched itself in her face. She knew she couldn't bodily throw him out the door, but she also knew that if he refused to leave—and it was pretty damn clear that he would—that she could not continue dating him. It was a terrible thing to realize, especially now when she felt so vulnerable, so achingly all alone.

And yet, what choice did she have? She could not surrender herself to another overbearing man who did his best to fill her with fear. She'd turned her whole life on its ear to escape that kind of oppression. She could not surrender to it now. She might as well be surrendering to Howard! At the moment, he didn't seem much different from Reed.

If he'd asked to stay, she would have been touched. But he'd been hollering commands since the moment Howard had called. And he was treating her like an infant!

Turning away from the memory of Reed's gentle embrace, she said firmly, "There are some extra blankets in the hall closet. I won't wake you up when I leave in the morning."

Reed glanced down, as though he wasn't at all sure he was glad he'd won the battle. Slowly now, he reached out for her beseechingly. "Ellen—"

"It's over, Reed," she told him briskly, fighting the powerful need to go into his arms. "Stay or go, it doesn't matter anymore."

He dropped his hand. He took a deep breath. The hurt on his face almost undid her.

She swallowed hard and struggled to get a grip on herself. More gently, she laid one hand on his wrist. "I'm sorry, Reed," she whispered, "but it's just not going to work. I know I gave you mixed messages, but that's not because I wanted to hurt you. It's just that I...lied to myself about who you really were."

"Ellen, please," he pleaded. "You've been through a hellish day. This is hardly the time to—"

"I moved two thousand miles to get away from this," she cut him off, knowing that her resistance would snap if she gave him even the tiniest bit of a chance. "Tonight you've proven you're more like Howard than I ever dreamed you could be. I fought too hard to become a complete person, Reed. I just can't risk getting involved with another man who won't let me breathe."

CHAPTER TEN

SHE WAS GONE when he got up in the morning.

"Some guard dog I turned out to be," Reed mumbled to himself, wondering if he would have slept through the sound of somebody breaking in to attack her.

Of course, he hadn't really slept until it was nearly daylight. Ellen had disappeared into her room shortly after thrusting the blankets at him and had never come out again. Her last words had haunted him all night.

When he spied a note on the kitchen table, he briefly took heart, but his flicker of hope was snuffed out almost instantly.

Dear Reed,

I'm sorry I hollered at you last night. I know you just want to help. I just wish you could understand that some things are more important than safety. I wish you understood the difference between an offer and a command.

It could have been so nice. I'll miss you so much. But I spent twenty-five years of my life in handcuffs, and I just can't surrender myself to another jail, no matter how beguiling the warden.

Ellen

Reed read the note three times before he tugged on his shoes and left. He didn't bother to take it with him.

He stopped at home to shower and change, glad that Catnip, at least, was glad to see him. At the office, Reed didn't really notice the several people who greeted him. He took the two messages Sandi handed him without a word. He didn't realize that while he robotically worked on the tasks the County paid him to do, his mind kept wandering back to Ellen and her safety. She'd ordered him out of her life, and there wasn't much he could do about that. He wasn't even sure he wanted to. He was angry, not just with himself but with Ellen, too. He'd had enough of her bedtime teasing, enough of her high and mighty independence. Hell, he was only trying to keep her alive! If she was so thorny and rigid that she couldn't see that, then maybe he was better off without her. He didn't want a shrinking violet for a woman, but neither did he want one who was ruled by pride.

No, there was nothing he could do to salvage the relationship that just days ago had looked so full of promise. But he could damn well solve Ellen's puzzle and find her tormentor. In fact, if he achieved the first, the second would take care of itself.

With Colonel Harrison's warnings in mind, Reed ran Bill Hazlett to earth in the County lunchroom during his midmorning break. At least, it was Reed's midmorning break. Chances were good that Bill had spent most of the morning there.

As nonchalantly as he was able, Reed grabbed a cup of coffee and slouched down beside Bill. It wasn't something he did very often these days, mainly because he rarely had time to listen to Bill's long-winded hunting tales. Even now, when he truly needed information, he found it difficult to play the necessary games with his old boss.

At last he found an opportune moment to say, "You remember, Bill, when you were asking me about a woman and a map last week?" When Bill nodded and grinned, Reed gave him a capsule summary of everything that had happened since Ellen had found the old coffee can. Then he said, "It seems to me that Ellen accidentally got her hands on some old secret that somebody would rather not have come to light. Now, I've racked my brain to think of any scandal we dealt with during the building of Manzanita Meadows, but I can't come up with anything. I know it was my project, but since you were my supervisor at the time, I was hoping that you might be able to come up with something."

Bill studied him with more sobriety than Reed had ever seen in the bearded man before. Slowly he answered, "Don't mess with this, Reed."

He felt a curious thrill of fear. At last, somebody knew something!

"What do you mean, Bill? What do you remember?"

Bill shook his head. "I don't remember anything, but I can see the writing on the wall. You two kids have had three warnings. How many do you need? Somebody wants you to stop poking around. I'd do it if I were you."

"Bill, I don't give a damn what's in that time capsule. All I want is for Ellen to be safe. And it seems to me that until I find out what hornet's nest she's stirred up—"

"Reed, Manzanita Meadows is practically a city. That Chumash Mountain development will practically be one, too. Somebody made a fortune on Manzanita Meadows, and somebody's also going to make a fortune on Chumash Mountain. People who are amassing fortunes do not appreciate anybody getting in the way. I bet that time capsule has information that affects some aspect of your current project, or the first Chumash Mountain project that makes somebody connected with the development very uneasy. And that narrows it down to, oh, fifty or so possible suspects." He shook his head. "On top of that, there's the Chumash Mountain project that Lars Lindroth's people were working on in the first place. That's the same time period, and that time capsule might have something buried that related to that as well. Have you bothered to check out *why* that development didn't pan out?"

Reed hadn't bothered; he hadn't even thought of it. He'd been so focused on Manzanita Meadows that he hadn't given much thought to Chumash Mountain at all. Granted, the material in the time capsule all appeared to be geared to Manzanita Meadows, but what if some part of it actually related to Chumash Mountain?

As he thanked Bill and said goodbye, Reed made a mental note to call Lars again to ask him why the original Chumash Mountain project had folded. It was the one question he *hadn't* asked Dale and Steve, and Ellen probably had not asked Sally. In the meantime, he stopped in the file room on the way back to his office to get the Manzanita Meadows master plan. He'd already examined the EIR, but he hadn't studied the original developer's proposal in much detail. He remembered that Jefferson Baxter had owned all the land at one time, back in his real estate heyday, but beyond that, he didn't remember much.

The assorted permits, records and correspondence relating to Manzanita Meadows now comprised about three feet of file space, and before it had been consolidated, it had taken up twice as much. Although Reed himself had originally constructed most of the files, now he couldn't lay his hands on the one thing he was looking for. Small wonder: nowadays he rarely bestirred himself to go collect a file. He was becoming entirely too dependent on his efficient secretary.

"Sandi," he greeted her bluntly when he returned to his office, "will you go down there and find that damn Manzanita Meadows master plan? I've spent ten minutes looking for it and—"

"It's right on my desk, Reed," she informed him impishly. "After all that fuss you made last week over the EIR, I figured you'd be asking for the master plan next, so I picked it up at the same time."

Reed ran a nervous hand through his hair. He gave his perky secretary a sheepish grin. "Sorry if I barked, Sandi. I'm . . . under a lot of stress today."

"So I've noticed," she said kindly. "Would you feel better if you unloaded a bit?"

He read the concern in her eyes and decided to tell her what had happened. After all, he did feel as though he were about to explode. Dropping his voice so no one could hear, he revealed, "Last night somebody broke into Ellen's place and tore up her kids' pictures. She was really spooked. When I got there she seemed to want to lean on me, but later she said I was in the way and wouldn't let her breathe." He sighed. "She broke it off, Sandi. I feel—well, I feel like somebody socked me in the jaw."

He suddenly noticed that Sandi was white-faced. She looked more shocked than sympathetic.

"He cut up her kids' pictures?" she whispered. "Reed, if anybody did that to Jennie's picture, I'd feel . . ." She broke off, looking so alarmed that Reed was sorry he'd mentioned it at all. Sandi's daughter, Jennie, was Jackie's age, and the two girls had been close friends for years. Reed had been upset about Ellen's pictures, not because he thought her boys were really in danger, but because he was certain that the destruction had been used to deliberately terrify her. He remembered Colonel Harrison's warning about his own children. Reed had called Nate the night before and the boy was fine; Jackie had dropped by on her way to work, all smiles. Still, Harrison's words left Reed uneasy.

"Reed, you don't think Ellen's children are really in danger, do you?" Sandi asked, her rose-tipped fingers twisting uneasily.

"No, not yet. I think Ellen may be in danger, though. I think that guy might not even know where her kids are. He probably just saw the pictures and made an intelligent guess. He wants her to stop trying to figure out the time capsule. Or else he wants her so scared that by the time he asks her to do something, she'll do it."

Sandi was trembling. "Reed, you've got to do something!"

"Dammit, Sandi, I'm trying! I called my old CO to see if there was any new trouble connected with my

work in the service, and *he* told me not to let Ellen out
of my sight. But when I told Ellen I wouldn't leave her
alone last night, she accused me of bulldozing her life
just like her ex-husband had done! How can I protect
her if she won't let me get close?''

''You've got to stay close, Reed! You can't take any
chances.''

Her urgency made Reed uneasy. Sandi was almost as
prosaic as Clara, and if even *she* felt he hadn't been
hovering, then Ellen must truly be in danger. And
Colonel Harrison was not a man who was easily
spooked, even under pressure.

He fought a sudden vision of Su Le's lovely face—
not as she had looked alive, but the way she had looked
when he'd last seen her.

He could live without Ellen; he had no choice. But
he would do everything in his power to make sure she
didn't end up like Su Le.

CHUMASH MOUNTAIN, Ellen mused, was a beautiful
spot. The Apache pines were dense and pungent, the
air was clear and the birds provided an ongoing free
concert for anybody who cared to listen. Listening
wasn't easy for Ellen today: all of her energy was focused on her warring emotions.

Before she'd left town, she'd called Shannon—who
apologetically admitted putting the tire story in the
paper—because she really did think it was the wisest
course. She had a powerful hunch that Reed would also
call Shannon, not trusting Ellen to deal with such crucial details herself. She also had a hunch that his own
inquiries into her safety might not end just because

she'd told him flatly that she didn't want to see him anymore.

It isn't that I don't want to, a tiny, wounded voice within her whispered. *It's that I just don't dare.*

She'd been methodically chewing on her bologna sandwich in ten minutes of deadly silence before John said, "I know I'm not the easiest guy in the world to get along with, Ellen, and I probably stuck my foot in my mouth again even though I don't remember doing so. But whatever I did to make you mad, I apologize. Now can you stop giving me the cold shoulder? It's hard enough being trapped up here all week with only one person to talk to without that person refusing to look you in the eye."

Ellen glanced up, startled at his honesty... and ashamed of her inadvertent behavior.

"John, I'm sorry. I'm not mad at you."

"Right," he replied sarcastically. "That's why you've looked ready to take my head off all morning."

She flushed. There was really no way out of this; she'd have to tell him the truth. "John, I'm very upset, but not with you. I'm sorry if I've been rude. The truth is, last night I had to break off a relationship with someone I care about a great deal, and I'm afraid I'm still off kilter. On top of that, I've been having some... other problems."

He eyed her warily. "What kind of problems? Physical? Mental? Legal? Are you likely to come after me with a hatchet in the dark?"

To Ellen's surprise, tears filled her eyes at his words, and she suddenly realized that what she'd been fighting all day wasn't nearly so much anger at Reed as

sheer terror. "You're not the one in danger, John!" she
blurted out, unable to stop either the words or the
tears.

John was the last person in the world she wanted to
admit her weaknesses to, and she flushed even more
with embarrassment. To her surprise, John leaned
forward and actually touched her arm.

"Ellen? Hey, I didn't mean to make you cry. If
something's really wrong...hell, it's okay if you're
bitchy. I just thought you were mad at me."

Still crying, she shook her head.

"You said I wasn't the one in danger, Ellen. Is
somebody else in trouble?"

She met his eyes, and saw a glimmer of honest concern. She nodded. "Ever since I found the time capsule, somebody has been doing strange things to me,
John."

His lips tightened. "How strange?"

She told him then: about the rock on Reed's dashboard, the slashed tires and the condition of her
apartment. She told him that the police couldn't help
and she didn't want anybody else babying her, but she
was a little afraid and that made her furious. She didn't
tell him anything more about Reed and he didn't ask,
which could have meant that he understood without
details or that he thought her tormentor was the only
person who'd incurred her wrath.

When she was done, John said, "Hell, Ellen, I can
see why you're upset. If somebody cut up my picture,
my mom would go berserk."

Ellen had always thought of John as her sons' age,
and yet she had never really thought of him as having

a mother. Quietly she asked, "Are you close to your mother, John?"

The question seemed to take him aback. He shrugged noncommittally and squirmed a bit as he replied, "Well, she lives in Utah, so I haven't seen her much since I left for college, you know, just Christmas and Easter and my birthday. But she's—" he swallowed in some embarrassment "—she's my mom, you know?"

Ellen was surprised to feel a sudden welling of genuine affection for the young man. She'd thought of him as rootless, selfish and shallow. But for all his superficial nonchalance to the world, he had a mother whom he loved and even if Ellen couldn't relate to him in any other way, she could relate to that.

By LUNCHTIME REED was feeling unbearably restless but not at all hungry. Although his cursory study of the Manzanita Meadows master plan had yielded neither new ideas nor information, he drove out to the development to have a look around.

The search was over; Ellen had said so. And yet, he wasn't at all convinced that whoever had smashed his windshield, slashed her tires and desecrated her children's photos was really going to be satisfied by a simple newspaper announcement that Ellen was no longer on his trail. And of course, the article wasn't coming out until Thursday. If somebody suspected that Ellen or Reed had uncovered information that the person desperately wanted to keep secret, he wasn't likely to rest until he had found a way to silence them. There was a reason why Reed's card was in that coffee can, a reason that had something to do with Manzanita

Meadows...or the Chumash Mountain project, old or new.

As he thought about his review of the Manzanita Meadows master plan, Reed realized that Jefferson Baxter, who had been the master developer for the entire project before he left real estate for politics, might remember the original participants in the development process. But Baxter was a very busy and very important public figure who wasn't likely to give Reed a lot of personal time; he had trouble even getting the man to return his calls on County business. Reed decided that the best course of action would be to corner Baxter in person right after the board of supervisors meeting on Wednesday.

He'd also try to catch up with Emmett Mercer then. Mercer was also on the board, but he was as friendly to everybody now as he'd been when Reed had first met him, back in the days when he'd been supplying furniture for the Manzanita Meadows model homes. Reed couldn't imagine bald, cheerful Emmett involved in some kind of a scandal! Besides, who would threaten a woman's kids over a bunch of sofas and chairs?

Reed had no trouble remembering the name of the general contractor for the project: George Haversham had made his name on Manzanita Meadows and had done very well for himself since then. Reed had met the man years ago, but there was no reason why Haversham should remember him. Yet Haversham would have supervised a number of subcontractors, any one of whom might know something, if indeed there was anything to know. Reed decided to give him a call as soon as he returned to the office.

He'd already picked Bill's brain, and he hoped that Lars, who was meeting Reed for lunch on Tuesday, might have some additional ideas. He was the perfect person to ask for help: not only had Lars been the project supervisor for the original Chumash Mountain survey, he'd been Reed's Z & E contact for Manzanita Meadows as well.

As he reached Manzanita Meadows, Reed turned his thoughts away from people and tried to focus on the physical landscape, searching for some elusive clue. He always found it gratifying to watch the development of a project on which he'd worked. In Manzanita Meadows, he'd worked especially hard to have miniparks for the children every few blocks and bus turnouts so the flow of traffic wouldn't be impeded. He'd insisted on more greenery in the apartment complexes than the builder had originally planned on, and as a result the complex looked light and airy despite the density. It was, he noted coolly, considerably more open than Ellen's neighborhood. No place for an intruder to hide.

Manzanita Meadows was a huge project, and a few lavish houses had been built in some areas of the community. But even the modest homes surrounding the apartment complex still showed pride of ownership after twenty-some years.

He circled the complex and drove on through the neighborhood, noticing the variety of landscaping in the yards. Some folks had used desert-cactus motifs to save water in drought-ridden southern California; others had lush valleys of tiny flowers and curved hills of grass. One on the corner nearest the the apartment complex had a handbuilt rock wall that gave the sloping property a dramatic two-tiered effect.

Reed drove almost a block before it struck him that something seemed very different about the wall. He circled back, pulled up in front of the house, and stared at it for a full five minutes before he got out and walked up to the front door and rang the bell.

Nobody was home, but he left his card and a note asking for somebody to call him at work. He didn't say why. It was too hard to explain in a few words why he'd reacted so powerfully to a hand-built wall of homely greenish-black rock.

But he was certain he'd found a clue to Ellen's trouble.

ELLEN SIPPED HER SOUP at the table while John consumed three cans of corned beef hash. He talked blithely about their research for the day, never letting the conversation pale. She wasn't sure whether he'd forgotten their earlier conversation or was indifferent to her feelings. It was possible that his incessant chatter was intended to cheer her up—after all, he'd never been very talkative before.

Against her will, her mind replayed the first moments after Reed had arrived the night before, eager to be with her, eager to soothe her fears. She'd anticipated the evening with such joy! And now, in hindsight, it was hard to summon up the righteous anger that had filled her the night before. Reed was wrong to be so protective, but... Surely he wasn't motivated by the same spirit that moved Howard. If Howard hadn't called, she wondered, might she have accepted Reed's plans without so much anger? If she'd said calmly, "Tell me your ideas, Reed, and I'll consider them; just don't tell me what to do," might they have found a compromise? After all, she didn't object to his concern, just his assuming control. She would have *welcomed* proof of his affection for her if only he hadn't offered it in such an overbearing manner!

Just a few days ago, she had felt so close to Reed! Too close, too soon, of course. And it had been foolish to get involved with a man when she was barely settled in her new world. Realistically, Ellen was sure it was better this way, better that she'd broken things off before he'd woven himself deeply into the fabric of her life.

And yet, a tiny voice within her kept crying, *If he wasn't already embedded in my heart, how could it hurt this bad?*

After the meal, John dug out the day's paperwork and spread it on the table. After he and Ellen compared notes, he drew a small straight line in the northwest corner of the site, signifying a tiny earthquake fault they had discovered that afternoon. It was so small, and so far from the proposed development area, that the developer would probably try to argue that it was inconsequential. But Ellen knew that a fault line, even a small one, could be a major concern in California. Granted, it *was* earthquake country, but nobody would buy a house smack dab on top of a fault.

Ellen and John had surveyed most of the site, but there were still half a dozen small slopes on the northern hillside left to examine. They hoped to wrap up the survey by the end of the week. Ellen knew she was getting much better at the job, and she also knew that she was getting a lot tougher physically. The days weren't so hard for her, and she didn't get up each morning feeling so hopelessly fatigued. Still, she was growing weary of this gypsy-like existence, and looked forward to her next project, which would keep her largely within the city's bounds.

They went over their progress and their upcoming plans for about an hour before John started folding the papers. Ellen was starting to relax—it seemed as though he might be planning to stay there for the evening—when he said, "Denise is going to wonder what happened to me if I don't get going."

He said the words awkwardly, so awkwardly that Ellen suddenly realized that he *had* been trying to comfort her—or at least keep her company. She was touched, yet almost irritated that she'd come across as needy enough for even *John* to feel that she needed coddling. She almost said, "Don't be silly, John. I'll be fine," but that seemed too obvious. Instead she told him, "Have a good time, John. I've got a great book here I've been trying to get to. I was too busy over the weekend."

He looked relieved. "Good. I, uh, I guess I'll see you in the morning, then."

"Right. Have a good time."

He studied her again, and for a moment he reminded her of Matthew on his way out to basketball practice without doing his homework.

But John wasn't Matthew. Matthew would not have left her feeling so disoriented, so scared. And it wasn't until John had been gone for a good twenty minutes that Ellen realized how scared she really was.

In fact, it wasn't until she was awakened hours later by footsteps padding softly toward the pitchdark cabin that true panic filled her. She thought of the other disasters that had occurred over the past few days and realized that there was no time for self-debate or second guessing. She'd told Reed there was nothing to worry about, and she'd tried to believe it. She had no weapon, no plan of action. She'd come to one of the most remote spots on the planet by herself, at night, totally unprepared.

She crept from her sleeping bag and kicked over the coffee can, which still contained the diabase. Instinctively, she picked up the rock and hurried to the lockless door. The instant it opened, she lifted the diabase with both hands and cracked the intruder on the back of the head.

CHAPTER ELEVEN

ELLEN STARED at the dark-clad body slumped at her feet, amazed and somehow proud that she'd been strong enough—mentally and physically—to knock-out a full grown man. He was out, at least for the moment, and she knew she had to make some quick decisions before he came to.

She hurried back to her sleeping bag to find her flashlight. She wanted to see her assailant clearly, and she knew she could use the light to make sure he couldn't really see her.

She shone it on him quickly, trying to assess his size. But in an instant Ellen's feelings of pride turned to panic.

She'd knocked out John.

As she rushed back to his side, a low moan told her he was coming around.

"John? Are you all right?" she begged him, feeling both guilty and imbecilic. "I'm so sorry! I had no idea you were coming back tonight. I never dreamed it was you!"

"That's a comfort," he replied sarcastically, rolling over on his back and staying there. Pain was etched in every line of his face. "I'd hate to think you killed me for some personal reason."

Ellen was too upset with herself to argue with him. "John, I'm sorry. Is there anything I can do? We don't have any ice or—"

"Never mind," he groused, clutching his head with both hands. "I know you didn't do it on purpose." His eyes narrowed. "Did you have some trouble while I was gone?"

"No. Nothing happened. When I heard the footsteps, I guess I..." It was obvious that she had panicked, but somehow she couldn't bear to say so. It made her feel even more vulnerable. Instead, she snapped, "Why'd you come back, anyway? If I'd been expecting you—"

"I don't need to ask permission to spend the night here!" John growled. "Denise had a headache. It just seemed like a good idea to come back."

He didn't look at Ellen while he said it, and she knew, deep in her heart, that Denise hadn't had a thing to do with his decision. Indifferent John hadn't wanted to leave Ellen alone! He'd seen through all her phony bravado; he knew how frightened she really was.

And so did Reed, she realized reluctantly. *He knew I was terrified, too terrified to admit it to anybody, especially to myself.*

The realization was too late to do her any good. She didn't need terror to handle her problems effectively. She needed courage, resolve and a clear plan of action. And maybe—*Oh, hell,* she thought, *I might as well admit it*—a true friend to stand beside her.

It was Reed she desperately wanted, but for the moment, she was grateful John had returned.

"What the hell did you hit me with?" he asked. "It was too damn heavy to be a flashlight or a coffeepot."

"It was a rock," she admitted ruefully. "The piece of diabase I found in the time capsule. It was right by the bed, and I couldn't think of anything else that was heavy."

John scowled as he sat up, spotting the rock and hefting it with both hands. "I'm lucky you didn't kill me. Hell, I bet that's why this thing was stuck in the can in the first place. It was probably a murder weapon and somebody just tried to bury the evidence."

The words rang out in the cabin as idle sarcasm, but in the ensuing silence John's eyes suddenly met Ellen's.

"My God," she whispered. "John, I think you may be right."

He opened his mouth, stared at her, then shut it again.

"What else makes sense? I mean, maybe the rock itself wasn't part of a crime, but the 'time capsule' could well be some kind of evidence. Reed's right! It all fits! Why else would somebody be so upset that I've been asking questions and digging up old memories? Something happened twenty years ago, something that somebody is ashamed of. He hid these clues hoping to forget it."

"Or else somebody else hid those clues, planning to come back later and reveal them to the world."

"Like a blackmailer?"

"I bet there's a good chance. And maybe the criminal is afraid that you'll try to blackmail him, too."

"How could I? I don't have any idea what these things mean."

"But when you do, this guy won't be safe any longer. I think he wants to make sure that you're too scared to do anything to him even if you do figure this thing out."

Ellen shook her head. "I think he's looking for it, John. Maybe he just wants to see what's in it. At my apartment it was pretty obvious he'd done some searching." She didn't add that on at least one other occasion, she'd had the feeling that something was not quite right when she'd returned to her apartment. Now she wondered if somebody had broken in then, too.

"Was the time capsule there?"

"No, I had it with me. Everything except the rock and the can. I took it to San Diego to show Sally Quinton." She shook her head, trying to put the pieces together. "I think you're on to something, John, but I still don't know how it all fits together."

"You don't know how any of this fits together, Ellen. And as long as that's true, you may be safe," John observed.

She knew he might be right, but her instincts told her that a smart woman never operates out of ignorance. It was one thing for the criminal to *think* she didn't know anything; another thing to be genuinely uninformed.

She'd promised Reed she was done sleuthing, but she knew—as she watched her young partner rub his throbbing head—that the freedom she sought would require more than forbidding Reed to protect her. She had to lick the fear, and that meant running her tormentor to ground.

No matter what the cost.

"HI, LARS. Glad you could meet me today," Reed greeted his old Z & E pal in the waiting area of the County employees' favorite pizza parlor.

"Hey, I was glad to have an excuse to get away. It's been awhile since we've done lunch. I got the impression on the phone that this wasn't, uh, purely social." Lars's broad red face creased into a grin. "I hope that doesn't mean we've got a problem with staff."

"Why do you think it's staff?" Reed asked as Lars led the way to a back booth.

"Because then you'll want to be subtle and diplomatic. Otherwise you'd just call me up and tell me my people wrote a report up wrong."

Reed chuckled, glad that he'd worked in the area long enough to have good friends. It was so much easier doing business with people he knew well.

"So," Lars asked after they'd ordered, "are we going to talk about Ellen Andrews, or are you mixing business and pleasure with another one of my employees?"

Reed hadn't quite decided what he was going to tell Ellen's supervisor about her—he'd ostensibly made this lunch date to talk about rocks and the original Chumash Mountain project—but once Lars opened the door, he couldn't seem to close it. "I don't think Ellen is interested in either business or pleasure where I'm concerned, Lars," he admitted reluctantly. "But I'm afraid that my concerns do involve her."

Lars looked a bit more sober now. "You're not going to ask me more questions about this time capsule thing, are you? Ellen was going to track down some of my people last weekend. The whole thing sounds a little bizarre if you ask me, especially the incidents with your cars.''

''The cars are the least of it, Lars,'' Reed told him, then gave a report on the events of the weekend, minus the personal results of his strong-arm tactics the night before. When he finished, he said, ''I'm sure that Ellen would not appreciate my reporting all this to you. She's determined to deal with her own problems in her own way. But she's not being realistic about the danger, Lars, and she won't let me help her. I'd feel a lot better if I knew you were keeping an eye on her.''

Lars stroked his chin thoughtfully. ''I don't like this. She's up there alone with John. Not that he isn't a tough cookie, but he doesn't even know he ought to look out for her.''

''Is there any way to get a message to him? Or can you think of some reason to bring Ellen back to the office and let somebody else help John finish the survey?''

Lars considered the question. ''Reed, if the police recommend it, I suppose I could do something. But you're suggesting that I tell an employee that she's in danger when she obviously doesn't think she is. It's paternalistic, patronizing and probably illegal, though I'd have to make a few calls to figure that out. When I talked to Ellen on Friday, she made it clear that she didn't want anybody to make a fuss.''

''On Friday she didn't know the bastard was going to break into her apartment and cut up her boys' pictures!''

Lars shook his snow-haloed head. ''Damn, that part makes me uneasy. Still, shooting at somebody or setting a bomb is life-threatening; cutting up pictures is just a sick prank. If Ellen went back up to Chumash Mountain without even checking in with me, I guess the break-in didn't upset her too much.'' He tapped nervous fingers on the table. ''You know she'd go right through the roof if she knew we were discussing her this way, Reed. She's not a child.''

Reed wasn't sure how to respond to that. He was probably out of line asking her boss to protect her. But after all, what did he have to lose? She'd made her feelings only too plain. But maybe it was just as well. In hindsight, he realized that he had jumped into the relationship a little too quickly. Ellen was too damn prickly; she fought him about everything. Maybe Howard *had* done a number on her, but did she have to keep taking it out on him?

''I wish you understood the difference between an offer and an order,'' she'd said in her note. He wondered if some subtle shift in his tone or phrasing last night might have made a difference. He doubted it. She didn't want him to be afraid for her, period. And he *was* afraid.

I really am better off without her, Reed rationalized. *If I hadn't been so concerned for her safety, I might have realized we were mismatched all along.*

Well, it was over now. But the mission was not over, and it would not be over until he was certain that whoever was badgering Ellen had been carted off in handcuffs.

Realizing he could push Lars no further at the moment, Reed said carefully, ''I'm wondering if we might be barking up the wrong tree here, worrying about Manzanita Meadows. It's possible that it's your project up there on Chumash Mountain that's stirred somebody up.''

''The survey?'' Lars's voice rang with incredulity.

''Well, maybe. Actually, I was thinking of the original survey, twenty or whatever years ago. Do you happen to recall why that project never came to pass?''

Lars thought a moment, then nodded. ''Sure. We did the survey, and the owner studied demographics and decided that the area was just too remote to be profitable. He hoped to build a resort later, but after a few years he sold the land.''

''And? Now?''

''Now there's a decent road up there, built by the state a while back. L.A. has sprawled even further north and east, so Chumash Mountain isn't so far away. I don't think there's any big mystery about it, Reed. The resort just wasn't financially feasible before. Now it is. It's as simple as that.''

On the surface it sounded so straightforward that Reed couldn't see any reason to pursue that line of questioning. ''I've got another idea, Lars, about how Ellen's situation might be linked to our original EIR at Manzanita Meadows. But I need some information about a type of rock, and I need to know which Z & E consultant did the geological study.''

''You mean twenty years ago?''

''Yes. I drove out to Manzanita Meadows yesterday and found a whole rock wall of diabase. But there's no mention of any igneous deposit in the EIR, and no diabase on the ground anywhere, even in the hollow that's been left undisturbed.''

''And you've never heard of anybody trucking in rock for a wall?''

"Not this kind. It's not very pretty. Besides, it's rare in this area. I called four landscape supply yards and two local quarries, and not one of them carries it or has heard of anybody else in the area who does. It's the same kind of rock that was used to smash my car, and Ellen found a piece in the time capsule."

"That could be a coincidence, Reed."

"Maybe, but I doubt it. That's why I'd like to talk to whoever did the geological part of the EIR. He might remember something that was too small to put in the report, or something that didn't seem relevant. For some reason," Reed added with a touch of irritation, "we don't seem to have his name in our billings records along with the other Z & E staff."

"Well, I'll try to dig up his name for you, along with any preliminary reports we may not have sent to the County," Lars offered. "You also might want to get the geologist's report from Baxter's firm."

"You mean the company Baxter sold out to when he went into politics?"

"Right. Watson Development, isn't it? Those records ought to be salted away somewhere."

It was an angle Reed hadn't thought of before. The law required that developers do environmental studies of their own, by hiring private consulting firms; then the County analyzed the studies for accuracy, bringing in objective alternative firms if County staff couldn't cover everything. As a result, Baxter's geologist had probably looked at the site before the Z & E geologist had checked it out. That person's notes or report might yet linger in the Baxter-Watson files.

Lars thought a moment, then added, "In the meantime, you might want to talk to Lucy Silverman. She's been our geologist for a good three years now. She could at least tell you a bit about diabase. Come to think of it, I think Ellen already talked to her.''

"Ellen doesn't know about the rock wall, Lars. I just found it yesterday," he explained. Then, reluctantly, he added, "I'm sure Lucy's good, but I'm sorry that you don't have the Manzanita Meadows geologist still on staff.''

"I don't even recall who it would be. We had a pretty brisk turnover during the war years. There was Sue Adamson, who was only here six months before she took maternity leave and never came back. And then that crazy hippie we called Rock Man, the flakiest guy ever to—''

"That's it! Rock Man. I remember him. Always wore a peace button and had hair down to here." Reed touched his shoulders. "I remember the first day he showed up out there at the site. I had to call Jefferson Baxter about something that afternoon, and Baxter said, 'Capwell, I know you folks at the County have to double-check my environmental assessment of the project, but how the hell does that wacko Z & E geologist expect to analyze soil densities and potential landslides by studying my astrological sign?' ''

Lars laughed heartily. "God, yes, that was Tim. He kept us all rolling our eyes. He was always whistling some half-baked rock tune or giving speeches against the war. And I'm no spiffy dresser, Reed, but honest to God, he came in to work looking like a refugee from the Salvation Army until I read him the riot act.''

"Yeah, he was an odd duck, but friendly enough, as I recall. And damned sharp when it came to geology.

Whatever happened to him, Lars? Did you have to let him go?"

"It would have come to that, I imagine. But he kept talking about building a cabin in Alaska, panning for gold and 'living off the land.' One day he just didn't show up for work. No answer at his apartment. A few weeks later the landlord called here looking for the rent. Opened his place and found it cleaned out except for some trash. Worse judgment call I ever made." Lars made a clicking sound. "But you're right about one thing, Reed: he knew his rocks. That's why we hired him. He was a geological genius. A demented genius, but..." He let the sentence trail off.

Reed wasn't sure how to answer. He was disappointed. Tim Reynolds had known his stuff, and he could have supplied some excellent information. But if he'd left no forwarding address twenty years ago, he'd be impossible to trace now. And Reed very much wanted to speak to the Manzanita Meadows' geologist in person.

The kind of questions he wanted to ask wouldn't be answered in a dusty report.

THE SUPERVISOR SAT at the dinner table, listening absentmindedly to his wife babble about her weekly women's service club. There were two new members today, she informed him. He didn't pay much attention until she mentioned Clara Capwell. Then his ears pricked up, but he strove to maintain his usual air of indifference. He listened with care as she rattled on about fundraisers and club politics until he was certain that she had no idea that the name Clara Capwell had any meaning for him, and no idea that he was at war with the Capwell woman's ex-husband.

She also had no idea that the supervisor was running out of time. He still didn't know what, if anything, Quinton had remembered or spilled to the Andrews broad. He'd snuck back to her apartment Sunday night, but he'd had to change his plans once he'd spotted the turquoise T-Bird outside. In an apartment complex, he didn't think he could take on the two of them together without making too much noise. He could strangle or stab an untrained woman; but Capwell had been trained in the service and probably couldn't be killed without a gun.

He couldn't wait any longer. The dike had too many holes; his clever fingers just couldn't dam them all. He had to get rid of Andrews and Capwell before they put any more pieces of the puzzle together.

By QUITTING TIME Ellen was tired. Not just working-hard-in-the-mountains tired, but bone-weary tired. The kind of tired that isn't helped by a frightened, sleepless night, let alone the belated realization that one has made a terrible mistake.

Yes, Reed was overly protective. No, she couldn't live with a man who tried to keep her on a short leash. And yes, Reed's cloying concern did remind her uncomfortably of Howard. Still, Reed was right about one thing: this was an extraordinary situation, and maybe some extraordinary precautions *were* advisable.

Besides, a whole catalog of Reed's shortcomings couldn't change the fact that she felt warm and happy and inexplicably excited when he was with her, and she'd felt tight and miserable and a little sick to her stomach ever since she'd told him they were through.

She also felt queasy when she thought about Howard's insistence that she hop the next flight to Kansas or he'd come fetch her. Surely he'd cooled down by now! Surely he wouldn't be foolish enough to fly out here and make a scene. Still, she wouldn't put it past him.

It threatened to be a long week. Shannon's article, which should take the pressure off her tormentor, would not come out until Thursday afternoon, and Ellen herself would not return to civilization until Thursday night. She didn't lie to herself that it was the chance to read the newspaper that had her counting the days. It was the chance to apologize to Reed—to give it another try if he were willing—which kept her so antsy.

That, and the fear that if he was right about the danger she was in, she might never see him again.

IT WAS ALMOST SIX when Reed returned to the rock wall house. He hoped that whoever lived there worked nine-to-five and had come home right after work today. If he didn't get an answer this time, he'd nose around and ask the neighbors questions. At least, he noticed his card was no longer in the door.

He knocked on it firmly, and to his relief it opened almost at once, revealing an elderly woman with her white hair in a bun. She did not use a cane or walker, but she gripped the open door heavily, as though for support.

"Hello, ma'am. My name is Reed Capwell. I'm with the Bentbow County Planning Division. I'd like to ask you a couple of questions about your property, if you can spare me a few minutes."

He handed her a card to verify his identify and offered her his best boy-next-door dimpled smile.

"Oh, you're the young man I tried to call," she said sweetly, beaming at him as though he were her favorite grandchild. "I found your card in the door yesterday."

Although he was gratified to be so eagerly received, Reed was irritated that his staff had once again lost a crucial phone call. He'd have to have Sandi give a piece of her mind to whoever filled in when she was on break. How many other important messages did he lose in the course of an average week?

But this was no time to discuss personnel problems. "Ma'am, the reason I'm here is that—"

"Please call me Vernalee," she told him. "Vernalee Lewis."

He took the frail hand she offered and squeezed it gently. "It's a pleasure to meet you, Vernalee. I had a dear aunt by that name."

It was true; she wasn't his favorite aunt and he hadn't seen her in twenty years, but Vernalee Lewis beamed at the disclosure just the same.

"Vernalee, I'm curious about this intriguing rock wall you've put in," he asked her casually. "It lends so much character to the property. Has it been here a long time?"

"Oh, my, yes. Henry built it the first year we moved in."

"Henry? Your husband?"

She nodded with muted sorrow that made it clear that Henry was no longer living.

"He loved to work with his hands, you know. Some of the neighbors paid to have their yards landscaped, but Henry planted every tree and bush himself."

"Did he build the wall with his own hands, too?"

"Oh, yes. Rock by rock."

"Where did he get the rocks? They're so . . . unusual for a garden wall."

"He found them down in the gulch," she said, pointing toward the undeveloped triangular lot between the apartment complex and the street that ran by her house. "We had a big black Lab then. Theodore was his name. We'd go for a walk every evening, Theodore and Henry and me. Henry would carry one big rock back every night. After about three months, he had just about all of them, and come spring he started building his wall." She sighed wistfully. "He was so proud of it!"

"And rightly so, Vernalee. It's beautifully done, and it's certainly stood the test of time."

Reed chatted to Vernalee for about ten minutes then checked over the now-rockless gulch before driving home slowly trying to make sense of what he'd learned. He was certain—well, nearly certain—that Ellen's rock had come from the pile in the gulch. He was also certain that the rock that had smashed his window had come from the same pile—or else had been used to symbolize the same pile.

The rocks did not belong here. They were not mentioned in the official EIR. But one of the rocks had been used to smash Reed's windshield, and one of them had been placed with a map, a newspaper page and Reed's business card in an old coffee can at the Z & E cabin.

It didn't make sense, but it was somehow connected; he was sure of it. He longed to talk over his facts with Ellen, but if she knew what he'd found, she'd be eager to start digging again. The question was, would she be safer doing nothing—alone—or digging with Reed right there beside her?

He'd pretty much decided on the former when he got home and spotted the red light flashing on his answering machine. Earlier in the afternoon, he'd called Watson Development and learned that Watson was out with the flu; the secretary had been quite adamant that no one else could help Reed. His luck with George Haversham was even worse: the contractor had been dead for about a year. But apparently his son had taken over the firm, and Reed was more hopeful about getting a quick return call from him. He'd left his home phone and the office number for both men.

When he rewound the tape, he realized that he'd received more than one call, or at least a very long message. The first voice was Jackie's, proudly reporting another successful evening on the job. The second voice was Sally Quinton's, expressing her frustration that she hadn't been able to reach Reed at work and her hope that an incident she'd belatedly recalled might be of value to him.

The third message contained no human voices. Only the sound of an explosion.

IT WAS NEARLY DUSK when Ellen, standing beside the cabin, heard a car chugging up the decrepit, distant road. Feeling on edge after all that had happened, she listened tensely to the sounds of arrival: an engine being cut off, a door slamming, a second door or trunk being closed. The sounds carried clearly in the forest stillness, making her wonder if the new arrival didn't care who heard him. Did that mean he was a friendly visitor, or did it mean that he knew she had nowhere to run and no way to get there?

She remembered the moment last night when she'd konked John on the head, and tried to tell herself not to be ridiculous. Then she remembered the sight of her sons' pictures ripped and strewn across her living room floor, and she knew she had every reason on the face of the earth to be afraid.

Rising abruptly as her heart began to thud, Ellen tried to call John and warn him of potential trouble. But then she remembered that he'd gone off to gather firewood and terror knotted her tongue.

CHAPTER TWELVE

ELLEN SLIPPED INTO the cabin and shut the door. Instantly she felt safer, though she wished there was a sturdy deadbolt to slide into place. She stood tensely by the window, trying to remember how long John had been gone. It didn't matter; time meant nothing to him. She could not shake her mounting terror. Nobody, but nobody, had a good reason to be approaching this secluded cabin! Yet wouldn't someone intent on doing her harm try to sneak up silently at night?

For several tense minutes she could only hear the scolding jays and one persistent woodpecker, but then, even within the cabin walls, she began to hear distant footsteps crunching over rocks and twigs. At last she could hear the panting of somebody who wasn't accustomed to the altitude. Somebody who was clearly making no attempt to conceal his presence.

The fear began to ebb from her body ever so slowly.

A new kind of tension seized her when she finally saw Reed's face.

He looked terrible. His brown eyes were haunted and a bit bloodshot. His five o'clock shadow gave the impression that he'd forgotten to shave. Even his shoulders seemed to hunch forward, and not from the weight of the pizza boxes he held in his hands.

He did not speak until he was about ten feet away from the cabin and Ellen had sheepishly returned to the front porch. Then he stopped, as though he'd come to a door, and met her eyes.

"Good evening, Ellen," he greeted her somewhat formally. Apprehension lined every syllable.

"Good evening, Reed." Her stiff tone mirrored his own—not because she wanted to sound distant, but because his own gravity did not invite warmth. Obviously he was still smarting from their last interaction. How could he know that the events of the last two days had caused her to sorely regret her parting words and that awful note? How could he know she wasn't angry that he'd overruled her directions and tracked her down? She was, against all logic, inexplicably thrilled to see him. Not just happy that he might have forgiven her for treating him so brusquely; not just thrilled that he might be willing to give her a second chance.

She was also relieved. A rainbow of safety seemed to surround her. In her heart she did not believe that any harm would come to her while Reed was with her.

"I thought you and John might like something that didn't come out of a can," he stiffly declared. "One's just got pepperoni; the other has everything but anchovies. I wasn't sure what you might like, so I tried to cover as many options as I could."

There was only one gracious reply she could make. "Thank you, Reed. That was very thoughtful of you." She was about to add hopefully, "But surely you didn't come all this way just to deliver a pizza," when a fresh set of footsteps crunching the sagebrush and twigs heralded John's arrival.

"I thought I smelled pizza!" he declared with more animation than she'd ever seen in him. "Whoever you are," he said to Reed, "you're always welcome here!"

He dumped the wood on the porch, took the pizzas with his left hand and offered Reed his right. "John Neff."

"Reed Capwell. I'm in charge of Residential Permits at the County."

"Right, right! I've heard your name. What the hell brings you up to this neck of the woods? This is a private project for Z & E. We're not even in Bentbow's jurisdiction."

Reed's lips tightened. "My, uh, interest here is... personal."

John stared at him as though he were speaking some other language. Then, belatedly, he glanced at Ellen—who had remained utterly silent during this exchange—and said, "Uh, right. Why don't I take this inside?" He vanished rather quickly, leaving Ellen to face Reed alone.

For a moment their eyes met uncertainly. Then Reed said, "If you had a phone, I would have called first. I know you don't want to see me anymore, but I have some information that you need to know. As soon as I give you my report, I'll be on my way."

A quiet voice of dread began to whisper to Ellen, *It's too late. He believed you when you said it was over. He doesn't want to give you another chance.*

Until that moment, Ellen had not been certain it was worth the risk of trying to patch things up. She always knew it would be a challenge. But she had believed that the future of her relationship with Reed lay in *her* hands. Hadn't he always told her how much he cared for her? And now...now...suddenly she felt as though she had lost him irrevocably, and she was reeling from the shock.

"There's...uh...no reason for you to rush off, Reed," she replied awkwardly. "Why don't you have some pizza with us? John usually gallops off to his girlfriend's after supper. Once he goes, we can talk."

Her eyes met his carefully, hopefully, uncertainly. Surely he'd just been waiting for some assurance! Surely he—

"It's a long drive back, Ellen. I wouldn't mind some of this pizza—the smell has been driving me crazy for miles—but I can bring you up to speed while I eat a piece or two. Then I better go."

His voice was civil, but unmistakably cool. Ellen felt slightly shaky. With all the pride she could muster, she said softly, "If you're sure that's how you want it, Reed."

For the first time she saw a glimmer of uncertainty in his eyes. "It would be the sensible thing to do."

"Maybe—" it was almost a plea "—we could play it by ear tonight."

She waited tensely for his answer, watched his kind brown eyes and longed to touch him. She remembered only too well the feel of her hands in his hair, the feel of his hands on her body. Why, oh why, had she destroyed that fragile new breath of love between them?

Slowly, sadly, Reed shook his head. "Ellen, we don't hear the same music."

She pleaded with her eyes. "We used to, Reed."

"No," he said crisply. "I only thought we did. I know better now."

Ellen swallowed hard as she turned away. He was serious. He really *had* come just to give her information. He didn't want her anymore, and that was the cold-hard truth.

When he trailed her into the house, John had already removed several pieces of pizza from one box and had piled them on his own plate. He hadn't even put extra plates on the table.

Ellen didn't comment; she just retrieved a couple of worn plates from the cupboard, handed one to Reed, and asked, "Do you want anything to drink? We've got some cola in here, I think."

Reed gave her a tight smile. "Anything is fine."

She grabbed two cans from the small refrigerator, tossed a third to John, then tugged a couple of pieces of pizza out of the pepperoni box for herself. She sat down near Reed and tried to look as though she weren't shriveling up inside.

"You said you had information," she prompted.

Reed glanced questioningly at John, then back at Ellen.

"It's okay, man. I know what's been going on," John answered. "I think the whole thing is a bit creepy, if you ask me."

"To say the least," Reed answered. Then he turned back to Ellen. "I drove out to Manzanita Meadows and found something interesting. One of the houses on the edge of the subdivision has a hand-built rock wall made of greenish-black rocks."

Ellen sat up straight. "Diabase?"

"That's what it looks like to me. I searched all around for some other rocks like that—even a stray one or two on the ground—but I couldn't find a thing."

"They could have been trucked in from some-where," said John.

"Sure, if anybody in the area sold them. But I called a few places, and they didn't even know what I was talking about. They sell all kinds of beautiful orna-mental rock or quarry staples, but nothing that looks like this. I mean, diabase isn't really pretty. The only reason a man—" he glanced at Ellen and corrected himself "—a *person* would use those rocks to build a wall is that they were nearby and plentiful."

"Cheap, you mean," said John.

"Exactly. But I couldn't find a trace of them."

"You talked to the owner of the house?" asked El-len.

"I talked to the widow of the man who built the wall. She says he collected each and every rock he could find from a gully next to the apartment complex, and she hasn't seen another rock there in fifteen or twenty years." He took a bite of pizza, then went on. "Today I talked to Lars about the geologist who worked on this thing. I remember him. A real weird guy named Tim Reynolds. We called him Rock Man."

"Do you know him, John?" Ellen asked.

John shook his head. "Name doesn't mean a thing to me."

"Well, it means something to me. I know this guy—well, I knew him back then. He was a flower child, who always wore jeans and ratty old T-shirts. He talked about rocks as though they were his best friends, and he was always dreaming about shucking it all to move to the wilds of Alaska. He showed up late about half the time, and even when he got there you had the feel-ing that he *wasn't* really there, if you know what I mean. We kept waiting for Lars to can him, but one day he just wandered off, never even gave notice, so it didn't come to that.''

"Well, personnel has a forwarding address, don't they?'' Ellen asked.

Reed shook his head. "They have zipso. He just didn't bother to show up one day, and nobody ever heard from him again. Lars is trying to find out who his best friends at Z & E were, though he was so weird I'm not sure he had any.''

John said, "If he wrote up a halfway decent report, the rocks ought to be mentioned. They're so atypical for the area.'' He looked at Reed, true interest shining in his eyes. "But you've checked the EIR, right? Ellen's been reading it for days.''

"There's nothing in the final report, but Lars is trying to dig up Tim's notes or at least an in-house preliminary report. In the meantime, I found out some very important information about Tim.''

Ellen watched him more closely, sensing fresh tension in his tone.

"I got a call today from Sally Quinton.''

He didn't look at Ellen, and she wasn't sure whether the gravity of his voice was caused by the mention of Sally or just his great discomfort being with Ellen. She had the feeling that there was something else he wasn't saying, something she really ought to know.

Reed briefly explained to John who Sally was, then continued, "She said she'd remembered something peculiar about the time period when she was working up here. One night she got a call from Tim Reynolds asking her to meet him. They agreed to rendezvous at this cabin.''

"Here?" John and Ellen echoed in unison.

Reed nodded. "Apparently Tim and Sally had been lovers at some point in the past. Although all that was long since over, according to Sally, she felt she owed it to him to find out what was troubling him. He was nervous, talking very fast, and that worried her." He took a bite of pizza and added, "Tim Reynolds was about as laid-back as you can get. He did everything in slow motion. For him to have acted frightened or excited about anything—except maybe a rock—is incomprehensible to me."

"And Sally thought it was odd, too?"

"Odd enough that she risked her fiancé's wrath to come up here and meet him. And her fiancé—well, husband now—has a really short fuse."

"And?" Ellen felt a bit breathless by now. She hadn't met Sally's husband, but now she wished she had. Might he fit into this odd puzzle somehow?

"And Rock Man never showed up."

John looked at Ellen, then at Reed. "What do you mean he never showed up? You mean he was late as usual, or called back the next day, or—"

"I mean, she never heard from him again. And as far as I can tell, neither did anybody at Z & E. He never came back to work."

For a long moment, silence simmered in the tiny cabin, silence seasoned with fear.

Then John said bluntly, "Maybe Tim didn't go to Alaska. Maybe he got bumped off by the guy who's after Ellen."

AN HOUR LATER, John stood up and said, "Gonna be cold tonight. You better bring in some more wood before it gets dark, Capwell."

The suggestion surprised Reed. From what he'd heard of John, the fellow wasn't particularly likely to think of anybody else's comfort. A week ago Reed would never have considered the possibility of asking a woman to carry wood, but now, as he glanced uneasily at Ellen, he felt as though he might be walking into a trap.

He was considering asking her if it would be all right for him to perform this simple act when he noticed that she was paying no attention whatsoever to his exchange with John. She was staring aimlessly out the solitary window, white-faced and trembling, and Reed wondered how her thoughtless partner could suggest that Tim Reynolds had been murdered by the very man who was stalking her, and then trot off to leave her up here alone. Of course, she wouldn't really be alone, but Reed wasn't sure how to let her know he'd packed a sleeping bag and had every intention of camping nearby.

Deciding to give the young man a piece of his mind before he left, Reed stood up and tugged on his old jacket. John was waiting for him at the door.

"I'll be right back, Ellen," Reed said softly.

She gave no sign that she heard.

He trailed John outside to the pile of logs he'd dumped on the porch. While he was deciding how to tell John exactly what he thought of him, the younger man asked without preamble, "Capwell, are you going to sleep with her tonight?"

Reed was astonished. Not even Jackie would have been so blunt! "I don't think that's any of your affair, John," he told the young man sharply. "Ellen's private—"

"Look, man, I'm not being nosy. I've just got to know. If you're sleeping with Ellen, I won't come back tonight. But if you're going back down the mountain, I'm sleeping *here*. I wouldn't want some jerk leaving my mom alone under the circumstances, and I'll be damned if I'll leave Ellen shaking in her boots till morning, not after what happened last night."

Reed was touched by the young man's unexpected thoughtfulness but alarmed by his last words.

"What do you mean, 'what happened last night'?" Reed asked sharply.

John glanced uneasily at the cabin, then gingerly touched the back of his head. "I could tell she was shook up when I left, so I decided to come back for the night. She heard me coming, but she didn't know it was me. When I opened the door, she was waiting with a rock and konked me on the head." He looked astounded. "I passed out cold! She tries to play it tough, Capwell, but I'm telling you, she was terrified."

Reed swore softly under his breath. He should never have let her spend even one night alone up here, no matter what she'd ordered him to do! The bomb threat was a warning, but it could just as easily have been a serious attempt on her life. He didn't want to tell Ellen about it if he could help it, but he decided that he'd have to at least tell John.

"I begged her to let me protect her," he explained. "I told her never to go anywhere without you while she's up here!'' He met John's eyes and confided softly, "Tonight I got a phone call. No voice—just the sound of an explosion. It sounded like a scene in a TV show when somebody blows up a car.''

John uttered an obscene word and closed his eyes. He looked as pale as Ellen. "Look man, maybe it's not my business, and Ellen's good in the woods—she can take care of herself. But this is *different*. I think somebody's trying to kill her—or at least scare the hell out of her. She's so scared she even confided in *me,* and let me tell you, man, that's one thing I thought she'd never do.''

Reed's eyes narrowed. "Why do you say that?''

"Hell, she thinks I'm some kid.''

Reed was too tense to fully appreciate the humor in the comment. Stiffly he replied, "You're all she's got up here, John. She won't let me protect her. Even in Bentbow, I'm not certain that she's . . . well, willing to have me around much right now. But she *can't* chase you off.'' His eyes met the younger man's. He wanted to give orders, but he knew how well Jackie or Nate would respond to such an approach, and he decided it would be smarter to let John make his own promises. "What do you think we should do?''

"I think we should make sure she's never alone until this thing is settled,'' he answered quickly. "Up here, I'll stay with her. When we get back to civilization, I'll let you know.''

Reed held out his hand. "Done.''

John shook it firmly, then asked, "So . . . about tonight?''

"I'll cover things at the cabin,'' Reed said. He could still sleep in the woods if it came to that—at least it wasn't raining—so there was really no reason for John to stay. And yet, there was no reason why he shouldn't just tell John to come back, either. He didn't really want the coast clear, did he, in case...in case...in case what? Ellen was giving him hints that she'd changed her mind again, but he was through playing her games. He'd decided he didn't want this relationship even if she did. Hadn't he?

Reed glanced through the cabin window and spotted her, shoulders slumped, still facing the fire. Alone, she did not try to mask her fear. Why couldn't she just admit to him that she was afraid? The thought of her terror tugged at something within Reed, something he'd hoped had died.

"I'll be staying here," he told John. "But I want you back here before I leave in the morning."

"Crack of dawn," John promised before he slipped away.

When Reed walked back into the cabin with an armload of wood, he found Ellen right where he'd left her. She glanced up at him, but she did not speak as he laid a fresh fire. When he was done, he sat down cross-legged by the fireplace, poking halfheartedly at the logs as the flames teased the kindling.

"So what do you think, Reed?" she asked, her voice low and husky. "Is John right? Was Tim killed?"

He met her eyes uncomfortably. "He was a flake, Ellen. That's why nobody ever went looking for him when he disappeared. Not even Sally. It was entirely reasonable for him to have decided to wander off without telling a soul. I still believe that could have happened."

She studied him silently, then asked, "But there might be more to it than that. He's the first unbroken link we've found between you, Manzanita Meadows and this cabin. He would have had your card, and he would have had access to a geological map of Manzanita Meadows. You found diabase there; he could have found it, too. And who better than a geologist to leave a rock as some sort of a clue?" She shook her head. "In fact, there's no good reason to think that Tim Reynolds *didn't* bury that time capsule. Or evidence, or whatever it was."

"We don't have proof that he did it, either. And we haven't a clue as to why."

Ellen ran nervous fingers through her dark hair. It was adorned with a leaf or two and looked as though it hadn't been combed in several hours, but there was something infinitely appealing about the casual way it waved across her nape. "I think Tim found out something that somebody didn't want him to know. When I dug up the time capsule, I discovered the same thing. I just don't know what it is yet." Her eyes filled with tears. "But whoever is trailing me knows. He thinks I'm going to expose him." Her voice dropped to a tremor. "He threatened my *children,* Reed!"

Reed tried not to think about how he'd feel if the bastard threatened his own kids; at the moment his job was to reassure this special woman that he kept telling himself he didn't really love. "He just wanted to frighten you, Ellen," he insisted, with far more assurance than he actually felt. "I don't think he even knows the names of your boys or where they live. Besides, if he wanted to use them to force you to do something, he would have issued his demands by now. He just wants you to keep quiet about what's in that coffee can.''

"But it's too late, Reed! I've told everybody what I saw! I let Shannon Waverly put it in the paper, for Pete's sake!''

"Ellen, if he were going to hurt you, I honestly think he would have done so by now.''

Her eyes met his. "Do you really think so, Reed?''

"Yes,'' he said with all the confidence he could muster. "I really do.''

He pushed from his mind the horrible sound of the explosion on his answering machine. He knew that Ellen was a competent adult and had a right to know about it. But she was already frightened, and he was going to make sure she wasn't alone. What good would it do to frighten her further? Besides, the call had come to *his* house. It might not have been meant for Ellen, after all.

If he or John stayed with her until Thursday afternoon, when the next edition of the *Westhope Herald* came out, she would be safe. She was already alert, frightened, watchful. How could terror improve her capacity to care for herself?

For a moment she was silent again, her eyes on the fire. Reed felt a curious warmth stir him, but it was a warmth filled with apprehension—about her safety, about her wishes, about his own desires.

Finally her eyes met his again. "Reed, last night I...I was afraid,'' she confessed in a tentative voice.

"John was gone for a while and I...realized why you were so adamant about staying at my apartment. I hardly know him but I still wanted him here.'' She smiled ruefully. "That sounds so odd. I've spent ten times the waking hours with him I've spent with you, and yet he's still a stranger. But you're..."

She studied him earnestly.

He felt weak and helpless against the tender need he read in those beautiful gray eyes.

Her voice grew husky as she whispered, "I was wrong, Reed. I was scared. I was proud. I was stubborn. I'm too uptight about men looking after me, I know that. If Howard hadn't called Sunday night, or you had *asked* me if I wanted your help instead of *ordering* me to follow your commands, I would have...I think things might have turned out differently. I mean, I wouldn't have wanted you to turn away as though you didn't care, Reed. I just wanted you to *offer* to help, not trample me."

Very slowly, he nodded. In hindsight, that was becoming more clear. "I didn't mean to be so abrasive, Ellen," he apologized, trying to decide if he dared to explain the reason he'd gone crazy Sunday night, the reason his fear had driven him out of control. But he'd never told a stateside soul about Su Le, not even Clara. He wasn't quite ready to share that grief with Ellen. At last he managed to murmur, "I just felt so desperate, Ellen. So terrified for you."

"I guess I felt a little desperate Sunday night, too, Reed," she answered softly. "I hated feeling so frightened, and I hated feeling that anybody else was frightened enough to feel the need to look out for me." Ellen lowered her voice and leaned toward him. "Reed, I don't want to believe that there's somebody out there trying to kill me!" She bit her lip, then faced him squarely. "And I don't want to believe I've lost you, either. Please tell me it's not too late, Reed. Please..."

She struggled for words and finally repeated with fresh anguish "...*please*."

While she waited for him to answer, Reed searched his heart for the strength to tell her no. A log crackled in the fireplace; an owl hooted outside. When Ellen finally closed her eyes and turned away, the pain on her lovely face all but broke him.

Reed rolled to his knees and crawled three paces until he reached her. Silently he took her hand.

She squeezed it. Hard. Swallowed a sob.

"What can I do to fix things, Reed? What can I do to make it right?"

Reed didn't answer. He pulled her toward him ever so slightly. A moment later she was in his arms.

He held her fiercely while she burrowed against his chest and surrendered to the weeping. His insides turned to mush.

"Reed—"

"Shh. It's okay."

And just like that, it was. He didn't remember why he'd been angry; he didn't care anymore. "On Sunday night I felt like you'd hit me with a two-by-four, Ellen," he huskily confessed. "I told myself it was over because I didn't want to give you the chance to hurt me all over again. But I love you, dammit, whether you want me to or not. I just hope to God that when this is all over, you'll give me a chance to show you I can adapt to your independence, and someday you might learn to love me, too."

Suddenly she pulled back, just far enough to meet his eyes. "Reed," she vowed, each word a dance in slow motion, "I already love you, whether or not we can ever work out the details between us."

He trembled as he listened to her confession. He felt deeply touched and profoundly aroused and so confused he could hardly remember why he'd come up here to Chumash Mountain. Yet he knew there were things that still had to be said. "Ellen, I'm trying to understand how you feel about your freedom. I know I hold on too tightly to the people I love. I'm so afraid something will happen to them. It's my problem, Ellen. It doesn't mean I don't think you're strong and capable." He took a deep breath and confessed, "It has to do with some things that happened overseas." There was more, much more, that he knew he'd need to tell her someday, but he couldn't bring himself to talk about it now.

Ellen nodded, as though she understood how much he'd left unsaid, but she did not press him for more explanation.

"If it weren't for all of these . . . threats, I honestly think I could find a way to back off, to give you breathing room, to let you find your own path. But I wasn't exaggerating when I said we're in a war of sorts here, Ellen. Not between you and me, but between *him* and *us*. Until we find out who's hounding you and the police take him into custody, I'm going to stick a lot closer to you than you might want me to. I just wish you could understand that it's not because I want to rob you of your independence. It's just that I want to keep you alive."

She studied him for a long moment, then used her free hand to gently stroke his face. "I know that, Reed. Really I do."

To his surprise, she kissed him. Just once, quite chastely, but he felt the warmth of her lips, then the ripple of her fingers through his hair. "It's a long drive down the mountain, Reed." Her voice was low and husky. "I'm not even sure it's passable in the dark."

Her words triggered a sudden inner jolt that made Reed realize he was feeling far more than relief that he wouldn't have to fight with her about spending the night as her protector. His heart was hoping for much, much more.

"Stay with me, Reed," she whispered.

Ellen's words shook him so hard he almost lost a grip on her. But then she was kissing him, kissing him in a way she'd never kissed him before.

At first there was a desperation in her touch, a desperation that called out for assurance that Reed really did want her, that he was done stonewalling, that everything between them might yet be all right. But when his arms swept around her and then dropped to the small of her back, he felt her shudder with a new kind of desperation, a desperation that echoed his own.

All of his resolutions vanished; all of Ellen's protests disappeared. When his fingertips claimed her breast, she whimpered and pressed herself against him. When he pulled her closer, trembling, she climbed onto his lap. In a matter of moments they were both breathless. Fire seemed to ring the room.

"Since John's not coming back, maybe I could sleep in his bag," Reed suggested unsteadily, unable to ask for more.

Ellen stroked his face again, kissed him with her tongue. "Since John's not coming back," she whispered urgently, "maybe you could sleep in mine."

He closed his eyes against the sudden swell of dizziness; his grip on Ellen tightened.

Reed's voice was nearly a croak as he answered, "It would be my greatest honor. But with all that's happened, Ellen, are you sure that—"

She covered his zipper with one hand. "I'm sure," she promised.

He did not ask again.

CHAPTER THIRTEEN

"THIS MEETING of the Bentbow County Board of Supervisors will now come to order."

The supervisor grimaced; the last thing he wanted to do was focus on another damn meeting. But his presence here was required, and if he missed the session too many people might ask where he'd been, and this was not a good time for anyone to be asking questions, even the routine ones favored by reporters. At the moment, he didn't much like the sight of Shannon Waverly sitting in the front row.

At least he had a good chance to study Capwell before things got underway. The last time he'd seen the man, Capwell had been on edge, coiled up like a diamondback. But this morning, despite the bags under his eyes, he was grinning ear to ear and laughing at lines that nobody else thought were funny. It wasn't too hard to guess how he'd spent last night. At least that bomb scare had gotten him out of his house long enough for the supervisor to search it thoroughly. He'd only had one close call—when Capwell's kid had shown up unexpectedly and scribbled him a note before she went off to work at a place called Blackman's. He'd read the note and chuckled. At twenty-three, she still called him "daddy."

He hadn't found a thing at Capwell's place, just as he'd come up dry at Ellen's. It was time to corner her at Chumash Mountain while Capwell was safely down in Bentbow. There were a great many places for a skilled marksman to hide on Chumash Mountain.

REED HAD LEFT THE CABIN at six in the morning to reach Bentbow in time for the board of supervisors meeting. Fortunately, John had returned in plenty of time. Ellen had been positively glowing, and John would have to have been just plain stupid to have missed the hot core of hunger that radiated throughout the cabin. When he gave Reed a man-to-man grin, Ellen looked embarrassed, but she didn't seem to guess that the two of them had agreed to watch over her. Reed shuddered to think what would happen if she ever did. A miracle had happened; she'd admitted that she loved him, and she'd taken him to bed. It was too wonderful to examine, too fragile to crush. He wanted it to last forever, but the voice of caution made him face the fact that until he nailed her tormentor, it wouldn't take much to rock the boat.

The board meeting had been uneventful. In the end, it was clear that the board was going to ignore the staff recommendation and vote for the new shopping center prudence opposed. Normally Reed took the protection of the public interest quite personally, but this time he couldn't seem to care. When he caught up with Supervisor Emmett Mercer, he didn't even mention the meeting. He asked him directly about his memory of Manzanita Meadows.

The bald fellow stopped, stared at Reed, and joked, "Capwell, I can't even remember what I was doing last week. How the hell do you expect me to remember something that happened twenty years ago?''

"Think about it," Reed urged him. "Is there anything you might remember, anything peculiar about that time—politically, socially, physically. The land—"

"I never had anything to do with the land, Reed." He grinned. "All I ever did was bring in the model home furniture. Now if that helped me get a few more customers, I'm grateful, son, but other than that..." He stopped and studied Reed for a moment. "What exactly are you getting at, Reed? Is there something wrong?"

Reed was certain he caught a look of apprehension in Mercer's eyes, but that could have been because the man was a politician, and he knew that questions about a politician's past almost always led to trouble. Reed couldn't believe that Mercer had done anything wrong, but he couldn't take any chances. "Emmett, do you remember a guy named Tim Reynolds?" he asked bluntly.

"Nope."

Mercer gave the answer too fast; he hadn't even had time to think about it.

"Are you sure? He was the geologist for Z & E, and he—"

"Reed, how the hell would I know a geologist back then? All I did was provide furniture for Baxter!" Pointedly he glanced at his watch. "I've got another meeting, son. Gotta run."

He winked as he bolted out the door.

Reed quickly turned to snag Jefferson Baxter before he disappeared, but he was already too late. The only supervisor left on the dais was Robert Robinson, who couldn't have had a thing to do with Manzanita Meadows. He'd been the mayor of Westhope when the development had begun, but the development was outside the city limits.

"Clara called," Sandi informed him when he reached the office. Before Reed could ask why, she explained, "She didn't say. But she didn't sound mad at you, if that's any clue."

Reed grinned. "It's not a clue, but it is good news. She doesn't usually call me without a good reason." As he started to dial his ex-wife's number, he realized that lately she'd called him a number of times for reasons that were less than critical. Granted, they usually ended up talking about Jackie, but Jackie was really doing quite well at the moment. She wasn't in need of the parental crisis-conferences that used to mark their lives.

"I dropped in on Jackie at work last night, Reed," Clara told him as soon as she said hello. "I wanted you to know that she—well, I wouldn't call her another person or anything, but I think she's actually taking this job seriously. I had the feeling—oh, call it mother's intuition, whatever—but I think she may be a few inches closer to adulthood than she was last week. I think it's just possible that she's finally going to grow up."

Reed breathed deeply. It was news he'd waited half of his life to hear. "So I didn't make a mistake buying her the car?"

"Well, I'm not sure that was necessary, but if it got her to take her responsibilities more seriously, it might have been worth it," Clara answered kindly. Suddenly her voice grew sober as she added, "You have always done the best you could, Reed. It's all Nathan could ever have asked of you." Before he could respond, she continued, "Jackie says you have a new friend of the female persuasion. She thinks Ellen is very special to you."

It was the first time Reed had ever discussed a woman with his ex-wife, and it felt very peculiar to him. "She is very special, Clara. It's new yet, but..." he wasn't sure how much of his happiness Clara could really appreciate "...but it feels very right."

There was an awkward silence. "I hope it works out for you, Reed. Honestly, I do. Just once in your life you ought to be able to marry a woman because you love her, and not because you promised your best friend you'd take care of his wife."

He didn't have an answer for that old lament, but he did have something he had to say on the subject of Ellen. Even though all the threats so far had been directed at Reed himself or at Ellen, the bomb threat had alarmed him too much to let embarrassment overrule caution. Colonel Harrison had reminded him that an old vendetta would be launched at his old alliances. In good conscience, he felt he had to warn Clara that she might be a potential target of violence, no matter how remote the possibility might seem. Hesitantly he said, "Clara, there's something I need to tell you."

She did not ask what it was; she just waited.

"I know you think I...worry too much. And maybe I do. But I have to tell you that several threats have been made on Ellen's life, or maybe on mine. One threat related to her children. I'm pretty sure the problem is the damn time capsule, but I can't swear to it. I don't think this is anything for you to worry about, but all the same, I'd take it as a personal favor if you'd be . . . well, especially careful for a while."

"Careful?" Her voice was half tense, half mocking. "Why, Reed, what makes you think I'm in any danger? I don't have anything to do with the time capsule."

Reed took a deep breath. "Clara, I think this person is trying to let me know that he'll hurt somebody close to me if I pursue this thing. I know we're divorced, but anybody could tell him that we're still . . . good friends."

After a dark silence, she answered, "That's all we ever were, Reed. Even when we were married."

Reed didn't have time to dwell on that thought; he had too much to do. Gently he wound up his call to Clara, reiterating his concern for her safety, and she promised to be careful.

Since he'd missed Baxter at the meeting, he placed a call to his office, which netted him the information that the supervisor had a full afternoon and would not be free to return his calls until morning. Since Reed hadn't received a call from the allegedly ailing Watson or healthy young Haversham, either, he decided not to sit idly by while the rest of the day slipped away. A contractor on site was somebody he could track down in person.

George Haversham, Jr. turned out to be a young man barely out of his teens. Tall and wiry with unkempt hair, he didn't seem the least bit interested in what Reed had to say. He just kept hollering orders and waving his clipboard at his crew. He claimed to know nothing about Manzanita Meadows except that his father had done a fine job and made a mint off the project.

Behind him, two carpenters were framing a living-room window. One of them, an elderly black fellow with a Dodgers cap, seemed to keep glancing at Reed with more than casual interest.

"I started working for my dad when I was seventeen," young Haversham told Reed nonchalantly. "He said he'd make me a full partner in five years. But he had a heart attack last year—died on the job—so I took over a little early. I wish I could help you, Capwell, but frankly, I don't know a thing beyond what's in our records, and I'm not even sure we have records that are twenty years old."

"If you did have records," Reed asked, "where would they be?"

Haversham shrugged indifferently. "In the shed in back of the office. But I haven't really sorted things out in there since Dad died, and I can't spare the time right now."

Gingerly Reed offered, "Maybe I could look myself."

The old black carpenter swore as he slammed his thumb with a hammer, and Haversham's friendliness grew strained. "My insurance wouldn't cover you if anything happened in that old building. I tell you what. When I get a break—you know, a rainy day or something—I'll see what I can do."

"It's raining today," Reed pointed out.

The young man scowled. "Not enough to stop my crew." He glanced at the two workers behind him, and the black man dropped some nails, then studiously looked away. "We've got some interior carpentry to do. Now, if you'll excuse me—"

Reed took the hint. He handed Haversham one of his business cards and thanked him for his help. On his way out the door, he tried to catch the old carpenter's eye, but he seemed intent on his work.

Reed casually dropped a business card on the floor beside him, as if by mistake, hoping against hope that the old man would pick it up and call him. He had a hunch that he knew something —something he didn't want to say in front of the kid—but if he didn't come forward on his own, there was nothing Reed could do.

ON THURSDAY MORNING, it drizzled on Chumash Mountain, but that didn't make any difference to Ellen. In fact, the sunshine was so bright in her heart that she had trouble concentrating on anything, especially the minor technicalities of the rest of the survey. She and John had agreed to work straight through lunch so they could go home today. There were only a few more measurements they had to double-check. By 7:00 a.m. they were hiking up the northern-most slope, where the hills were dense with oak and sagebrush and populated with mule deer.

It was eerily still in the woods at this time of day. Ellen loved the pristine silence, and she knew she'd miss these magical moments in this remote locale. But she also knew that she was too old to enjoy many more weeks like the last few, and as soon as she earned her stripes with Z & E, she'd ask Lars for a desk job, for some of the time at least.

One fringe benefit of the job was that she'd be able to see Reed pretty much whenever she wanted to. And

while she hadn't yet convinced herself that they'd
worked out all the tangles in their relationship, she was
certain that what she felt for him—and what he so obviously felt for her—was worth fighting for. She loved
him, pure and simple, and the memories of Howard's
oppression could not destroy her joy at the knowledge
that Reed loved her, too.

Their night together had been sensually rich beyond
Ellen's most creative fantasies. Reed had not forced her
to follow his lead; he'd simply devoted himself to
making her happy, and she'd found herself very happy
indeed.

"Ellen. Ellen!" John grumped, as though he'd been
trying to get her attention for some time. "Are you
with me here, or what?"

"Sorry." Inwardly she blushed, forcing herself to
attend to his directions. The last thing John needed was
a rodman whose head was in the clouds. There would
be enough time to think of Reed tonight. The minute
she and John finished up their work on the mountain,
she planned to fly to Reed like a homing pigeon.

"Ellen!" he shouted again. This time there was fury
in his voice. Or was it . . . fear?

An instant later, Ellen heard the sharp ping of
something zinging by her with the speed of an elec-
tronic bird. An instant later John hurled himself at her,
knocking her flat on the ground. In slow motion she
realized that it was a bullet that had just gone by; in
slow motion she realized that the second *zing* would
have gotten her right between the eyes.

Ellen closed her eyes and tried to breathe, aware of
only two things: John had saved her life, and if he

hadn't, she would have been the victim of a hunting accident.

But when John called out, "Hey, you idiot! You're shooting at people, not deer!" no red-faced hunter appeared to apologize or see if they'd been accidentally wounded.

A grip of terror made Ellen wonder if it had been a shooting accident after all.

ON THURSDAY AFTERNOON, Reed tried to figure out what Haversham, Sr. might have had to do with Rock Man's disappearance. As the contractor for such a huge operation he would have had intimate dealings with the project developer—Jefferson Baxter—and could easily have dealt with Reed's boss, Bill, as well as Reed himself. And of course, Tim's supervisor might have been involved; that would have been Lars, but Lars didn't know anything. Nor had he been able to dig up the information Reed had requested, either. Apparently he'd set Olga Rios, on the trail of the Manzanita Meadows house report, but so far she hadn't turned up a thing.

Reed had no better luck with his other potential sources. He placed a second call to Jefferson Baxter and avoided the secretary's attempt to pin down what he wanted. Impatiently he called Watson Development again and tried to get the secretary to check the old files, but she reiterated her position: he'd have to wait until Watson himself returned to the office. She wasn't nearly as courteous the second time around.

He was troubled by her attitude, troubled by Watson's alleged illness. The files he sought were normally readily available, yet he was having a devil of a time finding the name of the first geologist Baxter had hired for the project, let alone the in-house report. He wondered if Baxter's original geologist had found out something...or if he was missing, too. If only Reed had been able to study the Baxter-Watson geological report, he might have been able to pick up a clue. Instead he was growing more and more fearful. While all these people dawdled, Ellen remained in danger.

For the hundredth time he asked himself if he'd made a mistake keeping the news of the bomb threat from her, relying on John's protection instead. From a practical point of view, it had seemed like the best choice. Yet in hindsight he realized that Ellen, if she ever found out, would take his decision as a vote of no confidence in her abilities to deal with the situation. He did have faith in her; he just wanted to protect her. Still, he felt as if he was standing on shifting sands.

It occurred to Reed that he was also taking a chance pursuing leads when the article in the paper was supposed to assure Ellen's tormentor that she had dropped the search. But he'd tried to draw all attention to himself. Besides, after the bomb threat, he'd felt little confidence that the article was going to do much good. It was probably too late to bury his head in the sand. If he wanted to keep Ellen alive, he had to find out who was after her.

Late in the day, Reed finally got a call related to the time capsule, but it wasn't from anybody he'd been waiting to hear from. The caller was Shannon Waverly.

"Good news, Reed. I know today's edition of the paper says Ellen's not digging anymore on this time capsule thing, but I just came across a clue I thought she ought to know about. Do you know where I can reach her?''

''She's still up at Chumash Mountain, Shannon, but she's coming back tonight.'' Reed was thrilled to have any clue he could find, but he didn't want Shannon to share this one with Ellen. Ellen had to stop looking, or Ellen could end up dead. ''I'll be seeing her soon, Shannon. If you'll just tell me what you've found out, I'll pass on the message.''

''Great,'' Shannon replied. ''The last time I spoke to Ellen, I told her that Marylou Ruskin, who we think is in the basketball team photo, was out of town. She still is, but her sister tracked down her best friend, and the friend remembers two or three of the other girls in the team photo because they were all in the same class. So even without Marylou, that narrows things down to '70, '71 or '72. The team is ten-to-twelve-year-olds. The girl I talked to played all three years, and she can't remember which year this particular photo was taken. But she remembers something else that might be very important.''

''Which is?''

''The name of the coach.''

Reed took a deep breath. ''And the coach is—''

''Robert Robinson.''

''Robert Robinson? Supervisor Robert Robinson?''

''Supervisor now, mayor of Westhope then,'' Shannon crowed triumphantly. ''I've already started sniffing for dirty laundry back then, but so far I can't find a thing. The highlights of those years in the *Trailblazer*—you know the *Herald* wasn't in production then—seem to be a Vietnam protest, the San Fernando earthquake and some scandal involving a

Westhope High beauty queen named Sandra Carmichael who dated Robinson's son.''

It occurred to Reed that Shannon was probably looking for the typical under-the-table profits that a mayor might be in a position to make if he could somehow get tangled up in a development the size of Manzanita Meadows. But Reed was wondering if baby-kissing Robinson had ever met Tim Reynolds...or if Reynolds had somehow stumbled over some secret of Robinson's that Shannon had missed.

A secret worth killing to keep.

CHAPTER FOURTEEN

BY THE TIME Ellen reached Bentbow that evening, she was in no mood to play hard to get with Reed. She was still badly shaken from the hunting "accident"—if indeed that's what it had been—and despite her determination to stand on her own two feet, she was eager to spend a few moments in the shelter of Reed's arms. She wasn't sure if she should tell him what had happened. Either way, just being with him would help make the darkness go away.

John had said that a killer would have kept firing until they were both dead; a hunter, embarrassed by his faux pas, would have backed off once he'd realized what he'd done. Most likely, that was what had happened. Still, Ellen was relieved that she was not going to spend the night at the cabin, and glad that the newspaper had come out this afternoon. She stopped to pick up a copy on her way into Bentbow, and was pleased to see that Shannon had made Ellen's position perfectly clear. The headline was: Time Capsule Mystery Buried Forever. Even the most dense and determined tormentor would surely realize that his secret was still safe.

Ellen didn't even go home to shower and change; she just pulled into Reed's driveway and knocked on the front door.

He opened it almost at once, his brown eyes sparkling as he greeted her. "I used to think Friday was the high point of the week, but I'm beginning to think that maybe Thursday has just moved into first place."

Ellen walked in as though she lived there, feeling a blanket of warmth surround her. Reed closed the door behind her, then took her quickly in his arms.

At once the terror vanished. She felt whole again.

Reed's kiss was warm, urgent, as though he'd counted each and every minute since he'd said goodbye at Chumash Mountain.

Ellen kissed him back the same way.

She wrapped her arms around his neck and savored the comfortable intimacy of his embrace. It was different than the way he'd touched her in the cabin. That had been richly satisfying in a physical way, but it had been . . . well, tentative. As though he were feeling his way in the dark.

Now the sun was shining. They were sure of each other, ready to bond in a new way.

As Reed broke off the kiss to pull her closer, his lips pressed against her temple. "I missed you, Ellen," he said softly. "I worried some—forgive me, but I did—but mainly, I just missed you."

She hugged him tightly, trying to decide whether or not she really wanted to tell him about the incident with the hunter. She still wasn't sure whether or not it had been an accidental shooting. Besides, what could Reed do about it now but worry? The last thing she wanted to do was say anything to create hard feelings between them again.

"I missed you, too," she answered. "I think it was worse once I knew what I was missing."

He chuckled softly against her hair, then reached down to pat her bottom. "I know the feeling. Do you want to eat before we make up for lost time?"

She nibbled on his ear. "I had a hamburger on the way down. Unless you've fixed something special—"

"I've got steaks thawed that we can eat or leave in the fridge. To tell you the truth—"

Ellen dropped her hands to his thighs and trailed her fingers in a slow, sensual circle. "I'd love a steak," she teased him. "Tomorrow."

Reed's eyes shone with a new kind of feeling, and he gently pressed his lower body against hers. She leaned against him, savoring the unspoken promise... quivering as he aroused her barely dormant desire.

"Before dinner at dawn, would you like a tour of the house?" he whispered provocatively.

"Starting with the bedroom?"

He grinned. His dimples deepened. "I suppose there are other options."

Ellen's eyes met his provocatively. "Such as?"

He kissed her again. "The patio chaise lounge, the living room floor..."

She giggled, feeling almost girlish, as she kissed the hollow of his neck.

His legs pressed closer yet.

"I have a vague recollection of your skill on the floor, Reed, but the details elude me at the moment."

Reed laughed and turned toward the back of the house, one arm still tightly wrapped around Ellen. "Perhaps I could jog your memory a bit. You could give me a code word whenever I do something you like."

"Mmm. Like 'yes,' perhaps?"

"Something like that."

He stopped in the hall and kissed her again.

Ellen savored his lips, then whispered, "Yes."

He laughed once more. "You're easy to please."

"Yes," she repeated. They both chuckled, starting to feel good about almost everything. Then Ellen said, "Actually, it's not that I'm easy to please, Reed. It's just that you..." She couldn't quite figure out how to phrase it, so she kissed him again. It was a deep kiss, hotter than before, and before it finished one of Reed's warm hands had closed around her breast. She gasped slightly as his fingertips harnessed her taut nipple.

"Yes?" he whispered.

She smiled against his mouth. "Yes to everything."

He hugged her before he set off again for the bedroom. When they got there, he undressed her leisurely—exploring vital anatomical spots of interest in the course of the process—and then undressed himself a little breathlessly. He tossed his glasses on the bedstand, then stretched out his naked body next to Ellen's. She trembled as his ankles covered hers, then his knees and thighs. As he eased himself completely on top of her, Ellen's desperate fingers seized his hair.

She could feel the heat of Reed's strong body against every line of her own; she could feel the tenderness in his touch as he found delicious new ways to incite her mounting hunger.

When she started to press urgently against him, Reed teased her with a single word. "Yes?"

"Three thousand yesses," Ellen whispered, and welcomed him inside.

LATER, AS SHE LAY CURLED and sleeping in his arms, Reed tried to reconcile what he'd done. Yes, he'd gone behind Ellen's back; yes, he'd deliberately withheld information she'd think she had a right to know. But he'd kept her alive and reduced her terror. Could she really blame him for that? After everything they'd shared in the past few days, if she ever found out that John had been watching her for him and had made a surreptitious report about the "hunter," would she try to break things off all over again?

He should have told her about Shannon's discovery, but then he'd have to tell her that he'd already called Robinson, who'd shed no light on the subject but had sounded as edgy as hell with Reed's line of questioning. He still hadn't heard from Baxter, and he was trying to decide if he should track down Haversham's black carpenter to see if the elderly fellow might be willing to talk if he could get him alone.

Reed was frustrated; he was worried. He was doing a juggling act with too many unanswered questions that might have meant everything or nothing at all. And it was getting too hard to keep things from Ellen, especially when she'd given herself so irrevocably to him.

He knew what he had to do. He had to tell her the truth about the bomb threat, the truth about John. But if he did, he might lose her for sure. And if he didn't—this morning was living proof—he might lose her to the man who was stalking her. John had interceded; he'd done a good job. But Reed couldn't help but ask himself if Ellen would have been more alert, more careful, if she'd known all the facts. If anything had happened to her, he could not have forgiven himself.

Ellen had told him over and over again that she
could take care of herself. Maybe she was right. Maybe
he wasn't just crippling her freedom by his overprotection; maybe he was risking her life.

She wasn't Su Le, and this wasn't Vietnam. The circumstances were different, even if the danger was no
less real.

"I love you, Ellen Andrews," he whispered to her
sleeping form.

She didn't wake up, but she did snuggle closer to his
warmth. Even in her sleep, he was certain, she could
sense the power of his love.

He hoped she couldn't sense his fear.

"THEY SUSPECT that somebody killed Reynolds," the
woman squeaked over the phone. "But I'm certain
they don't know why he buried the stuff or what it
might mean."

"Capwell hasn't figured it out yet? I thought he was
brighter than that," the supervisor remarked with some
satisfaction.

It was a mistake. Almost at once the woman bleated,
"Please don't hurt him. He doesn't want to cause anybody any problems. He just wants to be sure that Ellen's safe. If you'd just leave her alone, he'd forget the
whole thing. I know he would. She isn't going to turn
over any more stones. She wants to forget the whole
thing. Please—"

"Save your theatrics for someone who cares," the
supervisor snapped, almost forgetting to disguise his
voice with his handkerchief and deliberate huskiness.
He wasn't fooled by that newspaper article. Andrews
might have given up the struggle, but he'd seen the de-

termination in Capwell's face. Ellen's lover wouldn't rest until he was certain it was over. But the poor sucker had a long way to go. Two decades had passed since Tim Reynolds's reports had been removed from Z & E's file, and the other Manzanita Meadows geologist had never known a thing. The trouble was that even without all the facts, Capwell was too damn close to putting it all together, too damn close to revealing the heart of it to the police. He was asking too many questions and causing too much trouble. Right now people viewed him as an annoying gnat, but sooner or later someone might take his accusations seriously. "You've already sold Capwell down the river," he told the spy who'd been so helpful. "It's too late to plead in his defense."

"Don't try to make me feel guilty!" she squealed. "You know I'd never hurt him on purpose! You gave me no choice!"

He chuckled, enjoying his power and the sure knowledge that the ax he held over her head would keep her from spilling her guts to Capwell. "I'm still giving you no choice," he snapped. "You'll keep reporting every move he makes to me unless you want to see your pretty girl's throat ringed in red."

She started to cry. She begged him to spare her "baby." Finally he told her to shut up; nothing would happen to the girl if she just kept her mouth shut and kept him informed. He didn't add that he was going to have enough bodies to worry about without leaving a path for the cops to follow straight to his door. And now, dammit, he couldn't just kill his two pigeons outright. They knew too much—maybe John did, too—and he'd have to get one of them to tell him how much damage had been done before he silenced them forever. Capwell was the one who had the most information, but he'd be the least likely to talk. Oh, he'd probably spill it all to save Ellen, but he'd already made sure that Ellen would be almost impossible to reach. The supervisor might be able to kill her from a distance, but after John's clever action this morning, he knew he'd be hard-pressed to kidnap her.

After his spy hung up, it occurred to him that he'd overlooked one of his most powerful weapons. Nothing had shaken Andrews until he'd threatened her kids; the only reason his mole—who really did love Reed Capwell, in her own way—was willing to betray him was because she loved her girl more. And Capwell— hell's bells, how could he have missed it?—loved his daughter more than anything on the face of the earth. Toss in all that guilt he had mixed up with her safety, and he'd go berserk if anything happened to *her*.

One way or another, he could use Jackie as bait. Damn good thing he thought of it. He was running out of time.

IT WAS DARK WHEN ELLEN woke up. Reed's long limbs were still closely wrapped around her body; something about the intimacy of sleep touched her deeply. She felt sated and cherished in a way she hadn't felt in a very long time. In fact, she decided as she brushed back Reed's brown-and-silver hair from his eyes, she wasn't sure she'd ever felt quite this way before.

He stirred in his sleep, pulled her closer. She pressed her lips against his cheek, hating to wake him up, but knowing that they had to talk.

"Reed," she said softly, "I have to go to the office in the morning. All my work clothes are at home." She didn't add that she was curious to see if there was any sign of an intruder...or an irate ex-husband from Kansas.

Reed opened one eye. "Ellen, it's the middle of the night. Just tell me what time to set the alarm for."

For a moment she just stared at him. Then she said, "Are you asking me to spend the night?"

He rolled up on one elbow and studied her carefully. He was still sleepy, but he was obviously trying to wake up. "Is this a trick question?"

"What do you mean?"

"I mean, if I ask you to stay, will you say I'm giving you orders and leave in a huff?"

"If I decide to leave, will you try to stop me?" It was a straightforward question, but Ellen knew it had no straightforward answer. She just wasn't sure what she wanted him to say. The truth was, she didn't want to spend the night alone in her apartment, not just because she felt warm and cozy here but also because she was still afraid. But she didn't want to admit that to Reed, didn't think she could without telling him about the hunter. And that was a decision she still hadn't made.

Reed sat up slowly, his back to her as he dropped his long legs over the edge of the bed. "Ellen," he said slowly, "I love you. You know that."

She laid one hand on the small of his back.

"I don't want to lose you. I don't want you to...walk out on me, and I don't want to wake up one morning and find you dead."

She stroked his skin gently. He hadn't answered her question, but at least he wasn't barking orders at her. He was trying to reach a compromise, and she wanted to reach one, too.

"Ellen, the truth is, I don't want you to leave here tonight," Reed said softly. "For many reasons. I'm hoping you'll decide to stay on your own."

She pondered his plea, then had to ask, "And if I don't?"

He turned around then, moving one knee back on the bed, and gently took her hand. "Ellen," he said tensely, "someone tried to kill you today. If someone had tried to kill *me,* I would be afraid."

It took her a minute to realize the importance of what he'd said. Nobody knew about the shooting but John and Ellen herself! And Ellen hadn't told a soul.

"John called you?" Ellen's voice was tense, but she tried to keep her frustration under control.

Reed nodded. Then, to her surprise, he confessed, "He's called me from the ranger station every night since I was up there."

Ellen's eyes opened wide. She withdrew her hand from Reed's. "John would never have taken such a step on his own! You came up to Chumash Mountain to tell him to watch over me!"

"Yes, I did," he said bluntly. "After I'd received a bomb threat, there was no way I was going to leave you alone up there if he hadn't agreed."

Ellen's lower jaw sagged. "A bomb threat? There was a *bomb* threat and you didn't tell me?"

Reed couldn't meet her eyes. "I thought it would have frightened you."

"Of course it would have frightened me! But it might have made me more cautious! Good God, Reed, I might have been killed this morning!"

He licked his lips. "I know, Ellen. That's why I decided that I had to tell you now...no matter what the consequences." Her rage cooled just slightly as he added, "I've always thought of protecting someone as doing the protecting myself. But maybe in this case, I can protect you best by giving you all the facts so you can deal with whatever happens when I'm not there."

Ellen tried to think how knowing about the bomb threat would have affected her behavior the past few days. Would it have made a difference, or would it simply have made her more afraid? She didn't know the answer. She only knew that Reed should have told her, and it hurt deeply that he'd chosen not to do so...until now.

"Please stay here tonight, Ellen," he urged her. "I don't want to be an ogre. I don't want to lose you, and I don't want to fight. I told you the truth. I've told you everything I know...except for a lead that Shannon shared with me just today, and it didn't pan out, anyway."

At first Ellen didn't answer; she was still hurt, still steaming. At last she said, "Reed, it's more than a matter of one evening. I don't want to go home tonight. I'm scared. I'd rather be with you." She hated to douse the fresh hope in his eyes, but she had to be completely honest. Her tone grew strained as she finished, "But I just can't see going into a long-term relationship with a man who keeps such things from me for my own good.'"

"I'm not keeping anything from you now," he said softly. "It's late, I know, but...I've told you everything." She was still pondering that when he added in a spectral whisper, "Well, almost everything."

"There's more?" New fear tightened her throat.

"Not about you, Ellen. About..." he swallowed hard "...about me."

"You've been threatened, Reed?" Her own fear for him was so great that she almost understood how he felt about her safety. But a moment later her feelings were tossed in the air and came down upside down.

"Ellen, I want to tell you a story." His voice was too soft now, too haunted. The look on his face was more than sad; it was eerie. "This is something I've never told to anybody since I left Vietnam. Not even Clara knows."

She sat up straighter, feeling tense and afraid. She'd always suspected that Reed harbored a deep and terrible secret that still wounded him. The fact that he chose to reveal it now filled her with gratitude and awe. But it also made her wonder what had prompted him to dig so deeply into his own past tonight. It was not an accidental or careless decision, she was sure; neither was his decision to reveal that he'd conspired with John.

"In Vietnam I was engaged to a girl named Su Le," Reed said quietly. His eyes met hers, eyes so full of agony that she knew she was seeing deep into Reed's soul for the first time. "She helped my CO set up a trap for a Viet Cong undercover operative who'd been systematically revealing our secrets. Nathan was part of the team."

Ellen was shaken, but she did not speak. It was a time for listening.

"Harrison assured me that Su Le would be safe. I promised her she'd be all right. I even went to see her grandmother, who wasn't at all happy about having her marry an American, and assured her that she had nothing to worry about."

His eyes were begging Ellen now, begging for a kind of understanding that went beyond her own situation. She was astonished and profoundly touched that Reed would share such pain with her.

"The mission was successful, but we never counted on revenge." Reed closed his eyes. "They tracked Nathan down two months later," he whispered. "They tortured him before he died."

Ellen tightened her grip on his hand.

"I'd never met Clara or Jackie, but I felt as though they were my own sister and niece. Nathan lived for them. So many guys lost their values over there, lived for the moment, slept with the whores. But all Nathan ever wanted was to come home to Clara and his baby girl. When I got back, I didn't have anybody, and I had to take care of Clara for Nathan. The easiest way was to marry her. Besides, I didn't think I'd ever want to marry anybody else, anyway."

No wonder Reed had married Clara, even though he acted as though he'd never felt any passion for her in the first place! No wonder he'd felt compelled to stay in the marriage. No wonder he'd always coddled Jackie.

Ellen slipped her fingers through Reed's, felt his pain in that tight grip. She wanted to be near him, but she didn't dare press closer, didn't know what to say.

"He said he could take care of himself. He was good. He was trained. He was careful." Reed's eyes beseeched her to understand. "I believed him. I respected his independence and I got out of the way." There was a long silence before he finished, "And he died."

Ellen felt so ill she could not speak. It was as though Reed's pain had become her own. She felt so callow. How heartlessly she'd dismissed his concerns as being chauvinist manifestations that mirrored Howard's! Her danger had triggered the deepest well of Reed's life-long pain.

Desperately she wanted to comfort him, to tell him that she understood his agony, his desire to protect her, his determination to protect her from Nathan's fate. And then it struck her that he hadn't finished his story. After all, he'd talked about Nathan's death before. But tonight was the first time he'd ever revealed that he'd been engaged in Vietnam, before he'd come home and married Clara. Had he given up the girl he loved as a form of self-flagellation after Nathan died? Or had she suffered the same fate?

In a near whisper she asked, "What happened to Su Le?"

Reed closed his eyes. His grip on her hand went slack.

"Oh, Reed." Ellen felt a wave of nausea, sickened that she'd asked.

Reed lifted his index finger and lightly touched a spot on his jaw. "I can still feel it here," he whispered. "He grandmother spit in my face when I told her how Su L died." He struggled for composure, his eyes unable to contain his pain. "I tried to keep my promise to bring them here. Her grandmother and her sister. I sent money; I sent letters. Everything came back unan

wered. I finally wrote to a friend still stationed over
here to go see them, make sure they were okay, to as-
ure them I hadn't forgotten them.'' He studied the
arpet. ''Su Le's grandmother said all that they wanted
rom me was to get out of their lives. Nothing I could
ver give them could make up for what I'd taken
way.''

Ellen wasn't sure if he was done, but she couldn't
tand it anymore. She leaned forward and pressed her-
elf against him. Lovingly she kissed the spot on his
hin that had haunted him for so many years.

''I never told Clara about Su Le,'' he whispered, his
rms closing around Ellen tightly. ''Once I got back in
he States, I never told anyone.''

For a long moment the two of them sat there, so
lose, yet so far apart. At least she understood the
orces that drove him, but she wasn't sure that under-
tanding was enough. Would he always cling to her so
ghtly? Would he always forget that she was not Su
Le? No matter how lovingly he shackled her, could she
eally bear to live once more in chains? She was more
han willing to stay with Reed tonight—she didn't even
ant to go home—but what about tomorrow night,
nd the night after that? Shannon's article wasn't likely
o stop a man who had tried to shoot her and resorted
o a bomb threat! What if they never found Ellen's
ormentor? Would she feel like a child with a nanny
orever? And how could their love grow if she felt like
hat?

They were questions she did not have time to an-
wer before the sound of a car in the street caused Reed
o stiffen. It lurched to a stop, and at once bold foot-
teps approached the house.

Reed snapped to attention and clapped one gentle hand over Ellen's mouth, signaling her to silence. At once he slipped away in the dark, peering through the bedroom window.

Ellen wasn't about to sit there cowering while she waited for somebody to kill her. It was far too late for casual company, but that didn't mean—please, God! —that the car heralded some new disaster.

Suddenly Reed whispered, "My God, it's the police!"

Instantly he tugged on his discarded jeans, and Ellen did the same. They were both barefoot but decently clad—and halfway down the hall—when they heard a firm rap on the front door a few moments later.

"I'm looking for Mr. Reed Capwell," said an older Hispanic policeman that Ellen had not met before.

"I'm Capwell," said Reed.

Ellen braced herself for some news about the man who'd been trailing her, some word that would either free her from further terror or render moot her arguments with Reed over protection when the police moved in to keep her safe. She could not have been more surprised by the officer's proclamation.

"I'm sorry to tell you, sir, that there's been a robbery at the convenience store where your daughter Jackie, works. She's been seriously injured, but she' still alive," the officer assured Reed. "If you'll come with us, my partner and I will take you to the hospital now."

Reed turned white.

It was Ellen who got his shoes, then firmly took his hand and led him toward the police cruiser. He was trembling violently as they slipped inside.

CHAPTER FIFTEEN

HE NEXT FEW HOURS were a nightmare. Ellen did her est to buoy Reed, but there wasn't a great deal she ould do while the doctors worked over his daughter. ll the way to the hospital he was deathly silent, and nce he got there he berated himself a dozen times for ulldozing Jackie into taking a job instead of just uying her a new car. Mercifully, he didn't seem to re- member that Ellen had urged him to encourage Jackie's dependence.

When Clara arrived, she and Reed clutched each ther, lost in their concern over their injured child. heir unspoken intimacy, in that moment, excluded llen. She tried to help them, bringing coffee, practi- ally force-feeding sandwiches, offering the sort of alm, practical support that she knew she'd want from friend if one of her own precious children was in cri- is.

It was the first time since she'd known Reed that he id not seem to be in charge of his life and trying to ke charge of the people around him. As the night ontinued, she almost felt as though she were the tronger one of them, a new experience that was not early as gratifying as she'd expected. She had always onged for the confidence of strength and indepen- ence, but not at the expense of someone she held dear.

It was almost four in the morning when a white-coated doctor appeared and said to Reed and Clara, "Mr. and Mrs. Capwell? I think your daughter is going to be all right. She lost consciousness due to a blow to the head, but she appears to have only a minor concussion. There was a lot of blood; at first it looked a lot worse than we think it's going to be. She's conscious, if you'd like to speak to her for just a few minutes."

Reed took Clara's hand and squeezed it hard, then stood up and followed the doctor. He'd gone about five steps when he stopped, turned around, and said softly to Ellen, "Wait for me."

She smiled as best she could, and Reed tried to smile back. For a man with all he had on his mind, it was a heroic gesture.

"HONEY?" REED WHISPERED in the eerie white stillness of the room. "Jackie?"

Big brown eyes opened as she held out both hands. "Oh, Daddy!" Tears pooled and dripped down. "Daddy, am I going to be all right?"

Reed gripped her hands but was afraid to embrace her for fear of injuring some bruised part of her frail body. "Honey, the doctor says you're going to be fine."

Clara circled around him and patted Jackie's hair as she had when Jackie had been a little girl. Clara had remained dry-eyed, face like a stone, for hours, but now large tears fell freely.

"What happened, Jackie?" Clara asked. "When the police first came, we thought you were shot. But the doctor said—"

"I got hit on the head with something hard as a rock. I guess they thought it was a gun because that's what robber usually uses. But I never saw it; I never saw who hit me. I'd gone to the back to get some more potato chips because the rack was almost empty, and the boss told me never to let it get down to one bag." She started to cry again. "I've tried so hard to do this job right, Daddy. I was so determined not to let you down this time."

"Hush, sweetie. You didn't let anybody down. Your boss won't hold it against you that you got robbed, and I sure won't, either. It could have happened to anybody."

"They why does it always happen to me? I only left the front for about a minute, and I checked first to make sure that nobody was driving up, because the boss told me never to leave the front while a customer was there. That's why I can't figure out what happened. I came right back out and somebody was waiting, I guess, because the instant I came through the door, I got clobbered. I can't quite tell where he hit me, because I felt the gun or whatever it was clear across the back of my head."

Reed studied his daughter carefully. Either she was exaggerating how long she'd been in the back—daydreaming or doing her nails—or someone had parked at a distance and quietly edged up to the building, waiting to catch her off guard. It seemed like a lot of careful planning for a thief who'd left without taking anything. Had the person who'd found Jackie and called 911 driven up at just that moment and scared him off? It was hard to tell. And it was also hard to tell whether this attack had really been an act of random violence in the course of a crime, or whether Jackie— Reed Capwell's daughter—had been deliberately targeted for reasons that had nothing whatsoever to do with her job at Blackman's.

It was the last notion that scared him the most.

"Jackie," he said quietly, "do you remember what time you went to the back of the store?"

"Reed, this is no time for an inquisition," Clara snapped. "She told you what happened. Just leave it alone."

It was odd for Clara to be defending Jackie while Reed pressed her to account for herself, and his ex-wife's comment told him how terrified Clara had truly been . . . and how desperately she loved her girl.

It also caused him to wonder how Clara could have forgotten his recent warning. Hadn't it even occurred to her that his involvement with the time capsule might be responsible for what had happened to her daughter?

He was too tired to sort out his own feelings from Clara's; what he needed to do was get some sleep and then try to figure out if the same man who'd been stalking Ellen was trying to get Jackie, too. He'd explained the situation briefly to the officer who'd driven him to the hospital, and the man had promised to notify Detective Newman as soon as he came on duty. Until then, Reed wasn't going to leave Jackie alone.

"Sweetheart, we love you and you're okay," he assured his white-faced daughter. "That's all that matters. You go ahead and rest now." He leaned over to kiss her cheek, squeezed her hand once more, then lead Clara away.

The instant they were out the door, Clara said, "What's wrong with you? Why are you badgering her like that? Don't you think she's been through enough?"

He studied her silently. "Clara, I wasn't badgering
er. I was . . . trying to get some information. I'm not
ıre I understand why she was attacked."

"What difference does it make? She's all right,
eed! That's all that matters."

She was trembling, still trying not to cry. Reed de-
ded it wasn't a good time to explain the depth of his
ars to her. He also decided that it wasn't a good time
 let her go home alone. But Clara had no interest in
aving the hospital just yet, which was just as well, he
ecided, because he didn't plan to leave yet, either, and
t the moment he wanted all of his loved ones safe and
ound in one place where he could keep an eye on
ıem.

When he returned to the lobby, he found Ellen sit-
ng quietly, her eyes weary and concerned. He knew
ıere were a thousand things he needed to say to her;
ıey had a crisis of their own that had been left unre-
olved. Still, Ellen had spent the night in the hospital
eside him, offering comfort to Clara, too, without
:owding her. With every passing moment his love for
llen grew greater. Somehow, he had to keep her alive.
omehow, he had to keep from losing her.

She stood at once when Reed reached her. "I called
 cab," she told him gently. "It's morning; now that
 m sure Jackie's okay, I need to go to work. I'm just
oing to go home long enough to shower and change,
nd I promise to lock the door and stay alert. Call me
 onight after you get some rest."

"Ellen—"

She laid one hand on his unshaven face.

"I love you, Reed. That's not going to change in the
ext few hours. Right now you need to concentrate on

Clara and Jackie. Then you need to get some sleep. We can work things out between us later.''

He was too tired to fight her. ''Can we, Ellen?'' was all he could say.

She hesitated, then stroked his neck. ''I want to, Reed. That's all I can promise you.''

Before he could remind her to be careful, she briskly walked away.

THE SUPERVISOR WAS steaming. How could he have been so stupid? He'd had the girl, had her outright, with the rock that would have served as a message to Capwell. He'd intended to set up a trade—the time capsule for the kid. Then some nincompoop had driven up at precisely the wrong moment. He'd intended to blindfold the girl before he took her with him, but he couldn't take the risk that she might recognize him, so he'd had to knock her out. He'd achieved nothing, except given Capwell fair warning to stay on his toes.

Then it occurred to him that he might have profited from the attack, after all. With Jackie injured and Clara distraught, Capwell was going to be concentrating on his family. He wasn't going to worry too much about his new woman in broad daylight when his ex-wife was sobbing on his chest about his child.

The supervisor grinned, slowly and with malice. Ellen Andrews was probably terrified by her near miss with his bullet, but chances were good that she didn't realize there was a connection between the attack on Capwell's kid and the attack on herself. She would be watchful, but she would not have enough sense to go to ground and hide. Sooner or later, she would leave the office on her own.

She might head for home, or for her class, or anywhere else. But Capwell would never find her there.

He would never find her anywhere, because by the time he remembered her, she would be dead.

T WAS SHORTLY AFTER lunch that Ellen got the call from the kindly old curator at the museum. It had been a busy but uneventful day at work. Mercifully, her brief stop at the apartment earlier had revealed no sign of any unwanted visitors... including Howard. She hadn't even received a belligerent note from him in the mail.

"How nice of you to call, Mr. Thompson," she assured him, wondering what information the old fellow could possibly have uncovered. "How is everything with you?"

"Just fine, missy. I had to look around a bit for your card, but I ran into Sara Mae Rafferty's youngest daughter the other day, and we got to talking about things. I mentioned that you'd come by and wanted to know about the clothes. Well, when the family gave them to us, you know."

"Yes, Mr. Thompson. How kind of you to remember." Under the circumstances, Ellen wanted to tell him to hurry up. She hadn't had any sleep and her patience was frayed, but she didn't want to hurt the nice old man's feelings, either.

Mercifully he said, "Well, she had to study on it a bit, but finally she recollected that the clothes were donated just before the big quake of 1971, because she'd planned to finish cleaning out the attic and give several other things to the museum, but the old house fell off its foundations during the earthquake and most of those things were crushed. She was glad they'd at least gotten the clothes out, but there was an old organ—''

Ellen didn't hear the rest. It was the word "earthquake" that filled her mind. It jogged her memory of something Lucy Silverman had told her—after tens of thousands of years, it would take something as cataclysmic as an earthquake to unearth those greenish-black rocks!

She listened as patiently as she was able to the rest of his friendly comments, but she was already pulling out her folder of information about the site: the EIR, Tim's personnel file, the original map and the articles she'd found in the coffee can.

And then she saw it, as plain as the nose on her face. The red crayon line at the edge of the subdivision ad in the newspaper—a line just like the one John had drawn on their survey map the other night! It wasn't a child's random mark! If she'd seen it on a County map in red pencil or ink, she would have recognized its significance in an instant. But she'd never thought of the subdivison ad—with only two or three main streets designated—as a genuine map, let alone a crayon as a proper cartographer's instrument. And yet, if it had been the only map at hand—and the crayon the only writing tool—somebody might have considered it better than nothing. Just as somebody might have used Reed's card as the nearest paper to write a message...or a statement of fact. *Has to stop...fault* Suddenly the message was perfectly clear.

Tim Reynolds—or whoever had buried that coffee can—had improvised to mark the site of an earthquake fault...a fault that ran right next to a major subdivision where thousands of people lived without the slightest clue that they were in danger. And wha about the people who lived directly on top of the fault? Had something been built there, too?

Ellen and Reed had gone over the environmental impact report with a fine-toothed comb; the possible seismic dangers had been mentioned in general terms due to the proximity of the state-long San Andreas Fault and dismissed. From what Sally had said, Tim was fastidious about geological events; he could not have missed something so obvious as a fault in the middle of the target area. And even if Tim could have been blackmailed into silence for some reason, Reed could not have missed anything so obvious... if he'd ever gotten all the original records. She wondered darkly what else he might have withheld from her, hoping that her ignorance would protect her.

She called Reed's office at once, but Sandi informed her that he was still at the hospital. Ellen left a message about her discovery in case he came in, deciding not to bother him while he was with Jackie. She'd leaned too much on Reed. It was time to check out the Manzanita Meadows site herself.

As she rushed from her office, Ellen tried to imagine just what had happened. She didn't think Tim had missed that fault; she didn't think Tim had been bought off. That fault had probably opened up during that 1971 earthquake—after Tim's report had been filed and after Reed had read it. Somehow Tim had found out about it, or gone back on his own to check the site. And the very next day—a quick check of the dates involved had confirmed it—Tim had disappeared.

John was right. The Rock Man had not wandered off to Alaska. There was at least a fifty-fifty chance that he had been murdered. And at least the same chance that the man who had killed him was trying to kill her, too.

BY MIDAFTERNOON, REED had dozed off a dozen times and come to realize that he was being downright irrational. The hospital was buzzing with people; nobody could possibly sneak in to do anything to Jackie in broad daylight. Detective Newman had dropped by to assure him that there had been other robberies in the neighborhood of Jackie's store, and he was reasonably convinced that the attack had nothing to do with Ellen's problems.

"Why don't you go home and get some sleep?" he'd suggested. "If you really feel the need to play watchdog, you ought to do it at night. And if you're not well rested, you know you won't hold out very long."

Reed decided he was right. He gave terse orders to the nurse on Jackie's floor and promised Clara that he'd be back by dark, when she could go home for the night. They'd both seen Jackie several times, and she seemed to be doing well. In fact, she was eager to go home. She'd even had enough energy to briefly speak to her brother when he'd called from Arizona.

Feeling restless despite his fatigue, Reed decided to drop by the office to see if Baxter or Watson had returned his calls. Even a call from Lars saying Olga had found Tim's notes would have been helpful. He could have called, but he knew that Sandi would be deeply worried about Jackie—he'd left a message for her with the switchboard operator this morning—and would feel better if he brought her up to date in person. He didn't want to admit that *he'd* feel better with a dose of Sandi's no-nonsense support, too.

As Reed reached the office, he realized that Jackie's condition wasn't the only reason he felt so unsettled. Just before the police officer had arrived the night before, Reed had spilled out his deepest secrets to Ellen. He had not planned to confide so much to her, not yet. But he couldn't let her leave and he couldn't let her hate him.

He didn't recall too much about her response. He'd been so welled up with his own fear and remembered pain! He knew she'd touched him; he knew she'd replaced the itch of Su Le's grandmother's twenty-year-old spit with the tenderness of new love. She understood—surely, she now understood—why he was willing to risk her love in order to protect her.

But understanding didn't mean she could live with it. Understanding didn't mean she could live with *him*.

He understood why she so desperately wanted to take care of herself, but that didn't mean he could live without *her*.

He'd just decided to call Ellen and ask her to keep him company at the hospital this evening when he got off the County elevator and ran into Bill Hazlett, who was wolfing down an afternoon donut. Crumbs dotted his gray beard.

"Reed! Heard about your daughter. Is everything okay?"

Reed shrugged uncomfortably. "I think so. I mean, she's recovering all right, no permanent damage. But it still gives me chills just thinking about it."

Bill nodded and clapped one sympathetic hand on his shoulder. "With all the other trouble you've been having, it is pretty spooky."

"You think Jackie was hurt as another warning? The police aren't so sure."

Bill shrugged. "I just assumed the two were related after what you said before. I warned you, Reed . . . this whole thing doesn't sound good."

"The police said the store wasn't in a very good part of town," Reed explained. "I guess there have been other robberies recently."

"Oh? She was robbed?"

"Well, no. But that's only because somebody drove up in the nick of time."

"Not in time to keep your kid from nearly getting her head split open. Must have been some firearm to pack that much of a wallop. Are they sure she was hit with a gun?"

Reed was about to answer that nobody was sure just what she'd been hit with, when Bill blurted out, "If somebody's trying to warn you off, Reed, it makes more sense to mess with Jackie than this Ellen gal. Anybody who knows the first thing about you knows you'd die for that little girl." He pondered his words for a moment, then muttered as he wandered off, "I sure hope she doesn't have to die for you."

Bill's haunting words stayed with Reed as he dragged the last few steps to his office, hoping he'd be spared any more "concern" from well-meaning friends. He knew Bill meant well, but he'd only succeeded in getting him all upset again. Was Detective Newman wrong? Was Jackie truly in danger? Newman had never been very concerned about Ellen, either. And somebody had tried to kill her. At least, he thought somebody had. He didn't really buy the theory of the inept hunter.

He found Sandi on the phone as he reached her desk. She stood at once, as though to rush to his side, all the while trying to shake the caller. As she talked, sh anded him a pink message that said: "Supervisor Baxter returned your call. Will try again Monday."

To the caller she said, "No, I don't know when Mr. Capwell will be in, and if you won't leave me your name and number, I can't very well have him call you. If it really is a matter of life and death, I suggest you call the police. I—"

Suddenly Reed touched her hand. "Give me the phone."

She covered the mouthpiece. "Reed, it's just some kook. He—"

"Give me the phone." Despite her wide-eyed surprise, Reed didn't take the time to explain. The caller might have been a kook, but he also might be the killer...or somebody who knew something that could keep Ellen or Jackie alive. Reed had missed too many important calls relating to the time capsule in the past few days...and was still waiting on several others. Now he wondered if they'd all gotten lost in the shuffle when Sandi had been out of the office. Perhaps her judicious protection of his time had inadvertently denied him access to crucial information.

"This is Reed Capwell," he said crisply into the phone. "How can I help you?"

There was a long pause. Then a crusty old voice said, "I heard you askin' questions at Haversham's construction site. The young boss ain't lyin' to you. He don't know a thing."

Reed tried to still the wild surge of adrenaline that the man's opening words shot through him. "Go on," he managed to say.

There was a long, painful silence. Then, in a near whisper, the voice revealed, "I was there, me and two other guys, the day of the big quake. It opened up a hole the size of Texas. Old Haversham told us to fill it in by mornin'.''

Reed was too shocked to speak. He couldn't even intelligently process the information; he was paralyzed by the monstrous nature of what this man confessed to having done.

''I knew it was wrong, and so help me, God, I'm sorry I did it. But he paid me a thousand dollars, tax-free, and my youngest son was dying of leukemia. I needed every penny I could lay my hands on to try to save him—''

He broke off abruptly. ''Point is, we had 'dozers on the site, and we smoothed out the whole thing. All them rocks you was askin' about—the place was full of 'em. He didn't tell us to get rid of 'em, exactly, just smooth things out. A pile of rocks rolled down the hill beyond the fault where the ground was solid, so we left 'em. But the land was flat as a pancake by morning.''

''My God,'' Reed finally managed to utter. ''What's on that land now? Houses?''

''The apartment building. We started construction right away. We'd gotten all the permits ahead of time. Nobody ever knew about the fault except the hippie.''

''Tim Reynolds?''

''I don't know his name. But he was somebody official. I'd seen him there before. He went nuts when he saw the hole in the ground, and he kept waving this greenish-black rock around at old man Haversham. Not like he wanted to hit him, but like it proved somethin', or would prove somethin' when he showed it to his own boss or some bigwig. Haversham hollered back some pretty ugly things and told him to get off the site. That hippie-boy was fit to be tied when he left, cursing up and down. When Haversham told us to fill it he hole before anybody else saw it, one of the guys said, 'But what about the hippie? Somebody's gotta shut his mouth.' And Haversham said, 'The big man'll take care of it.' I figured he meant somebody would pay the kid off, somebody with money to burn. I mean, I knew that's where the extra money for the bulldozin' probably came from." Now shame colored his deep tone. "I swear to you, Mr. Capwell, 'til you showed up yesterday, it never occurred to me that that long-hair could have disappeared for any other reason. That's why I called you. I don't feel too good about covering up that fault, but to help my little boy, I thought it was worth it. But nothin's worth covering up the death of somebody else's little boy, if you get my drift. If some fatcat killed that hippie or paid somebody else to do it, he should be strung up."

"What fatcat?" Reed demanded, mentally running through the list of the men he'd questioned in the past few days.

"I don't know. I never heard his name. All I know is old man Haversham called him the 'big man,' and sometimes 'the boss.' Somebody's always the boss, ain't he? Somebody's always in charge of somethin'. Don't you got nobody in charge of you?"

A sudden vision of Bill's face—and Bill's insistent warning—electrified Reed. Was it possible that his own supervisor twenty years ago had been involved in this terrible event? Is that why Tim had left Reed's business card in the time capsule? Had he intended to report the fault to Reed—or to Bill? Why didn't he report it to his own supervisor?

Oh, God, he recalled sickly. *Tim Reynolds's supervisor was Lars.* Lars, who'd mentioned the possibility of a bomb before Reed had even heard the bomb on the phone!

It was not possible that Lars was involved! But neither could he see tired old Bill as a killer. But Bill Hazlett hadn't always been a broken-down planner. When Reed had first arrived, he'd been a crackerjack workhorse, eager and bright and completely in charge. He'd always wondered what had happened to Bill. Everybody thought he'd just burned out over time. Now Reed wondered if something far more dramatic might have shaped his change of heart.

Still, there were other bosses involved in the project. Haversham's boss was Jefferson Baxter, and who but Baxter—or old Haversham himself—would have had the most to gain from suppressing evidence of an earthquake fault in the middle of an approved development? Even if somebody else had been paid to look the other way, wouldn't Baxter have to be at the heart of this mess?

It was time to call Detective Newman. Reed finally had something more than guesses to offer to the investigator.

"You're a brave man to tell me this," he told the black carpenter, desperately wishing he knew the man's name. "Once you tell the police, they'll be able to pin down who the killer is, and they'll put him away. And you may save the life of—"

"No way. No cops. I'm just telling you to get it off my chest. I hope you get him, but I can't talk to no cops."

"For God's sake, a murder has been committed! And another may be about to—"

"No cops! I'd lose my job, and it'd break my wife's heart! After all she's been through losing that boy..."

e broke off, struggling for words. "Good luck to you, r. Capwell. I figure now that you know what direc- on to look, you can solve this without me."

"But he may have tried to kill my little—"

He was talking to himself. Reed slammed down the ⁙one, then started to dial the police station at once.

He was lucky. Detective Newman was in the office, ⁙d within a few minutes he got him on the line.

Before he could even blurt out the essence of the ⁙one call, Newman said, "Capwell, I was just about call you. Seems I was wrong. That trouble with El- ⁙ Andrews might have something to do with that time ⁙psule after all...and something to do with you. One my boys just happened to notice that last night's re- ⁙rt mentions a rock lying in the middle of the floor at ⁙at convenience store. I checked it out. It's greenish- ⁙ack. Our office rockhound says it's diabase."

"Dear Lord," Reed whispered. It was his worst fear ⁙me true. "*Now* will you put a guard on Jackie? And ⁙ Ellen? And my ex-wife?"

"Your ex is still at the hospital with your daughter, ⁙d I've already placed a guard. But I can't find Ms. ⁙ndrews. I talked to her partner at Zamazanic & Ea- ⁙ton a few moments ago, and he says she took off ⁙hile he wasn't looking, right after she got a call from ⁙me old geezer. I guess she told her supervisor where ⁙e was going, but he zipped off right after that and ⁙body seems to know where he is, either."

Reed felt ill. It couldn't be Lars! And yet...who ⁙tter to cover up whatever Tim had found, and what- ⁙er had happened to Tim himself? But why would ⁙rs involve himself in murder? Just for money? He ⁙uldn't believe it. He *wouldn't* believe it! Lars Lin- ⁙oth was his friend.

But what he felt for Lars was a wisp of smoke com
pared to what he felt for Ellen.

"Look, Capwell, I'm going to put out an APB o
Ms. Andrews, but I still don't know who's trailing he
If you've got any ideas you've been holding bac
now's the time to let me know."

Reed reported what the old black man had told hir
and he relayed his own suspicions, especially those i
volving the men he hadn't been able to run to grour
yet.

With great reluctance, he even mentioned Bill ar
Lars.

"We'll get right on it, Capwell," Newman pror
ised. "And you might want to try to find Ms. A
drews yourself. You might think of some special pla
that we'll miss, or spot some personal clue."

"I'll find her," Reed vowed, terror lashing its ta
against his heart. "I'll find her however long it takes

CHAPTER SIXTEEN

HE MADE IT TWO STEPS, maybe three, before he found Sandi hanging on his elbow.

"Reed, come into your office for a moment. I have to tell you something."

"For Pete's sake, Sandi!" he barked, sharply dragging his arm away. "Whatever it is, it's going to have to wait till Monday! Ellen could be—"

"It's about Ellen!" she whispered with astonishing anguish. "There are some things you've got to know before you rush to Manzanita Meadows! I'm sure that's where she's gone!"

Her desperation was so apparent that Reed had to stop, had to study her pinched face. Despite the fact that her fingernails were digging into his arm, she wasn't quite looking at him. Nausea engulfed him. The certain instinct that something was terribly wrong slithered through him with rising terror. "Good God, Sandi, if anything's happened—"

"Reed, there's so much I haven't told you!" She was starting to cry. Again she tugged on his arm. He didn't want to go back inside; he didn't want to hear her awful revelation. But he couldn't seem to get her to talk in the hallway, and he had to know what had shredded his normally calm and rational secretary, his longtime friend.

He had to know what Sandi's hysteria had to do with Ellen.

They walked briskly back to his office. Waving a manila folder, young Ian Hawkson called out a greeting to Reed just before they reached sanctuary, but he hollered crisply, "Not now, Ian!" and slammed the door.

Sandi was weeping uncontrollably now. Under any other circumstances, he would have given her his utmost sympathy and bent over backward to find out what was troubling her. But this was no time to take a sobbing woman in his arms. Ellen was in danger, and Sandi—somehow—had contributed to her peril.

"Tell me," he commanded. "There's no time to lose! Ellen may be alone out there with—"

"The night of the big quake in '71 you got three calls from Tim Reynolds, each one wild, urgent. He sounded crazy, but he didn't say why he had to talk to you. I put the messages on your desk. I didn't think anything about it."

"Sandi, how could you have forgotten this until now? You know how hard I've been working on this thing, trying to figure it out! How could you—"

"Reed—" tears washed down her face "—I didn't forget. I was terrified!"

"Of what?" he asked incredulously.

"This man called my house that same night. His voice was muffled, angry. He told me that he knew where Jennie went to nursery school and what bedroom she slept in at home. He said nothing would happen to her if I made sure you never knew that Tim had tried to reach you. All I had to do was come in early and tear up those pink messages. If I didn't, he said he'd kill my baby, Reed."

For a long, hard moment he did not speak. Too any questions were darting through his mind. Earthuake. Geologist. Lost messages.

"Who was the man?"

"I didn't know then. I didn't want to know. He told e she'd be safe as long as I forgot the whole thing, id he told me that nothing was going to happen to im because he'd found a very 'green' reason to keep uiet. I figured he'd bought Tim's silence about...well, hatever it was. So I wasn't surprised when Tim took f, Reed. Never for a moment did I think he was ead!"

"Who was the man?" he repeated. At the moment, othing else mattered. If he couldn't find Ellen, he uld find the man who wanted to kill her.

But Sandi seemed intent on clearing her own conience with all the sordid details. "I forgot about it, eed. All of it. It's been over twenty years! And then ght after that article came out in the *Westhope Herd,* he called again. He knew where Jennie worked, here she lived, who she was dating. All I had to do as tell him what you knew. Keep him informed as you ncovered more clues. He promised nothing would appen to you, Reed. All I could think of was Jene."

She was sobbing now, sobbing so hard he could ardly understand her words. In any other situation he ight have been generous and forgiving. Right now he ad to get the facts. He had to find Ellen before it was o late.

"Sandi," he commanded coldly, *"who is this man?"*

"It's Supervisor Baxter," she whispered. "I didn't now until this morning! When he called you back, I nswered the phone. He'd threatened me again just the

night before. He always used a different voice—sort
a gruff scary whisper—but something about the c
dence gave him away.'' She shivered uncontrollably. '
think he murdered Tim.''

''Did he tell you he killed him? Has he admitted
trying to kill Ellen and Jackie?''

She shook her head. ''Not exactly. But after what
said this morning I think that Baxter was desperate
keep Tim from telling anybody about the fault—he
invested too much in Manzanita Meadows, and if t
development had been shut down, it would have d
stroyed him. Still, I don't think he really planned to k
Tim. I think he tried to buy him off and Tim would
be bought. Things got out of hand.'' She batted at
tear with one hand. ''When you and Ellen start
poking around, he made it clear that he couldn't let y
find out anything important about what happened. F
wanted to know every move you made, but I swear
you, Reed, I never told him anything that I thoug
could do you any harm. Besides, I thought he w
only trying to frighten you. But Jackie—he could ha
killed her! She's like my own precious daughte
and—''

''Call back Detective Newman and tell him what y
just told me,'' he ordered. ''Word for word.''

''But Reed—''

''Do it!'' he shouted. ''I've got to go find Ellen. I'
going to Manzanita Meadows, and if she's not ther
I'll keep looking till I track her down.''

Sandi was still sobbing when he left the office, b
he waited until she started dialing the phone. He li
tened to her first words to Detective Newman. She w
quoting Baxter, who apparently had said something
Sandi like, ''She might be too slippery to catch in t

ountains, but the minute she hits civilization, I'll be
aiting to hunt her down.''

LLEN WASN'T AT Manzanita Meadows. Reed found a
ouple of kids playing catch in the street who remem-
ered seeing a woman prowling around with a clip-
oard, but she'd been gone awhile. As Reed studied the
partment complex—and looked down the slope to-
ard the house where he'd found the rock wall—he felt
shiver as he realized the danger the children were in.
a a major earthquake, the people who lived on top of
is fault wouldn't have a chance. The earth would just
vallow them whole.

Reed drove to her apartment; she wasn't there. He
ressed his face against the windows in every room he
ould, but he could see no trace of trouble. Feeling
antic, he drove back to his own house to check his
nswering machine. It was after five by now; after all
aat had happened the night before, he wouldn't have
een surprised to find Ellen at his door.

There was no sign of her, but there was a red light
lowing on his answering machine. There were four
essages: two from Clara, one from Nate, and one
om the woman he loved.

"I think I've figured out the puzzle, Reed, but I've
ot to check something out at the cabin to be sure,"
llen's beloved voice reported. "I called Clara at the
ospital and it sounds like your little girl is going to be
ne, so I think you'd be better off spending the eve-
ing with her and not worrying about me until morn-
ag. I think we'll have a lot more to talk about once we
ut this thing to rest." There was a long pause, but no
lick. At last she added, "I really do love you, Reed. I
ant to make it work.''

Once he'd called the police, he tried to take comfort from her words. But his heart battled terror as he jumped in his old T-Bird and drove like a madman to Chumash Mountain, desperately hoping he'd get there in time.

THE LATE AFTERNOON SUN was starting to fade when the supervisor heard her coming, then watched her trim form hike into view. He could tell she knew what she was looking for; she didn't even bother to go into the cabin, despite the fact that it was starting to rain. She headed right for the spot where he'd found that coffee-can-sized hole in the ground and started walking over the area with slow and cautious deliberation.

It was obvious that she was looking for the hippie's body. But she was nowhere close to it; Reynolds was buried on the other side of the cabin. Still, for the thousandth time the supervisor wished he'd been able to hide him further away from the house. But Sally Quinton had arrived just moments after he'd first shot Tim in the struggle—apparently just moments after Reynolds had buried that damn coffee can—and the supervisor didn't dare make any noise or leave any trail by dragging him through the chaparral. Quinton had waited there all night while he'd shivered silently near the body in the dark, and even after she'd finally left he was afraid to risk moving it very far in case she came back.

This time he'd planned ahead; a couple of pack mules were waiting out of sight to carry the Andrew woman's body miles away from here. He would get her to tell him what she knew and who she'd blabbered to and then he would silence her forever. The only thing he hadn't decided yet was how long to wait for Cap

ll. If it weren't for the girl, he'd tail Ellen up here for
re. But since Jackie was still in the hospital, Capwell
ight wait until morning.

Whether or not he did, it would be the last morning
e would ever see.

Ellen Andrews, on the other hand, would not even
e to see dusk.

STARTED TO RAIN while Ellen searched the ground
ound the cabin; dark storm clouds hung low in the
y. She was tugging out a flashlight from her back-
ck when she heard the gunshot, subconsciously reg-
ering the *whisk!* of a speeding projectile rushing past
r arm.

This time she didn't need Reed to warn her that she
asn't the accidental target of an overzealous hunter;
e didn't need John to push her to the ground. *Some-
ne is trying to kill me!* With haunting hindsight she
alized that she should not have returned to the cabin
one. The article in the paper had made it clear that
e'd stopped looking for clues, but if her killer had
me other means of keeping tabs on her, he might re-
ize that Edwin Thompson's call had set her into ac-
on again.

When another bullet whizzed by, Ellen crouched like
rabbit, terrified. Reed had warned her time and time
ain; even John had told her to be careful. Still, she
d believed—hadn't she?—that someone was merely
ying to frighten her, just as Howard had always done.

Suddenly she understood that Reed had been right.
his *was* war. This had nothing to do with Howard,
d everything to do with the kind of trouble Reed had
en in Vietnam. Had she refused to see the depth of
e danger because of her pride, she wondered, or her

long search for self-respect and freedom? Or was
perhaps for another reason, one neither she nor Reed
had ever considered? Was the real truth—that she'
been targeted for murder—simply too awful a notio
to even entertain? Had she lied to herself in a desper
ate quest to dodge the truth?

As the second bullet whizzed by, an even more ter
rifying realization hit her. She had asked for freedom
begged Reed for the opportunity to solve her prob
lems by herself. She'd been granted her wish. There wa
nobody here to help her now—no Howard, no John
no Reed. There was only a man who'd already kille
once to protect his secret and was surely ready to ki
again. He was armed and hidden; Ellen was standin
in the open and had no weapon.

Worse yet, she hadn't the slightest idea what to do

She ran. At first she ran toward the cabin with som
vague intention of hiding inside. But he cut her off wit
another bullet, and she had to dart up the muddy hil
The chaparral was dense there, and with the rapidl
falling night as her ally, she might—maybe—find a wa
to hide from him.

The next bullet caught her in the arm. The surpris
was fierce; the pain much fiercer.

At first she was too overwhelmed to think. But the
something unexpected happened. The pain made th
fear turn to anger, and with the anger came a clea
headed rage.

She spotted a small, sprawling oak not too far awa
It had low branches, enmeshed with sagebrush that wa
almost as high as the youngest Apache pines. Sh
bolted toward the clump and crouched down, sti
gripping her arm. But she did not stay still, crouchin
in her hidden spot. She quickly crawled out of sigh

around the trunk of the wet oak, until she found a long low branch only a few feet off the ground. While the shots continued, she grabbed the slippery branch with both hands—ignoring the blood that was sweeping down over one of them—and hoisted herself up into the sparse shelter of the nearly leafless tree.

She heard another shot. It was below her. He couldn't see her; he still thought she was crouched on the ground.

Ellen was buoyed by a thrill of relief, coupled with a flush of victory. She had outwitted him! She had not been felled by the first bullet to cut her flesh!

It was a short-lived relief. Within moments he was up the hill, circling the tree, still shooting into the bush. Suddenly he was right below her. If he lifted his eyes a good three inches, he'd be staring right into her hiking boots.

It came to her then, like a cue card held up in big letters across a TV studio. One to one, he would defeat her; gun hand to weaponless fist, she'd be powerless. But June had told her just last week, "A woman's true power lies in her legs." Once, Ellen had thought that meant she could run like hell when she had to, but suddenly she realized that she could kick like a demon, too. She hadn't done weekly battle with that hellish leg press for nothing!

The concept of kicking a human being in the face violated everything she believed in. The notion of letting this madman know where she was frightened her even more. But she'd be damned if she'd hide in the shadows like a gone-to-ground gopher, waiting for him to gun her down! And if she gave him another minute, that's exactly what he'd do.

Ellen hurled herself at him with all her force, kick
ing both feet squarely at his head. One foot missed him
altogether, but the other caught him right in the jaw
The force of her body knocked him backward.

He gave one terrible groan as he collapsed into the
sagebrush. Ellen could hear the gun go flying. She had
two choices: try to pin him down or try to find the gun
It was nearly dark by now and she'd never held a gun
in her life, but she knew that the only way she could
overpower this man again was if he grew dizzy or
passed out cold, and if that was the case—for a few
minutes, at least—she'd be better off using the time to
find the gun.

He lay still as she calculated that he was probably
right-handed, so the gun had most likely flown off to
her left. She crawled on her hands and knees, finger
ing the soggy soil in the dark, listening to him moan as
he began to thrash and roll.

She felt his hand on her ankle just as her finger
bucked cold steel. She seized the gun with both hands
trying to figure out which end was the handle. She'd
held a water pistol once, as a kid, and it seemed to her
that it fit into her hand about like this. She felt for the
hammer and tugged it toward her with her free hand
It made a ripping noise in the darkness. At first she was
afraid she'd broken it, or rainwater had gotten inside
but the sudden stillness at her ankle told her that the
murderer knew the sound and clearly understood his
peril.

With all the force she was able to muster, she
growled, "It's pointed at your head. You touch me
again and you are dead."

She was trembling, but she meant it. He seemed to
understand.

"I'm not moving," he said, his voice still a low moan.

He was an older man, perhaps in his sixties, with a trim haircut and small hazel eyes. She had never seen him before.

She wasn't sure how long she could hold him at bay. He was twice her size, her arm throbbed and she was terribly tired—she'd had a hellish sleepless night even before all this trouble started—but she was not about to go down without a fight. After all, she had nobody but herself to count on.

And then she remembered: she'd left a message for Reed. She'd told him not to follow her, to let her do this herself. She'd implied that the whole future of their relationship rested upon his staying out of the way. What a fool she'd been! Ellen suddenly realized that she had never needed Reed's overprotectiveness more in her life.

There was a time to stand on your own, and a time to lean on your friends. This was one of those times when she would have given a great deal to have had a choice.

A moment later she heard the footsteps, heard Reed's beloved voice, heard two men identifying themselves as county sheriffs.

"Don't shoot!" Ellen called out. "We're up here. I've got a gun on him. I don't think he's stupid enough to move."

It seemed to take a long while for the first sheriff to reach her, longer yet for him to put handcuffs on the gunman, read him his rights and lead him roughly down the slope, ignoring his pleas that he was an important man, a supervisor for Bentbow County, and he had people in important places who would raise the roof when they found out that the police had hauled him away when he was injured.

"Are you all right, ma'am?" asked the other sheriff, after he'd explained who Baxter was and how the Chumash Mountain patrol had been notified by Detective Newman in Bentbow that they were needed on the spot. "Is there anything I can get you, anybody I should call?"

That's when Ellen saw Reed. He was standing by the cabin in the rain, both hands thrust fiercely in his pockets as though the motion alone would keep him from rushing toward her. He was absolutely white and absolutely still, and it was obvious that it was killing him not to rush in and take care of her. It was equally clear that he feared she'd be furious because he'd ignored her orders and brought the cavalry to the rescue.

Ellen crawled out from under the dripping oak and hiked toward him, gripping her arm below the wound.

Reed tensed as he watched her, but he did not take a step in Ellen's direction, or even hold out his arms.

When she was just a few inches away, she asked softly, "How long have you been here, Reed?"

"Since you first cocked the hammer. I was afraid that if I moved, I'd distract you. And then I realized that...you really didn't need my help at all."

Suddenly all the courage washed out of her. Tears filled her eyes. "Oh, Reed," Ellen whispered, "there may be times when I don't need your help, but I think I'm always going to need *you*."

He blinked hard, as though he might have a tear or two of his own. Still he held back. "Ellen," he said softly, "might this be one of those times?"

In a rush she threw her arms around him. Only then did Reed fiercely cradle her against his chest, heedless of the rain, heedless of the flow of blood all over his shirt. In the aching tenderness of that embrace, she could feel his anguish, his love, his powerful respect for her. She would never doubt it again.

"It's the hardest thing I've ever done," Reed whispered.

"I think it's the hardest thing I've ever done, as well," Ellen confessed. "Next time we play cops and robbers, let's corner the murderer together, okay?"

He kissed her temple and pulled her closer yet. "It's a deal, partner." His hands were trembling. His voice was hoarse and dry.

Ellen clung to him, weeping freely, until it was nearly dark on the mountain and they were both soaked to the skin. When all the sorrow had been washed from their hearts, Reed took a step back and stroked Ellen's wet hair. He kissed her once. Lovingly she laced her fingers through his.

Then they started toward the cabin, shoulder to shoulder, hand in hand.

Harlequin Superromance®

Family ties...

SEVENTH HEAVEN

In the introduction to the Osborne family trilogy, Kate Osborne finds her destiny with Police Commissioner Donovan Cade.

Available in December

ON CLOUD NINE

Juliet Osborne's old-fashioned values are tested when she meets jazz musician Ross Stafford, the object of her younger sister's affections. Can Juliet only achieve her heart's desire at the cost of her integrity?

Available in January

SWINGING ON A STAR

Meridee is Kate's oldest daughter, but very much her own person. Determined to climb the corporate ladder, she has never had time for love. But her life is turned upside down when Zeb Farrell storms into town determined to eliminate jobs in her company— her sister's among them! Meridee is prepared to do battle, but for once she's met her match.

Available in February

my VALENTINE 1992

Celebrate the most romantic day of the year with
MY VALENTINE 1992—a sexy new collection of four
romantic stories written by our famous Temptation
authors:

GINA WILKINS
KRISTINE ROLOFSON
JOANN ROSS
VICKI LEWIS THOMPSON

My Valentine 1992—an exquisite escape into a romantic
and sensuous world.

 Harlequin Books ®

VA